THE OLD BUGGERS' BRIGADE

Phil Lawder

ISBN: 978-1-9997129-1-4

Cover design by Colin Robinson

My thanks to Matthew Branton and Siobhan Curham for their editing skills and support.

Dedicated to everyone
who would like life
to be just a little
more exciting

Outside – December 22nd 9.45pm

He runs.

They let him go. A few feet. Catch him easily. Circle round him.

He breaks away. Trips over an extended leg.

Falls.

'Bit unsteady on your pins, are you?'

Strangely well-spoken voice. He'd been expecting street rough.

He feels the damp pavement against his face. Sees the reflection of the streetlight spread and shatter. Sees graffiti on the wall, *OLD minus GOLD = GOOD*

Hands grab him, haul him to his feet.

'Up you come.'

He feels anger, fury. His breath comes in short gasps.

'You young bastards.'

'You're dead right. We're bastards, but we're young bastards. Whereas you,' the face comes right up to his, 'you are an old bastard. An oxygen stealer, a grey rotting gnome sitting on your little pile of gold. Well, your gold's no good to you now, old man.'

He winces as the younger man spits in his face.

He wants to tell them, there is no gold. He's not even old. Sixty-nine. That's nothing these days. The words don't form. A policeman's lifetime of instructions and persuasion desert him. When he most needs them.

His glasses are snatched from his face. He blinks, darkness turns to fog.

The first blow hits the back of his head. He staggers. The second, a boot to the stomach. He's down. Breath gone. Incoherent.

They come fast then. He screams. Once. Loud. No one comes.

Chapter 1 – December 26th 2.30pm

Bill

'Another one, Bill? On the house. Compliments of the season.'

'Don't mind if I do, George. Oh, for a draft of vintage that hath been cooled a long age in the deep delved earth, something, something, that I might drink and leave the world unseen.'

'Sorry?'

'Keats, George. Died young, lucky bugger.'

'Right.'

George is looking at me with that 'how come he knows poetry and stuff' look. I do like to surprise people, even now. Oh, yes, full of surprises, me.

I let the last of the old pint slide down my throat and pick up the full glass. 'Never touched the sides,' Gerry used to say. Used to? Steady on, he's not dead yet. I hope. I raise the glass in a silent toast to an old colleague and good friend.

'Calmed down a bit now,' I say to George. 'Bit of a rush before lunch, wasn't it? You'd think they hadn't had a drink for a year the way they dashed in. You've only been shut for one day, for God's sake. Must have been that promise of free crisps. And the chance to get away from their families for a few minutes. Or the family's chance to be rid of them, of course. Silly buggers, don't know how lucky they are.'

George grunts.

I look at the remnants of the crisps on the bar. Wouldn't touch them myself. Mary always warned me off them, read some report about what they find in them. 'If you want some, buy them yourself. Then you know who's fingered them. The day men wash their hands after going to the loo is the day I'll eat crisps off a bar.'

'What did you get up to yesterday, Bill?' George asks. He doesn't really want to know, probably a bit embarrassed now he's asked. Thinks I'll start crying, or something. Not me, not here.

'You know the Patels next door to me?'

George shrugs.

'They obviously heard about Gerry and that I'd be on my own, so they sent the little one round on Christmas Eve, never can remember his name, Sashi, Sasi, something like that.

'Mummy and Daddy are wondering if you would like to join us for a meal tomorrow.' Little singsong voice, all very formal, the way they are. 'They suggest twelve thirty, if that would suit.''

George grins.

'Was going to refuse but I thought they might misunderstand, think it's a racist thing, so I said yes.'

'Yeah, can't be too careful.'

'No idea what to take. Mary always took care of that sort of thing. Couldn't take booze in case they're teetotalers; lot of them are, I understand. Anyway, dashed down to the supermarket before it closed and got flowers for her, chocolates for the kids and that seemed to go down well. They did it nicely, I have to say. Seemed a bit strange, yesterday, sitting around the table with all the usual stuff – turkey, all the trimmings – and a row of black, well, brown faces. Mrs P said she hoped I didn't mind the curry smell in the house. I explained to her that I liked a good curry and that, anyway, it was her house. She seemed pleased about that, said I should come round and try a real curry some time. I tried to sound enthusiastic.'

'Careful what you let yourself in for. You'll be wearing a burqa soon.'

People are basically nice. Spent most of my life chasing villains and even some of them were OK. God, who is this sentimental old bugger in my head? People, nice? What a load of crap. Thirty-five years on the force told me that's bull. Bunch of toe rags. Don't start wearing the rose-tinted now, Bill, you'll be smiling at vicars next.

'So, Bill,' George's voice breaks in, 'What's the latest on Gerry, then?'

'Much the same, to be honest. They're keeping him in Intensive for now.'

'Odd, not seeing him over there with you. Part of the furniture.'

'I'll go and see him after this. Late in the evening can be a lonely time when you're in hospital. Do you know if the buses are running? Can't take the car. Wouldn't look good, *Former Chief Inspector up on Drink Drive Charges.*'

'Think so. I saw a Number Twelve earlier. But you mind out for yourself, wandering around after dark's not a great idea nowadays.'

'George, I've been walking these streets since I was a kid. No-one's going to keep me off them.'

He grins but I can see he thinks I'm a fool. Maybe I am. But he knows better than to try to lecture me.

'Have they got the young bastards who jumped him?' George asks.

'Not a sniff. Wonder if they're really trying.'

'How do you mean?'

'Well, if you were a young copper, would you really want to make your name chasing kids who beat up old men, what with everything else going on? You're just as likely to think they've got a point and go for the big stuff.'

'Yeah, all a bit of a mess, isn't it? I heard on the news this morning there were eighty-six attacks across the country in the week up to Christmas. And there's some bearded psychologist fellow saying it's all because they can't get free flats and the government don't dare cut pensions. I ask you.'

'Yes, the Daily Express was saying they should export all the young unemployed to India. Then we oldies can walk the streets free from fear. All it needs, frankly, is a few more police on the streets and courts that back them up, rather than constantly painting them as the aggressors.'

'You don't seem to think much of our justice system. Bit odd, that, for a retired copper.'

Careful, Bill. Don't show your cards, even to George. I shrug it off.

'To be honest, I never thought it was that good. Used to make our own justice, in the days before CCTV cameras and tape recorders. Rough justice, if you like, but there's a few lads walking the straight and narrow today thanks to a good hiding and a scare at the right time. Nowadays, you sneeze on some kid and he'll sue you.'

'What have we come to, eh? It's a sorry world. Still, only one we've got. Anyway, give Gerry my best when you see him later.'

The pint's empty. Time to face the outside world.

'Certainly will. Cheers, George. Probably see you tomorrow.'

Chapter 2 – December 26th 8.45pm

Jenny

It's that time of the day. The Christmas lunch has finally been conquered, the table is littered with the detritus of nutshells, empty bottles and dead crackers with their strangely breakable gifts, it's getting dark outside and conversation has lapsed into what we all hope is a comfortable silence. I look around Nick's flat, or do I now have to call it Nick and Cressida's? Familiar bits of furniture, a sideboard that used to be in our dining room, that chair from the spare bedroom, all temporary here, no doubt, until he, or they, find something that is more their thing. All temporary, all passing through. Yes, aren't we just.

Compliments are due.

'Lovely turkey, Cressida. Where did you find it?'

'Oh, Nicky got it,' she replies brightly, smoothing an arm across his shoulders. Nicky? Suddenly my son's a chorus boy. 'He found it at Smithfield, didn't you, Tiger?'

Tiger. Right. Silence best.

'Your great grandfather used to get his turkey at Smithfield.' That's David, clambering up the rather shaky family tree again. I look across at him. It's one of those moments when I just can't understand why I've spent the last thirty-four years with him. It's the combination of pink shirt, (I shouldn't have insisted), bow tie, paper hat. He's an Easter egg. Confused his festivals, poor lamb.

Some men are born only to wear suits, white shirts, sober ties. David's one of them. Always looks lost in bathing trunks. Incomplete, somehow, like one of those horrible hairless cats.

He ploughs on. 'Your grandmother – she was just a little child at the time, of course – used to tell me that they would always go up on Christmas Eve and choose the bird, bring it back for Bridie to pluck and cook.'

Lucky old Bridie, how she must have whooped with joy.

David's brow furrows. 'Now tell me, you two,' His serious voice, company director. As was. 'I want to ask what you think about all these attacks in the street. I mean, I know times are a bit hard but really, beating people up just because they're older. You know, I was reading in the Telegraph that there's been two hundred this month alone. Bit steep.'

'Well, Dad,' Nick leans forward, pushing fingertips together to emphasise his point. Do I see the beginnings of a jowl forming under that fine square chin? I do hope not. Not yet. His hair flops over one eye, reminding me of the serious schoolboy explaining equilateral triangles to me.

'Of course, there should never be the need for violence in a civilised society.' I wait for the however. 'However,' yup, there it is, 'you can understand why they feel so hard done by.'

'Can you? Damned if I can.' David takes another swig of wine. Obviously, I'm driving home.

I look across at the darkened window. Just a pane of glass separating our cosy world from the streets. Will they ever get back to being the places we wandered and explored? Or are we always going to be looking over our shoulders, the fear of the baseball bat to the head, the kicks avalanching in on you?

'Look, Dad,' Nick's voice brings me back. 'your generation got it all, paid off mortgage, nice big house, money in the bank, retired at fifty-five with a full index-linked pension.'

'Fifty-six, actually.'

'OK, whatever, but look at us. We're going to be working at least till we're seventy, probably have a fifty year mortgage, if we can ever get one, and for something a lot smaller than your Holly Lodge. And at least we have jobs, for heaven's sake.

There's more than two and a half million out there who've got nothing. It's been ten years since the last financial crisis and nothing's getting any better. Worse, if anything. Can't blame them for being a tad envious, can you?'

'Actually, yes, I can. I worked bloody hard to get what we've got.'

Yes, all that chewing and swallowing. All that 'Sorry, dear, it looks lovely but I had to take a client out for lunch,' night after night.

'I put you and your sister through decent schools, paid all the bills, gave you nice holidays.'

I wait.

'And looked after your mother.'

Thanks. Even as an afterthought.

'And don't think we're not grateful, Dad. You gave us a really good start, helped us to be where we are today, well, where I am.'

Well corrected, Nick, I don't think your sister's way of life is quite what your father had planned. Making shell necklaces in some Cornish tourist trap, dressed up as a Pierrot: seems good to me. The one that got away; the one who didn't become a lawyer or banker. Good for you, Fiona. But what do I know?

'It's just that, somehow,' Nick pushes on, 'it feels like your generation had all the goodies and we're left with the scraps. And the never-ending debt.'

'And that's a good reason to go round beating people up? Nearly forty have died, you know.'

'No, of course it's not a good reason. I'm explaining, not justifying.'

I think of old Mr Byers, caught on the tube one Saturday night about a month ago. Lived just up the road from us. Can't call him a neighbour, really. Couldn't stand him, cantankerous old sod. Hard to know what to feel when I heard. All that clichéd nonsense about hearts going out. Mine stayed firmly where it was. Still, shouldn't have happened. Even to him.

I sense Nick's coming to the boil so decide to change the subject.

'What do you think about that awful Dominic Evans and his Generate gang?' I chip in. 'Do you think he's behind all this violence?'

I look round the table. David frowns as he tries to remember who Dominic Evans is. Nothing new there, but there's an awkward silence from Nick and Cressida. I raise an inquiring eyebrow.

'Did I say something wrong?'

Nick clears his throat. 'Er, Mum, actually Cressida works for Dominic Evans.'

Whoops. 'Cressida, I'm so sorry. I didn't mean to embarrass you.'

'No, no, really, that's OK. I'm on his organising team, the Generate rallies, not, you know, the parliamentary lot. I know he tends to get a rather bad press but, if you could just see him working, I mean, the man's amazing and he's really, really trying to make things better.'

'Really, really?' I get a scowl from Nick for that. 'So, not behind these street attacks, then?'

'God, no. He wouldn't sanction anything like that. And Generate is all about helping young people get back their self-respect. Really, I mean, honestly, he wouldn't. No, he's amazing, just so, you know, charismatic. I think he'll go far.'

I think I detect a bit of a crush. Time to leave it alone, even though I remain unconvinced. Nick breaks the silence.

'Dad, coming back to the point, I'm sure that your generation didn't realise, even though there were plenty of people telling you. And, personally, we don't blame you.'

'Blame? I should jolly well think not.'

'But the attacks. Like I say, there's a lot of younger people nowadays who've got absolutely nothing and frankly nothing to look forward to either. You, with what you've got, you can't know what that feels like. They look at older people and think 'they've got all that stuff and I'm never going to get it'. They just see higher rent and taxes on whatever they can earn taking their future away, day-by-day. Well, you can see how things happen. I'm not saying it's right, but it is understandable.'

'It's just typical jealousy. They can't be arsed to put in the hours so they take it out on those who can.' This from the man who was always on the 5.26 home. 'And, incidentally I pay taxes too. I'm paying for pensions as much as you are. I mean, are we supposed to say sorry and give them all our money?'

I see Nick and Cressida exchange a glance, an imperceptible nod from her. I smell ambush. David doesn't.

Nick takes a breath. 'Well, in a way, yes.'

'What?' David's face gets even redder.

'No, hear me out. I mean, look at the way it works now. People hang onto their money, live in their big houses, have their big holidays and then, when they die, the government gets a giant slug of what's left. That money just disappears into the bottomless debt pit. Gone. It's crazy. There should be a way, some system for older people to recycle their wealth so that everyone can benefit.'

Ah, I think I see where this is going. I turn to Cressida.

'Shall we clear away while the men sort out the world and its problems?'

Nick half rises. 'Don't worry, Mum. We'll do that later.'

'No, Nick, you stay. I don't mind a bit of gender stereotyping and I'm sure Cressida ought to be getting used to it by now.'

And anyway, that heavy smell of turkey is getting to me. Like drying plaster.

'Cressida, shall we?'

We take the plates through to the kitchen. I decide to mend fences.

'Look, sorry again for the crack about Evans. I guess I've been reading the wrong papers.'

She looks at me with a serious expression, and I see instantly that she must have been head girl. I guess this is why we've been relegated to Boxing Day. 'He really is something special, you know, Jenny. I think he might save this country, really.'

Yes, but who for, I wonder. Not the time to say that.

'Well,' I say, determined to have the last word, 'someone's behind it, it's getting worse, and no-one seems too keen to stop it, either.'

She looks around, embarrassed, trying to change the subject.

'Bit of a mess in here, I'm afraid.'

'All good cooks should have messy kitchens, in my view. Shows that something creative has happened.'

'I do hope so. Somehow, Christmas dinner doesn't feel very creative, just like some mammoth time trial full of nasty traps, that you have to negotiate with everyone watching.'

I'm starting to like this girl. Suppose it's just what I expected Nick to go for, even if she's not my ideal. Perfectly cut glossy middle class hair, pulled back into a bow. Pale blue eyes that say I'm not as demure as I look. I should be pleased, I suppose, perfect daughter-in-law material. Not yet though. Not in the proper married, change of name, shared secrets and shopping trips sense. I suppose that will come. That's going to be hard.

She's watching me, waiting for a reply.

'You did well,' I offer. 'It's one of those meals that just keeps on coming, isn't it, right down to the last sprout.'

'God, yes, what am I going to do with all those sprouts?'

'Throw them away. They make a lovely sound going down the waste disposal. They're one of the great myths of Christmas, started no doubt by some enterprising marketing man who found he had a pile of stunted cabbages that he couldn't shift.'

'Sounds like wise advice.'

Time for a body swerve.

'So,' I ask, 'do you think Nick will get what he wants from David?'

'Sorry?'

'All that nonsense about the government getting too much inheritance tax. Didn't make sense, fiscal or logical. I assume that he's working up to asking us to give you the deposit on a flat.'

Cressida looks at me. It's good to see respect in with the embarrassment.

'You're very bright, Jenny. It's a pity you never worked.'

'But I did.' I'll ignore the condescension for now. 'I worked at the bank with David. That's where we met. I was running part of the foreign exchange department. I only left when I was expecting Nick.'

'And never went back? Didn't you want to?'

'God, yes. You cannot imagine how boring children are. Does that shock you? Has my image as earth mother and dutiful wife flown out of the window? I do hope so.'

She laughs, thank God. Such matters are far too important to be taken seriously.

'You could get back to it now. I mean, you're a lot younger than David.'

'Not a lot, but thank you for that. Is this leading up to the "you're never too old to be what you want to be" bollocks?'

Good, shocked her.

'But that's true. Surely.'

'Cressida, you're, what, twenty-six, twenty-seven? The only thing it's too late for with you is winning the kindergarten egg and spoon race.'

'Actually, I did win that. Got the little trophy somewhere at home, at my parents' home.'

I bet you did. And captain of hockey. Let it pass, it's Christmas, after all.

'So, coming back to the conversation that you've steered us so cleverly away from, I think you should have that deposit. We've got plenty and, frankly, if we have to do without the third holiday next year, so be it. Maybe your Generate friends won't be so envious then.' I talk over her attempted riposte. 'Best if you stop Nick actually asking for it now, though. David gets a bit confused if he has to make a decision. I'll sort it for you.'

She kisses me on the cheek, like she means it, not the abrupt face bang that we got on the way in, and goes back into the living room. I look around. Given the choice of starting the washing-up or rejoining the table, I go for the washing-up.

Chapter 3 – December 26th 10.15pm

David

Thought I'd let Jenny drive home. Had a few, probably be over the limit. Still be OK to drive, I'm sure, but Jenny worries, what with the rain too. So, put her mind at rest. Frankly, in the Volvo, hardly matters. Built like a tank, we'd always come off best.

Good thing about Nick's place, you can park off the road, behind a fence. Can't leave a car anywhere nowadays, it seems. Bloody nuisance. Pinner's still OK, just about, but even there it's getting risky. Pal up at the golf club had his car keyed in the station car park last week. In broad daylight. Like I was explaining to Nick, everyone's jealous of someone else nowadays. Well, they're certainly not going to make me feel guilty.

'I thought Nick was on good form today,' I venture. 'And Cressida produced a lovely meal.'

She glances over at me as she drives. That look. Seem to be getting a lot of that nowadays. Obviously trying to tell me something. No idea what.

'They both did the cooking, actually, and I thought Nick looked a bit drawn. I think he's worried about his job.'

'Well, plenty more where that came from. I could always call up a few old contacts if it came to it.'

'I don't think there's plenty of anything any more, and I think you'll find your old contacts have all gone.'

God, probably have, too. Bit of a clear out in the last few years. Got out just in time. Didn't feel like it then, though. Funny how things work out.

'I thought she'd made the place look nice,' Jenny volunteers. Good to hear her say something positive. 'Better than when

Nick was on his own. I noticed a couple of new prints on the wall, those bright cushions on the sofa. A woman's touch. I mean, why is it that men can be so obsessed about every detail of their car or their phone or whatever, yet be happy to live in a completely anonymous room?'

OK, not quite so positive.

'She seems a permanent fixture now,' I say, trying to move on to a safer subject.

'Permanent fixture, like a fridge, you mean, or a washing machine?'

Oh, hell. Can't say anything right today. Something's still puzzling me, though. I have one last go.

'Not sure what that diatribe about how we'd had all the cream and there was nothing left for them was all about. Probably the wine talking. Damn good, that St Emilion I brought. Better call the wine merchant, make sure I get a few more before the price goes up again. Yes, he was probably emboldened by liquor, as they say.'

'As who say?' She always does that. It's just an expression, for God's sake. Best to close my eyes for a while.

Get jolted awake. 'Steady on, love.' Women can't handle big cars, I find. Should have driven after all. She's stopped, staring at something. I focus. Try to.

'What's going on? Why have we stopped?'
'Over there. Look.'

I look through the slapping wipers. Open space, uneven paving stones. Couple of beaten up trees. A crowd of people. Bit of a scuffle.

'So? Nothing to do with us. Let's go.'
'No. Someone's being attacked.'
'So? It's no-one we know.'

I hear the sound of a whistle being blown. 'There, you see, someone will hear that.'

'Wait.' She's getting out of the car. Oh, Christ, now what?

'Don't be so silly. Get back in. It could be dangerous.'

She leans back in. 'Next time it might be one of us. Would you want someone to just drive past?'

I really don't see the connection. I mean, it's not going to be me. I drive everywhere. You wouldn't find me walking around in… wherever it is that we are right now.

She reaches across me, grabs the torch from the glove compartment, starts walking towards them. She's only left the bloody door open. Lean over to close it. And have an idea. Ease myself over into the driving seat. May need a quick getaway. Better lock the doors as well.

She's walking across towards them, shouting at them. Suddenly she thinks she's Wyatt Earp. Oh, God, they've seen her. Coming towards her. Must be five, six of them. What the hell do I do?

I know. Saw it in a film. Start her up. Into gear. Charge at them. Scatter them. No problem. Here goes. Foot down, give them a bit of Swedish metal. Just check the doors are locked first. And charge. Wow, quite fun, this. Mind the wife. Go for the kid on the left. This will put the wind up him. The skinny figure, caught by the headlights, jinks one way, then another. Out of the way, you bloody idiot. Jump. Oh, God, oh bugger.

A green hoodie with someone inside it flies over the bonnet, crashes into the windscreen. Not part of the plan. I slam on the brakes. Look round. Can't see clearly, back windows all steamed up. Got the others running, anyway. Jenny's coming round to the door, pulling on the handle, shouting something. Great soundproofing, these Volvos. I unlock. She drags the door open.

'What the fuck do you think you're doing? You've probably killed him.'

'Doing? I was rescuing you, you silly cow.' I'm shocked. I think that's the first time I've ever heard Jenny use the f-word.

'I didn't need rescuing. That's the guy over there who needs rescuing.' She points to a pile of overcoat on the ground and starts towards it. 'Now, put the car over there, well away, and come and help me.'

I park the car, get out, lock it and cautiously go over, feeling this is not the time to explain that, just because one person needs rescuing, it doesn't mean that another one doesn't. I think that's right.

She bends down. I look around carefully, seems all clear, edge closer. It's a man, oldish, by the looks of it, older than me, anyway. I lean in, to see if he's conscious. He's looking back at me but it's hard to tell if anyone's home.

'What's your name? Do you remember your name?' I ask, remembering the drill from *Holby City*.

He stares back at me. Doesn't look good. Finally, he takes a deep breath.

'Course I bloody do. Bill Johnson. Who the hell are you?'

Chapter 4 – December 26th 10.25pm

Jenny

Scary moment. Not that I'd ever admit that to David. When those thugs started to come at me. What would I have done? Taken a swing with the torch, I suppose, hoped to make contact. I guess he saved me; I really should thank him. Later, maybe.

This old man's looking pretty beaten up. Need to get him into the light, see what's damaged.

'Oh, God, now what?' I hear David mutter. I look up. Policeman arriving, just in the nick of too late. He runs up, out of breath, more pudding than stick. They really don't make them like they used to.

'Now then, what's going on here?'

Not much change to the script, then. 'This man was being beaten up, officer. You probably heard his whistle. Looks like another age attack. Thanks for coming, you must have been some way off.'

'What makes you say that?'

'The time it took you to arrive.'

'Oh, yes, right. I was down by the Market Place.'

Rain drips down my neck. I shiver. Need to get out of here.

'Anyway, enough of the chat,' I announce, 'We'd better check him out.'

David is leaning over him still. The man is glaring back at him.

'How's he looking, David?'

'He seems a bit groggy.'

The man eases himself up onto one elbow. 'I can speak for myself, thank you very much. I have been thumped around the head three times and kicked in the stomach six times.' The voice comes out in sardonic gasps. 'Nothing broken, far as I can tell, no damage to anything important. "A bit groggy" doesn't really capture it, does it, but it'll do for now.'

The policeman is over beside him. 'Can you stand?'

'With a bit of help, I think so.'

David and the policeman help him to his feet. He's tall, bigger than both of them.

'I think I'd better call for an ambulance.' The policeman takes his radio out.

'And dump me in A&E on Boxing Day evening? I don't think so, son. I have no desire to be manhandled by some ten-year-old student who thinks he's a doctor just because he's got a white coat and has watched five episodes of *Casualty*. Anyway, think about the forms you'll have to fill in later.'

'Forms?'

'IRFs, lad. Incident report forms. Best just forget about it.'

I suddenly remember David's flamboyant gesture with the car. 'I'm afraid you'll have to fill in some forms anyway. There's another casualty.' Leaving David to support the old man, I lead the policeman across to the green hoodie, still sprawled on the ground. He looks young, maybe fifteen. Limbs all seem to be pointing in roughly the right direction, so I'm hopeful.

The policeman shows a puzzling lack of surprise at the sight. He kneels down.

'Still breathing, at least. Want to tell me what happened here?'

'I'm really not sure. I was a bit engaged with those lads, as you can imagine and my husband was in the car over there, where it's parked, miles away from the boy. So I can only guess it was a completely separate incident.'

He's staring at me, saying nothing, doubt all over his face. Or indecision. God, he must have seen. But if he saw that, he must have been waiting, lurking over there.

Well, attack is always the best form of defence, I find. 'Such a pity you didn't get here just a moment earlier or you might have seen something.' Still he says nothing. Either very calculating or very thick. I favour the latter at the moment.

'So,' take the initiative, get bossy. Most Englishmen are scared of women anyway, 'I suggest that you call for an ambulance for this chap and we'll be on our way. I'm sure our friend over there needs to get home as quickly as possible.'

He is suddenly animated, as if someone's rammed a cattle prod up him. He presses buttons on his radio, a long pause before a bored response. The ambulance is finally ordered. We return to the others, leaving the crumpled hoodie boy where he is. Probably should put a blanket over him or something but, what the hell, he's young. And he's a shit. Laying into an old man like that.

David is sitting with the man, what was his name, Bill something, on a graffiti-scarred bench. He's retrieved a brolly from the car and the two of them sit like weathermen. I'd forgotten it was raining. Funny thing, adrenaline.

'How are you feeling now, sir?'

'I'll live, constable.'

'Sergeant, actually.'

The old man looks at him with raised eyebroww. 'Good God. Are you based at Hillman St?'

'That's right.'

'How's Jack Williamson?'

'You know CI Williamson?'

'I trained him. Taught him all he's forgotten. Give him my regards.'

'Who shall I say sends them?'

'Bill Johnson. Former Chief Inspector Bill Johnson.'

'I think I've heard that name mentioned a few times. It's good to meet you.' He suddenly looks embarrassed, seems to realise this is not a social occasion. 'Do you want to tell me what happened now, sir, or shall I make an appointment to send one of our liaison officers round?'

'Neither.'

'Sorry?'

'What's your name, lad?'

'Carolson. Barry Carolson.' I get the impression that he's working very hard at not finishing each sentence with 'sir'.

'Well, Sergeant Barry Carolson,' he makes the name sound somehow fake, 'if you interview me now, we will either have to sit here in the cold and wet or I will have to trail over to Hillman Street, neither of which I want. If you send one of those dreadful liaison officers round, I will have to put up with two hours of sympathetic nods, more than any sane man can stand. It's not as if there's any chance of the police following this up and actually catching someone. If there were, I'd probably put up with it. As it is, there isn't and I won't.'

'I can assure you, sir, that every case...'

Bill holds up his hand. I notice the grazed knuckles. 'Yes, yes, that's what I used to say too. Forget it.'

'Well, there is the matter of the injured party over there.'

'Traffic accident.'

'Sorry?'

'Look, you can spend two hours filling in papers about who did what, to whom and how, or you can just get him carted off to hospital and patched up. With a bit of luck he won't be able to do this again for a few weeks. Call it community service.'

The policeman, Barry whatever, nods slowly. He could clearly see the difference between a free evening and a pile of paperwork. So, this is how the law is applied. Good to know.

'Now, I think I hear an ambulance coming. So, if you kind people could just give me a lift home – it's just around the corner – I can get away before the paramedics get their hands on me.'

We help Bill to the car, still parked in the middle of this bleak space. He settles into the seat, leans back and closes his eyes.

'Where to?' I ask hastily.

The eyes open. 'Anywhere other than this hellhole. And preferably 43 Selchurch Avenue. I'll direct you.'

We pull away as the ambulance arrives. The rain gets heavier again.

Chapter 5 – December 26th 10.45pm

Bill

She's a good driver. Funny how you can tell within just a few yards. Confident. In touch.

God, it's going to hurt tomorrow. Hurts pretty badly now. Still, I'd know if something was really damaged. Lucky they were wearing trainers. Probably not one of the professional gangs, just a bunch of lads high on something.

'You bring it on yourself,' Mary used to say. Well, yes, but what else do you do? Stand and watch? Walk by, averting the eyes? Once a policeman, always a policeman. Those girls they were hassling, they just seemed to disappear. Hope they're OK. Shouldn't be out after dark nowadays. Nor should I, but bugger that.

It was seeing Gerry, I suppose, in hospital. All wired up like that. Didn't recognise me, after twenty years working together. Well, that's going to make anyone want to take on the world, isn't it?

Interesting couple. Especially her. Could be useful. We'll see.

'Just here on the right. That's it, number 43's about half way up on the left.'

They help me in. I can see that he wants to get away. I'll hold them back for a while.

'I wonder if you could just help me settle in. It's all a bit…' I stagger slightly and she's at my arm, guiding me to a chair.

'Thank you. I think a small whisky is called for after such an adventure. I wonder if you … I'm sorry, I don't even know your names yet.'

'Jenny, I'm Jenny and this is David.'

'Bill Johnson, but I've already told you that, haven't I? David, would you do the honours? You'll find glasses in the cupboard to the left of the kitchen sink and the whisky is in that cabinet over there.'

Well, that's got some life into him. Obviously likes a drink.

She waves a dismissive hand. 'I won't if you don't mind, as I'm driving, but I'm sure that David will join you. Now, let's take a look at you. Do you have a first aid kit here?'

'Oh, don't bother, I'll be OK.'

'Nonsense. I've spent half of my life sorting my son's rugby injuries and scrapes and scratches. We need to get your face cleaned up and it'll be really difficult for you to try to do it in a mirror.'

I'm grateful for the subtle way she's letting me know my face is a mess. I tell her where the kit is and let her get on with it. David helps himself to a whisky, puts one in my hand and goes to stand in the corner. Obviously the squeamish type.

'Why don't you make your wife a cup of tea?'

'Um, OK. Where's the, um…'

'Just look for it, David, for heaven's sake.' Snappy. Strange, after he saved her like that. Something's up.

'OK, I'll just….'

'Tea's in the caddie by the kettle, milk's in the fridge and the cups are next to the glasses.'

'Right. Thanks.'

'This is going to be interesting,' she mutters. I feel it best not to respond. Never a good idea to encourage anger in someone who is applying TCP to your face.

She gets a bowl of water from the kitchen, says nothing to him in the process. I watch as she squeezes out tissues and the water changes colour. I feel as if my face is on fire. I hold up my hand to stop her and take a good swig at the whisky. Better.

'Do you live here alone?'

I nod, carefully.

'We'd better come in tomorrow and check up on you.'

I don't object. He's back with the tea. She takes it without a word, winces before she's even tasted it.

'That OK?' I ask innocently.

'Actually, yes. Thanks, David, good to know you can do something in the kitchen. I'll remember.'

He frowns. 'I can do a lot more, if you'd just let me.'

I really don't have the energy for a domestic.

'Jenny here has kindly said you'll come in tomorrow and check up on me.'

He turns to her, though doesn't quite look at her. 'I've got golf at nine with the gang.'

'So, we'll come after that.' The voice is rising again. 'Unless you have an action-packed day planned that you haven't told me about.'

'Why don't you come for lunch?' I suggest. 'Then I can repay your kindness.'

'But will you be able to get things together?' asks David. Interesting, he's the one who's concerned. 'You may not feel too good tomorrow, you know.'

Don't I know it. 'No, that's OK. There's things here I can put together.'

'Look,' David insists, 'we've got plenty of food at home. Always buy too much at Christmas. We'll bring some of our bits and we can pool resources.'

Good sense of self-preservation, this chap. 'That's a deal, then.'

Jenny leans back. 'That's as much as I can do for now. I don't think you'll need any stitches.'

'No, tough old hide.' I force a smile.

She drains the tea, he drains the whisky.

'Now, off you go. And thank you again for all you've done. I'm sure I'll be all right now.' I heave myself out of the chair to see them off.

As soon as they are gone, I'm on the phone. Get Chas to drop in casually tomorrow lunchtime.

Chapter 6 – December 26th 11.15pm

Barry

It's still raining.

It's still raining and I'm getting wet.

It's still raining, I'm getting wet and it's Christmas.

Oh, tidings of comfort and bloody joy.

OK, it's Boxing Day but it's still the Christmas break. For some. For just about everyone, in fact, except Muggins here and a few key workers. And the shop assistants doing the sales. And the bus drivers. And the tube, I suppose. OK, quite a lot actually but they're all probably back home, indoors, warm and dry by now. Not out patrolling the streets, keeping the world safe for humanity. Or something.

This isn't what I signed up for. I wanted computers and fast cars and solving complicated problems, frauds and such. There's enough of them about, after all.

'Family men get first bite at Christmas,' that's what the desk sergeant said. What he didn't say was, 'Tough shit, Barry, you're going to be on foot patrol all through the festives.' Foot patrol. When I could be at home playing Grand Theft Auto. OK, not the ideal game for a young(ish), upwardly mobile(ish) policeman. But better than this.

Bloody streets are deserted now anyway. What is the point? Another forty-five minutes of this before I can head back. Now, decisions, decisions. Along Upper Street or down Worthington Way. Both dismal, both dark, no doubt both smelling vaguely of vomit. Upper Street, I think, see if there's more graffiti added to that wall by Boots. No, maybe not. Worthington Way, check if anyone's tried to set fire to the Job Centre again. Or maybe…

Hell fire, Barry, just get on with it. You're a policeman. Supposed to make decisions.

Still, at least something happened. That old guy, Johnson, I've heard his name a good few times around the station. He's like some mantra, some evocation of a glorious rule-free past – Bill Johnson wouldn't have put up with this, Bill Johnson would sort that his own way, that sort of thing. I can see why.

What would the glorious Bill Johnson say if he knew I'd stood back and watched him being beaten up? He wouldn't be impressed, that's for sure. That woman seemed to know, the way she was looking at me. And her husband, there was something shifty about him. Not sure what that was all about; I'll check it all again tomorrow.

Bugger, didn't get their names. Just have to take potluck with Johnson, and hope he knows. I know just how he will look at me.

Cressida

Gosh, it's difficult talking to your boss when you're naked.

Thank God we're not FaceTiming. Usually Dominic's preferred form of communication. 'See the whites of their eyes.' I think you need to be switched to it at each end to make it work. I hope so.

Nicky wanted me to ignore the call. I can see his point, it's still Christmas holidays and we have just had the morning in bed. But we'd done all the good stuff; now that I've shown him all my important little places he's pretty good, and we were into the comfortable snuggling bit. To be honest, I was ready to get on with something else. Though the idea of tackling the last of the dishes from yesterday is far from enticing. Seemed to go well, though, the Christmas meal. Jenny looked as though she was enjoying it and that's important. Always get on the right side of the mother. And she's sharper than she looks. Better than that dreadful session with my lot on Christmas Day. Lunch with my mother rates about the same level as having your toenails extracted to the sound of Wagner. And once Daddy established that Nicky knew nothing about golf or stocks and shares, that was him staring out of the window for three hours.

'Cressida, I need you in the office tomorrow.' No 'how was your Christmas, sorry to disturb'. That's what I like about Dominic, no messing about.

'What time?' Nicky's reaching across, stroking my bottom. I don't stop him.

'Ten o'clock. We need to get everything organised for the youth rally on Thursday.'

Nicky's hand is creeping up and round. I try to keep my voice as steady as possible. 'I thought that was all under control.'

'It's got to be perfect. We need to go over all the detail.'

'OK. I'll be there.' Nicky is nibbling at my neck.

'Right, I'll let you get back to that hunky boyfriend of yours.'

My God, he can see us. Or maybe just a good guess.

He laughs. 'Judging by the silence, I seem to be clairvoyant. See you tomorrow, if you can still walk.'

I ring off and turn to Nicky. 'You are a very naughty boy and you are going to have to pay for that.'

He grins. Men are so easy to please.

Chapter 8 – December 27th 11.45am

David

That's better, blown away the old cobwebs. Nothing like a round in the morning to get everything working properly again. Shame I had to slip away so quickly, though, to get back to that old boy.

Still, duty calls. Not such a bad old stick, I suppose. What a palaver that was, though. Still think Jenny was crazy to take them on like that. Tried to explain on the way home but she wasn't having it. Talked to the guys about it this morning and they agreed. Funny thing was, none of them seemed very surprised at Jenny doing something like that. Wonder why.

Didn't tell the lads the other bit, though. Doesn't do to talk about that sort of thing. Not at our age. But, gosh, she was, well, there's no other word for it, just incredibly randy when we got home. Didn't know what hit me. Lucky I stopped at just the one whisky, really. No mention of it this morning, though. With it being a bit of a rare occurrence, you'd think... Never going to understand women.

Anyway, here we are, trekking back into Queen's Park again, with a boot full of goodies. I don't begrudge it. What else would we have done with the day? That's the trouble with the bit after Christmas. It's OK, I suppose if you've got loads of kids around, or if it's part of your precious holiday allowance. But for us, well, one day's very like another. I think Jenny's a bit bored. Probably am myself, if I'm honest. Never thought that would happen. We'll plan another holiday. That'll help.

Silence getting a bit heavy. Start the conversation. 'I wonder how he'll be today.'

'Mm.'

Had hoped for a bit more of a response, to be honest.

Try again. 'Could have been a lot worse, I suppose. Must have a solid skull.'

Nothing.

We're driving past the spot where it all happened. Wonder how that lad is they took off in the ambulance. Hope he's OK. Or do I? Not sure, really.

Jenny glances over to me. 'Look, thank you for coming to my rescue yesterday.' I shrug. 'I mean, I'm not saying I was wrong to do what I did but it could have got nasty. So, anyway, thanks.'

I decide to take the olive branch. 'You're welcome. I think you were right too, for what it's worth. And I couldn't just leave you to it, could I? Not ready to lose you just yet.'

'Aren't you?' The question is sharp but, when I look across, there's a small smile. Dangerous territory though, we'll be into the whole relationship discussion in a minute.

'No. Oh, look,' I add quickly, 'we're here.' I turn into the road. In the daylight, his house looks a littler tattier. Still quite imposing, big house on a policeman's salary, I'd have thought, but who knows? Maybe he had an inheritance or something.

He's at the door, talking to an Indian chap. I guess there's a lot round here. There's a lot everywhere. Certainly in banking now. The Asian invasion, they call it. Probably what did for me.

Jenny's out of the car and up the path almost before I've stopped. I start to pull the cold boxes out of the boot. As I join them, the Indian man is talking.

'It's a scandal. It really is. Of course, it used to be us. Still is occasionally.'

Bill interrupts. 'And this is my other rescuer, David. David, Mr Patel, my neighbour.'

A soft handshake from him. 'Karan.'

I look at him blankly.

'Karan, my name.'

'Ah, er, David. But you know that. Sorry.'

He ploughs on. 'I was just saying to your wife that these attacks really are a scandal. No one seems to be doing anything about it. And that dreadful Dominic Evans fellow, inciting them the way he does.'

'Well,' I reply, 'I don't have much time for him myself – don't have much time for any politician, frankly – but I don't think he's actually inciting anyone. We know someone who works for him, says he's jolly bright.'

'Then whoever it is should be putting strychnine in his tea. Believe me, my parents went through this with Enoch Powell. It's all part of a plan.'

I feel it's time to change the subject. 'How are you feeling, Bill?'

'Like I've been beaten up by five youths. My heart aches and a drowsy numbness pains my sense, but I'll live.'

Jenny looks up. 'Keats?'

'Another aficionado! Excellent.'

'Ode to a Nightingale,' Jenny says. 'It was my favourite at school. Just right for spotty teenage angst.'

So, how is it that I never knew that? She's barely met this man and he's finding stuff out about her. Time to intervene.

'Well, shall we take the goodies in? It's getting on towards lunchtime. Good to meet you, er, Mr Patel.'

'Karan. Good to meet you too. You look after him, now.'

I nod and we head into the house. 'Where do you want everything?'

Bill looks around. 'I thought we would make it special and eat in the dining room, through there, on the right.'

I head into the room, where the table is laid and a fire is burning in the grate. Nice table, too. Looks antique. Definitely inheritance. I start to unload everything while Jenny busies herself checking up on him and his injuries. I hear them talking.

'So, Jenny, what's your opinion about all these attacks?'

'Worrying, to be honest. I mean, we're fairly immune out where we are. At the moment, at least. But you do wonder where it will all end.'

'It will end where we let it end.'

'How do you mean?'

'Well, do we just let it happen, stand silent like stout Cortez on his peak in Darien, or do we do something about it?'

I'm beginning to feel that they're speaking some kind of secret language. I call out. 'Bill, where do I find serving plates?

He comes into the room. 'I'm sorry, we're leaving you to do all the hard work. There's plates in the sideboard there. This all looks wonderful. I've got some cheeses and a salad in the fridge. I'll get them out, then we can feast.'

'Sounds good. Are you up to some wine?'

'Absolutely. Ambrosia of the Gods.'

'I think you'll like this.' I uncork the St Emilion. I may not know about poetry but I do know about wine.

Chapter 9 – December 27th 1.45pm

Bill

They live well, these two. Going to have to burst them out of their comfortable little cocoon.

'Well,' I say, 'That was a veritable feast. I always thought goose was really fatty but you've cooked it to perfection.'

Jenny knows how to take a compliment. The head nods in response. 'Thank you, Bill. It's all in the speed of roasting. I can give you the recipe if you're interested.'

I hold my hands up in mock surrender. 'While I pride myself on not being totally incompetent in the kitchen, I don't think I'm quite up to this. Not just yet. Anyway, with just me, there'd be a hell of a lot of leftovers.'

She looks at me, the way only women dare to, full emotional connection, leans in. 'Is this your first Christmas on your own?' The voice has dropped from sprightly sax to mellow clarinet.

'Second. Though, to be honest, last year's went by in a bit of a blur. Mary, my wife, she died in November, so it was all a bit raw. Anyway, how did you know I wasn't just a crusty old bachelor?'

She laughs. Nice sound. 'This isn't the home of a bachelor. Too soft.'

Good, observant too. I start to reel them in.

'I was due to spend this year with Gerry Smith, an old pal of mine, we were in the police together. But he was attacked last Wednesday.'

'Attacked?' David chimes in, puts down his wine glass. Got him.

'Yes, not far from where you came to my rescue, in fact. Nearer the Market Place. Five or six of them cornered him.

Unlike my lot, unfortunately, they were the real thing. Probably shouting slogans as they put the steel-toed boots in. You know the stuff, Kill the Parasites, Ditch the Rich, all that deathless prose. As if Gerry could be described as rich, on a copper's pension.'

'Bloody outrageous.' I'm guessing he has a blood pressure problem, or maybe it's just the wine. 'Where are the police when you need them, eh?' He looks suddenly embarrassed and stares at the empty plate in front of him. I let the silence hang for a moment as she glares at him.

'It's OK, David's right. It's not like it was before the crunch. You hear it on the news every day. The police do what they're told now and my guess is that they have been told that this is not a priority for them.'

'But that's awful,' Jenny cries. 'How is your friend?'

I have an image from yesterday evening of the inert body, almost invisible behind tubes and bandages. I shrug. 'Time will tell. I don't think he'll be dancing again. Mind you, he was always a bloody awful dancer.'

They laugh, relieved that the atmosphere is eased. The doorbell rings. Right on time.

'I wonder who that can be. Do excuse me.'

I open the door. There is Chas, wrapped in leather, short grey hair immaculately brushed, as always, grinning at me.

'Bloody hell, William. You've been in the wars, my old mate.' I lead him in. He follows, preceded by a bow wave of aftershave. He does the double-take. 'I'm sorry. I didn't realise you had company.'

'Chas, this is Jenny and David, my rescuers from last night. Jenny, David, this is Chas, a friend and business associate.' I feel a discreet dig in the ribs.

'Well, if you're the guys who got Bill out of his little bit of bother, I'm delighted to meet you. We need more of your sort around nowadays.'

Everyone shakes hands. I see David wince; Chas must have given him one of his bone crushers.

'Do sit down, Chas. I was just telling them about Gerry.'

Chas sits and reaches for the wine bottle, carefully checking the label. 'Ah, yes. I called the hospital just now, on my way over. No change, not yet. Nice wine. You bring this, Dave?'

'Well, yes, actually.' I enjoy watching him swell up under the laser of Chas's charm offensive. 'Got it from my local man. I can give you the –'

Jenny starts to rise from her chair. 'Well, perhaps I'd better start clearing –'

'Not a bit of it,' I interrupt. 'I'll do it all later. I've plenty of time for that.' Don't want her slipping away. Not now.

'So, Chas,' I ask, 'how was your Christmas?'

'Oh, good. Great, in fact.' He goes to the sideboard and pulls out glass. 'Had the grandchildren round, all six of them. Riot. Stayed home yesterday just enjoying the silence. Usual sermon from the son and daughter about sharing the money, of course. Told them they'd already had a good chunk, plus a business each and that would have to do. Bit of an atmosphere.'

Jenny straightens up. 'Yes, we had a similar discussion, with our son. It's a tricky one, isn't it? I mean, I know we have been a lucky generation, living through the boom times and all that, but, on the other hand, you can't spoon feed them.'

'Too right.' Chas is warming to his theme. 'When I was their age, I was working all the hours that God gave to get started, and some He didn't. Taking any work that came my way.'

Jenny is nodding hard. I get the feeling that hers was not an easy route either. Good.

Chas swirls the wine round the glass, then takes a drink. Nods his approval.

'Nice.'

David beams even more.

'Then with the big wobble a few years back,' Chas ploughs on, 'it looked as if it was all going to go in a puff of smoke, didn't it? Well, what we've got has been hard won, and I for one am not about to throw it away, not even to my own kith and kin.'

My turn. 'Yes, and these kids seem to think that they can just take it off us. If it's not attacks on the street, it's money disappearing from accounts. Glad to see they've pulled in some of those banking crooks, though there's a lot more where they came from. They're all at it. And that bugger, pardon me, Jenny, Dominic Evans, behind them, getting everyone excited. Did I hear you say you knew someone in his office, David?'

David seems to wake up. 'My, our son's partner, female partner, that is, works for Evans. She says he's a very hardworking MP. I think people are a bit harsh about him. You can't say that Evans is behind the banking scandals, can you?'

I concentrate on staying calm. Someone in Evans' office would be the ultimate prize. 'Really? Well, I'm sure he's hard working but what's he working hard at? Are you telling me that you've found a politician who's not looking to climb the greasy pole?'

'Well, no, wouldn't go that far. I mean, we all know they're a bunch of shysters, don't we? It's just, I mean, well, I'm sure he's not … I mean, I've never felt threatened by anything he says.'

I see Jenny looking at him, that straight look that I used to get from Mary whenever I was talking bollocks.

'What do you think about him, Jenny?'

She pauses, then her words are measured. 'I think that he is using the situation to rise up the ranks and eventually take over his confused and God-forsaken party. Or maybe start his own. I think he sees all the resentment of the undereducated and underemployed and he gives their thuggery a legitimacy that hasn't been seen since Moseley in the thirties. In short, I think he's a complete shit, even by the standards of politicians.'

Chas claps loudly. 'Well said, girl. I for one don't want to be categorised as, what was his phrase last week, a "doddering drain on society". I would dearly like to punch him in his far too pretty face.'

I look at David. 'David, think we're being unfair?'

'Well, yes, to be honest.' Quiet snort from Jenny. 'He has said some things that could have been open to misinterpretation, which is silly of him but I think it's more cock-up than conspiracy. I mean, you're not suggesting he runs these gangs, are you, or organises the bank swindles?'

'No,' I respond. 'He's keeping his distance from all that. He's far too clever to have any connection showing. Anyway, my point is this…' Time for the close. 'As far as I'm concerned, this has all gone too far. I refuse to feel that I daren't go out. I refuse to allow people to play around with my hard-earned money without telling me. And there are a lot who think like me. So, tell me, do you think I'm just being an old moaner or do you think I'm right?'

David and Jenny look at each other. He's looking confused, she's looking excited. She speaks first.

'When you say that there's a lot who think like you, what do you mean?'

'Just that. A lot, and ready to fight back.'

'Are you suggesting,' David butts in, 'That a bunch of oldies are going to go out and pick fights with these young thugs?' He looks from me to Chas. We look back. He bursts out laughing. 'It's absurd. I'm sorry, but this really has gone too far. There's nothing seriously wrong here, just a few local skirmishes.'

'A few local skirmishes,' Jenny interrupts dangerously softly, 'that landed Bill's friend and a couple of hundred more in hospital right across the country. And that's not what you were saying yesterday.'

The doorbell rings again. I'm not expecting anyone else. Bad timing. I excuse myself and answer it. There, on the doorstep, is the useless young policeman from last night.

Chapter 10 – December 27th 2.15pm

David

Well, my mind is reeling. One minute, a perfectly pleasant conversation after a damned good meal, the next we're planning street battles. They are, not me. No, not me. And now he's here, that Barry Whatever chap. Don't know where to look. Sooner we're out of here, the better. He's looking pretty puzzled too.

Bill breaks the ice. 'David, Jenny, you remember the constable from last night. I'm sorry, lad, I forget your name.

'Carolson, sir, and it's Sergeant Carolson.' He looks a bit peed off. So would I be, being demoted like that.

'Sorry, son, must have been the bumps on the head. Oh, and this is Chas.' A curt nod from Chas, who backs away into a corner. 'Anyway, *Sergeant*,' slightly unnecessary emphasis from Bill, 'what can we do for you?'

'Well, sir, it's good that you are all here, actually, as I was going to ask you if you had this other gentleman's contact details.'

He nods at me. Uncomfortable.

'Yes, you see, sir,' the sergeant continues. Bit of dramatic effect going on here, clearly knows he's got something juicy to share and wants to make the most of it. 'You see, the young man who was injured last night, a…' he consults his notebook. '… Mr Sean Delling, died this morning in hospital.'

Oh, shit. I feel winded, as if he has punched me in the stomach. I look across at Jenny, who is staring wide-eyed at him. She won't catch my eye. A feeling like an electric current runs through me. Clasp hands together to stop them from shaking. How could this have happened? I was doing the right thing, for God's sake.

Bill is looking politely concerned. 'I'm very sorry to hear that. In what way can I help you?'

'Well, sir, you may recall your advice to me that I report it as an unwitnessed traffic accident.'

'Sorry, no. Bit of a blank on that conversation.'

'Well, you did.' He sounds like Nick when he was a kid. 'Sir. You suggested it would save a lot of paperwork.'

'Really?' Bill's eyebrows rise in innocent surprise.

'Well, I took your advice,' the sergeant ploughs on. 'Only now, of course, things are a bit different.' He looks across at me. 'Are you all right, sir? You look pale.'

'What? No, no, I'm fine thanks, absolutely fine. Tickety boo. Probably just a bit of post-Christmas overindulgence catching up. You know how it is.'

'Not really, sir, I've been working all Christmas.'

Wouldn't you bloody know it? A martyr.

'I'm sorry to hear that. Though good to know we can sleep safe in our beds, ha ha ha.'

That seemed to come out a bit loud. Everyone is looking at me. I can feel the blood rushing to my face. Feel like a schoolboy caught pinching sweets from the tuck shop.

'I'll just clear some dishes,' I cry and jump up and gather up some plates. Some bread and meat spill onto the table. I head as nonchalantly as I can towards the kitchen, feeling gravy drip down my sleeve. I find myself starting to hum softly and stop immediately. The constable turns back to Bill as I go out.

'So, sir, coming back to what we were saying. Clearly, I have to investigate this carefully and ascertain as many facts as I can.'

I peer back in and see that Bill's nodding in a fatherly way. 'Inspector Williamson been on your back, then, son?'

'No, sir.' His moon face has gone bright red. He turns towards me. 'I wonder if you'd mind rejoining us, sir.' I move back reluctantly, find I still have the plates in my hand and put them down on the sideboard.

'Now, sir, would you be kind enough to tell me what you saw.'

'What I saw?' I reply. 'How do you mean?'

'How the young man, Mr Delling, came to be knocked down.'

'Knocked down? Um, no, can't say I can help you on that, officer. No, um, didn't see a thing.' I look across at Jenny but she's giving me the poker face. Can't tell what she'd want me to say.

The policeman, Carlson, or whatever he's called, is staring at me. 'Are you sure you don't remember more than that, sir?'

'Sure. We were concerned with helping Bill here, weren't we, dear?' I turn to Jenny for rescue. She is looking at her fingernails. The pause seems to go on forever.

'That's right,' she finally chips in, 'our concern was to stop the attack on Bill, so I suppose we were all facing that way.'

Now the policeman's eyebrows go up. 'I see. And the fact that your car was on a pedestrianised area had nothing to do with it.'

Jenny frowns at him. 'I don't know what you're implying, officer, but if you're suggesting that we somehow attacked this boy, I find that very offensive.'

He recoils under Jenny's attack; most people do. 'Not at all, madam. I mean, sometimes things happen in the rush of the moment, unintentionally, so to speak. No-one's fault.'

A heavy silence hangs in the room like a fart at a wedding, as my old Uncle Gerald used to say. Eventually, Bill speaks.

'Well, that seems to have covered the ground. Was there anything else we could do for you, before you go?'

The boy in blue hesitates, takes a deep breath. 'No, I think that will do for now, but I will need your details; I'm sure there will be further questions at a later date.' He's staring at me while he says this. I look nonchalant, give him my name, address and phone number.

'Right then,' Bill stands and moves to the door. After a moment, thingummy follows. Bill closes the door behind him.

Chas winks at me. 'Well, David, my son,' he whispers, 'I think he's got you deep in the doo-doo.'

'What? No, I thought I saw him off quite well.'

'Did you? Well, far be it for me to disillusion you.'

'Jenny, what did you think?'

The straight look. Oh, God. 'What do I think? I think that you might have done better if your face hadn't been the colour of a surprised beetroot.'

'Well, you try being interviewed by the police. It's not what I'm used to. And may I remind you, by the way, that I was actually saving you at the time.'

Bill comes back in. He grins across at me but the eyes are hard. I can imagine what it must have felt like to have had your collar felt by him. He knows I need his co-operation.

'Well, David,' his voice is soft and calm, 'looks as if you're involved whether you want it or not. Welcome to the Old Buggers' Brigade.'

Chapter 11 – December 27th 2.45pm

Barry

Bugger, bugger, bugger. What a cock up. The Inspector's going to have my guts on this one. Bang goes any chance of CID now. It's clear as daylight what happened. I saw it, for heaven's sake, but with them all sticking together…

Why? Why stick together? I suppose the old man's grateful for being saved and doesn't want to drop them in it. I'll check back with him when he's on his own. Policeman to policeman, see if I can get him to change. Fat chance. At least I've got their contact details now.

And who was that other guy? I'm sure I've seen him somewhere before.

Radio's going. Better answer it. Can't pretend I'm not here.

'Carolson.'

'Hey, Baz. How's it going?' Alan Jones. Sergeant Alan Jones. Professional Welshman and pain in the butt. They should put immigration controls on the Severn Bridge.

'Hi, Taff.' He hates that.

'Williamson wants to know what you've got on the Delling case. I think he's in a hurry.'

'I'm on my way. Should be back in about twenty.'

'Want to give me a heads up?'

'No, I'll be there soon enough.' And I'm not telling you, you little toad, not having you running to sir.

Chapter 12 – December 27th 4.30pm

Jenny

'David, it is not a stupid idea and watch where you're driving.' Even after a couple of glasses he's all over the place.

'Jenny.' Funny how married people only use the partner's name when they're cross with them. 'These people are crazy, cracked, loopy. What do they think they will achieve? They can't win. They're just going to get beaten into oblivion.'

'They're getting beaten into oblivion anyway.'

'Don't exaggerate. A few random attacks. Hardly oblivion.'

'A few random attacks? Couple of hundred a month, call it a few if you like. A few marches and demos in the big cities, with more to come. You're right, David, it could be all random, coincidence. But what if it's not? What if there's a pattern here?'

'Conspiracy theories. You'll be telling me next that the Americans never landed on the moon and that Elvis is still alive and working in Sainsbury's.'

There are times, increasingly frequently, when I would just love to stick a skewer up his arse.

'OK, you do what you want. Carry on going to the golf club with your buddies, drinking your St bloody Emilion. But I'm following this up.'

He glances over to me. It's not a look I see often, worried, vulnerable. 'Are you very bored with me?' He sounds like a little boy who's been told he's failed his spelling test. Poor sod, having to put up with me.

I take a deep breath. 'No, David, it's not that. Of course I'm not.' I'm lying; I wonder why. 'It's just that, I think I need something to get my teeth into. You know, I don't want to be just wandering around the house for the rest of my life, however long that might be, being cook and gardener.'

'We've got a gardener.'

'Exactly. I can't even do that. I just need something bigger than Pinner, frankly.'

'Well, there's plenty you could do. The W.I. are always looking for people and, with your organising skills, you could get that Oxfam shop really buzzing.'

I suppress a shudder. I'm sure he means well. 'But, don't you see, David, This matters. It's important.'

'You mean *if* it's important, if there's a real problem, if that man Bill is not just a crazy old copper with too much time on his hands, if there's even something you could do. That's what you mean.'

'Don't tell me what I mean. I have a brain and I can work these things out for myself, thank you very much. I'm going back tomorrow and that's that.'

'Fine. Good luck to you. I'll be at the golf club.'

Silence hangs like a metal wall between us. David crashes the gears at the next roundabout, swears. It surprises me. I realise how rarely he swears. I've become adept at judging the depth of his anger from the size of the sigh, the set of the shoulders, how long he will stare at a television screen. Are we going to end up as a doddery old couple shouting obscenities at each other from either side of the kitchen? Are we going to end up as a doddery old couple at all?

We turn into our driveway. Straight away it's clear there's something wrong. The security lights don't come on. The front door's slightly ajar. He sees it too. Stops the car. Turns off the engine and the lights. We sit in silence. Then he sighs, undoes his seatbelt.

'Wait here.' He starts to get out.

'David, wait.' I put my hand on his arm. 'I don't think you should go in. Maybe we should call the police.'

'Don't worry, you're just spooked by the conversation this afternoon. It'll be fine.'

He climbs out before I can say anything else, gives me a little smile. It's not reassuring.

'Be careful,' I whisper, though I don't think he hears. I watch him as he walks almost casually across the drive. Goes to the door and, after a moment's hesitation, eases it open. Disappears inside.

I wait. Can't wait. Can't just sit here. Climb out my side. Round the back of the car. Edge towards the door. Funny how I was so brave yesterday and so scared today. A shout. Noises. I move towards the door. I can feel my heart trying to get out through my ribs.

Two men burst out. I'm sent flying against the big flowerpots in front of the house. Crash down, everything falling around me. Soil on my face. I'm coughing, spluttering. Footsteps running away. Silence.

I get onto all fours. Wait till my vision clears. Specs have gone flying but I can see enough. Up with the help of the door jamb. Into the hall, find the light switch.

David's on the floor, face down. Creeping towards me across the well-polished parquet is a pool of bright blood.

Chapter 13 – Dec 27th 4.45pm

Barry

That hurt. Inspector Williamson certainly knows how to put the boot in.

'So, let me get this right, lad.' Lad, one word but overflowing with meanings; wet behind the ears, gullible, stupid. 'Let me get this right. So far, we have a dead body, one Sean Delling, who appears to have been knocked down by a phantom car, since no car existed at the scene, otherwise you would have reported something last night. And you didn't report anything last night, am I right?'

I shake my head. Bugger that old man and his condescending advice.

'We also have a man beaten up, an old pal of mine, as it happens, except that he clearly wasn't beaten up as you did not report any such incident.'

'He requested that I did not do so.'

'Did he? He requested it, did he? So, if a man's house burns down and he requests you not to report it, you wouldn't? If a girl jumps off a high building and, on the way down, requests you not to report it, you would comply? Am I right?'

'No, sir. Though, to be fair, those are not really parallel cases.'

'Aren't they? Thank you for correcting me on a point of law. I bow to your greater knowledge. And I certainly would hate to be unfair to you.'

'No, sir, sorry, sir.'

'Carolson, you're an idiot. And, worse than that, you're a lazy idiot. Now, give me one good reason why I shouldn't take you off this straight away and give it to Taff Jones.'

'No, sir, I'm sure that won't be necessary. I know what happened, sir. I just need to trap the assailant.'

'Is that the assailant that beat up Bill Johnson or the assailant that killed Sean Delling?'

'Delling, sir.'

'Tell me more.'

'When Mr Jones was attacked, sir, he was rescued by a couple, a Mr and Mrs Belsworth.'

'Who the hell are they?'

'They just happened to be passing and got stuck in.'

'Did they indeed? Go on.'

'Well, sir, it is my belief that Delling was struck by Mr Belsworth's car.'

'I see. And what evidence do you have for this Holmes-like conclusion? Did you see this happen?'

Stay calm. He's just guessing. 'No, sir, as I have told you, I came to the scene after the event.'

'Hm. And have you discussed this with Mr Belsworth?'

'Yes, sir. They were at Mr Johnson's house today. He seemed very shifty, Mr Belsworth, that is, not Mr Johnson.'

'Ladies and gentlemen of the jury, this man is clearly guilty of this crime and probably several others because he seems a bit shifty. You'll have to do better than that, lad.'

'Let me check the car, sir. See if there are any traces.'

He stares at me. Making sure he's got his arse covered, no doubt.

'I'll give you twenty-four hours, then it's with Jones.'

So, first thing tomorrow it's out to the suburbs with forensics, see what I can get from that fat cat Volvo he was driving.

I reckon I've got him cornered.

Chapter 14 – Dec 27th 9.00pm

Cressida

'We got the call about seven thirty this evening. My boyfriend, Nicky, that's him sitting over there with his mum, Nicky Belsworth, one L, he took the call.' I look across at the policewoman who is nodding away, trying to combine sympathy and efficiency in one nod, then look across the waiting room at the two forlorn figures opposite.

I think back to that moment. Hardly need to think back; it's not going to go away. We're in the sitting room, watching some slushy film. Phone rings. Then he's standing there, looking at me, as if he's trying to get something to me telepathically. Eyes wide out of this deathly pale face. I've always heard people talk about the colour draining from someone's face but I'd never actually seen it until I looked across at Nicky. He's talking into the receiver but looking at me.

'Are you OK?' 'We'll be right there.' I'm desperate by now, trying to understand what's happening. He puts down the phone.

'What?'

'It's mum. They've had break-in. Dad's been hurt.'

I grab my coat, find the car keys and we are out within thirty seconds.

No need to tell this policewoman all that. None of her business, frankly. I'll just give her the facts then she can get on with her job.

She's talking to me. I try to tune back in.

'Sorry, what?'

'What did you find when you got to the house?'

'By the time we got there, the ambulance had collected Mr Belsworth. There was a lot of blood on the hall floor and there was the writing on the walls. It seemed to have been sprayed on. You know, with those paint cans.'

No need to mention that Nicky threw up when he saw it all.

'Did you see what it said?'

'Well, we were hardly going to stand around and read it, were we? We had to get here.'

She takes a breath. I watch as her training works against her desire to snap at me.

'What I mean, madam, is did anything strike you? Do you remember any particular words?'

'No. Sorry. Mrs Belsworth had left a note for us to follow. Seems she couldn't find her phone at the critical moment. Understandable, I suppose.'

Still, not too clever, in the circumstances.

The policewoman nods again. 'I'm sure Mrs Belsworth will remember.'

'I don't want you talking to her at the moment. Not while her husband's having emergency surgery.

'Well, the quicker we can get onto this, the more chance we have of finding who did it.'

I look at her insistent face. 'Tell me, what are the statistics of you finding the perpetrators of something like this? Fifty to one? A hundred to one? You're not going to find who did it. You might as well wait. Anyway, you've got people at the house now.'

Clearly wants to get one up on the others, find the magic clue. She knows she's been rumbled. She puts away her notebook.

'By the way,' she says, 'does the name Delling mean anything to you?'

I see Jenny's head jerk up. So does she. 'Delling? No, I don't think so. Why?'

'Oh, nothing. Just that it's the name written all over the walls of the house.' She stands up. 'Perhaps I will have a quick word with Mrs Belsworth.'

Chapter 15 – December 27th 9.30pm

David

Where the hell am I?

Trapped.

I should be on the golf course. They'll be waiting for me.

Strapped in, falling.

If I can just get this thing off me.

Bells ringing.

They're pushing me back. Where's Jenny?

Ouch, that hurt.

Sleepy.

Getting darker.

Chapter 16 – December 27ᵗʰ 11.00pm

Jenny

They won't let me go home. 'It's a crime scene,' that policewoman said. She seemed rather proud of the fact. It's not, it's my home. She doesn't understand. The one place anyone wants to be with something like this is home, among the familiar things. Be able to walk around and touch stuff. Pretend it's all normal.

Not so normal, I suppose, at the moment. All that paint everywhere, like seeing an old friend slashed across the face. And that blood. David's blood. Oh, God. Yes, God, I've been talking to you a lot in the last few hours. We'll see if you've been listening.

You look at someone normally and they seem so whole, so, I don't know, impermeable. The system works, they move, talk, stand up, sit down, eat, fart, whatever. Then someone does something to them, breaks the machine. One hole and everything stops working. All the other bits are fine but the whole thing closes down.

And they won't let me see him. It seems they have to keep infection away. Never thought of myself as infection.

It's like with Mum. She'd only gone down to the corner for some milk. 'Stop squabbling and get on with your homework,' she yelled at me and Harry. And the door slammed shut. Next thing there's Joe from No. 23 hammering on the glass panes in the front door. 'Stay here,' shouts Dad and then he's gone. Harry runs upstairs to see what's happening from the top window. Says there's people gathering at the end of the street, some van sideways on across the pavement.

At least then we were at home. I remember how we sat together in the kitchen that night, people coming and going, talking softly to Dad and looking at Harry and me as if we were drowned kittens.

But they wouldn't let me see her either. Nothing about infection. Just wouldn't let me. For years I kept expecting her to come back in through the door, shake the rain off her hair the way she did. 'Sorry it took me so long, love. Dreadful queue.'

Is David going to walk back in through the door? 'Sorry I'm late, dear, ran into Jack at the clubhouse.' Not quite the same. I want to be back behind my front door. I want to go home.

Found myself thinking about Christmas Day, only two days ago. Seems so much more. Her parents, Cressida's, got them then. While David and I sat at home. I cooked goose. Tried to make it special. He chose a fine wine. And drank most of it. I refused to do crackers and silly hats. Think that would have made me cry. And David doesn't like that. Always that rabbit look of panic. 'No need for waterworks, love. The world isn't ending.' I remember thinking, that's because it already has. Not with a bang, no certainly not a bang. Not a whimper either. Did you whimper, David and I didn't hear you?

Well, David, maybe you'll allow a little waterworks now. Not ready yet, though. Strange, when there's plenty of reason. You cry over a broken cup but when something like this comes along, dry eyes.

'Delling.' That's what that policewoman said. He was that boy, the one that David hit. What was his first name? Wonder if he's got a mum somewhere. How would I feel if it were Nick?

Poor Nick. He looked so shocked. I can understand him being sick. That hall was his refuge, coming back from that dreadful boarding school. I could see he'd been bullied but David was having none of it. 'Good for him. Put some iron in his spine.' Ice in his soul, more like. I'd find him sitting on the stairs on his first days back, curled into where they curved, a book on his lap but not reading, just being there.

Anyway, Cressida's taken charge now. Surprise, surprise.

We're back at the flat and she's making up the sofa bed. I've found my phone again; in my handbag all the time. So they can call me, the hospital. They've promised they will if there's any... well, if necessary.

I've got a brandy in one hand and a hot cup of tea in the other – that hospital tea was so disgusting, you'd think they'd do better, considering what a comfort a good cup of tea can be. I've been instructed to relax.

Maybe they'll let me go home tomorrow.

Chapter 17 – December 28th 9.30am

Cressida

'Cressida, get that pert bottom of yours in here.'

That's the thing about Dominic, he can say things that no-one else would get away with. I go into his office. Andy Woodham is sitting there too, leering as usual. He soon learned that there were things I'd put up with from Dominic that I would not put up with from anyone else. A firm slap to put him back in his basket. Being short and round didn't improve his chances anyway. But he's a good speechwriter, to give him his due.

'So,' I get the full Dominic Evans grin, which means that something outrageous is coming. 'Good of you to climb off your exhausted boyfriend for a few hours. He phoned to thank me for bringing you in, by the way.'

Andy titters. I decide enough is enough. 'Where do you want to start?' Andy titters again, then stops suddenly as he realises that things have moved on.

'The arena. Is the speaker system up to it?'

'The Foo Fighters played there a month ago. I went and heard every word.'

'They would have brought their own system. Check it out. We are going to have two and a half thousand cheering people there. I want to be heard. And on the subject of cheering, have we peppered the space with our own people to lead them?'

'There's fifty of our core team there.'

'Not enough. Get more. And brief them. They're mostly too stupid to know when to cheer.'

'OK.'

'Placards?'

'Ordered.'

'Saying?'

'The usual. Forty with your name on, twenty "Justice for All" and twenty "Let's Do it".'

'Nice and vague. Good.'

'Anything else?'

'No, not at the moment. Get those things sorted and stay close. Now, Andy, that passage about financial justice stinks, sounds like a manifesto from a building society.'

I realise my moment is over and go back to my desk. This is going to mean bringing in a lot of people from their holidays but fine, it's important.

I was so lucky to get this job. Junior researchers are two a penny in the House. I asked Dominic once what made him chose me. Of course, he cracked some joke about the size of my breasts but then he looked at me and said, 'You were captain of school, weren't you?'

'Yes, why?'

'I bet there were other girls who wanted that post.'

'Well, yes, a few.'

'That's why. You get what you want. So do I.'

I like that. There's so many people round here who are just wishy washy, yes men who do what they're told in the hope that someone will eventually toss them some scrap of a position. Dominic goes for broke. He's like what I've read about Margaret Thatcher. He doesn't care a jot for what other people think; he just goes for it. And he's going to get it. He's onto a great theme here, a real vote catcher. The rest of the party would be mad to ignore him. After the rally, they'll see.

Captain of School. Yes, there were others in the frame, Gill Braithwaite for one. Caught with a spliff in her gym locker. I remember her crying so much she threw up but she couldn't deny the evidence. That did for her chances. It meant that I had to go without my dope for a week but worth the investment. That seems a long time ago now. Only, what, eight years, but so much has happened, what with travelling and university and now this. And Nicky, of course.

Better call Jenny and Nicky after I've got all this done, see if they've been able to get back into Holly Cottage. Poor loves. I've heard of people who could never go back into their house after a break-in. I find that a bit wimpy to be honest but I can understand it. I'd hate the idea of someone going through my things. I'll see if anywhere's open after work and get some flowers to take to the hospital. Not sure if they allow flowers in Intensive Care but if not, Jenny can take them back with her.

Now, on with the work. Time and tide wait for no man, as Daddy says. Or woman.

Chapter 18 – December 28th 10.30am

Bill

No reply from their number. May be nothing, of course, he could be out on the golf course, she could be at the shops. But it's the old copper's instinct; something doesn't feel right. I'd have thought that Jenny would have been on the phone first thing but nothing. It's already half past ten. I'll try her mobile. Don't like doing that normally, no knowing where they are or who's listening but I need to know.

Phone's ringing. Wonder what her ring tone is. Doesn't seem like a Ride of the Valkyrie type.

A male voice answers. 'Hello, er, Jenny Belsworth's phone.'

Something's definitely up. 'Hello, is Jenny there, please? This is Bill Johnson speaking.'

'She's not really taking any calls at the moment.'

Not really? Does that mean she is or she isn't or she's only taking imaginary calls? 'Please tell her it's Bill Johnson. She might want to talk to me.'

Muffled conversation. A hand over the phone. Finally a clatter as it's picked up. 'Hello, Bill.'
The voice sounds twenty years older than the woman I met. 'Jenny, what's the matter?'

'Long story but there were people at the house when we got back yesterday. They stabbed David, he's in Intensive Care, and they'd painted all over the walls. It's to do with that boy. It was his name they painted up.' She's fighting hard to stay calm. Plucky, just as I would expect. No need to make it harder.

'Jenny, listen, I won't bother you any more at the moment. Just give me a call when you want to. You know where to find me.'

'Thanks, Bill. Be sure I'll get back to you. Bye.'

Yes, I'm sure you will, but not for a while. If you needed any further persuading, not that you did, this would be it. 'Just a few local skirmishes,' that's what he said. Well, David, how does it feel to be skirmish?

One more call to make. This one's the Gladiator theme, I know that.

'Chas, it's Bill.'

'Hi, how you feeling today?'

'Better, thanks but listen, I just spoke to Jenny.'

'Good. Is she in?'

'They had a break-in, they were in the house when they got back.'

'Oh.'

'David was stabbed, he's in the ICU.'

'Bugger me.'

'Chas, was this anything to do with you?'

'What? Come on, that's not my style.'

'Well, I know you. Sometimes feel people need a bit more persuading.'

'Come on, Bill. I'm not going to go out of order without telling you.'

'Has been known.'

'Granted, but not this time. She was in the bag anyway and, frankly, he didn't matter.'

'They'd spray painted the name of that boy that Belsworth killed.'

'Well, there you go, then.'

'Things are not always what they seem, Chas.'

'How true, oh master, how true. You seem very concerned about this lass. Has she got under that thick and beaten skin of yours?'

Cheeky sod. Never knows where the line is drawn.

'She's a potentially useful recruit. That's it.'

'Fair enough. So, do you think we have to look for someone else now to take Gerry's place?'

'Let's wait and see. My feeling is she's even more in now because of this.'

'OK. So, what happens now?'

'Business as usual. Get everything ready for the rally.'

Chapter 19 – December 28th 10.45am

Jenny

'What boy?'

'Hm?'

'Mum, what boy? You said something about a boy to that guy on the phone just now. The graffiti.'

'Oh, yes.'

'So, are you going to tell me?'

'No, Nick. Not now.'

'So, who's this Bill guy?'

I look around the waiting room. Cheery paintings on the walls of country scenes and Victorian happy family life fail totally to make the room any more cheerful. Dreary blues and creams, chosen, no doubt, by some psychologist who was paid a fortune to decide that they are restful and calming. Not money well spent.

What do I say to Nick? He deserves to be told something but not too much. Cressida does work for the enemy, after all. I wonder how Bill would handle it and find myself wishing he were here. I have to give Nick something.

'When we left you on Boxing Day, we found that man who phoned, Bill Johnson, by the road. He'd been beaten up, not badly but shaken. We took him to his home,' a twinge of pain from that word; I must, must get back, 'and he kindly invited us back for lunch yesterday as a thank you. I guess he was just phoning to have a chat, the way old people do.'

'Still doesn't explain the boy.'

I wave the question away. In some ways, it's a shame that Nick is not more pushy, but right now it suits me fine.

I change the subject.

'You'll need to phone your sister, tell her what's happened.'

Nick winces. 'I've already tried but you know Fiona. Refuses to have a mobile because they fry your brain. I've left a message at the post office but they say she's away for a couple of days.'

'Well, you've done what you can. Thank you. We'll just have to wait for her to get in touch, I suppose. Any more from the police about the house?'

'Nothing. We'll go round after... well, later if you want.'

'OK, that would be nice. How's Cressida getting on?'

'Haven't heard. To be honest, once she's in that office she's in another world.'

The doctor comes in. God, so young. If he didn't have the white coat I'd be telling him to wash his hands before supper. He's got that face on, the one that says this may be bad news.

'Mrs Belsworth?'

I nod, suddenly unable to talk.

'Shall we sit down?' He guides me to chairs.

I sit. And wait.

'Mrs Belsworth, your husband is still on the critical list and, to be honest, he'll be there for some time. The knife luckily missed most of the vital organs but it caught the spleen. That's why there was so much blood. We had to remove the spleen but that shouldn't have any major long-term effect. It's one of those organs, like the appendix, that we can do without, with a bit of medication.

We got to him just in time, I'd say. It probably helped that he was, is, shall we say a little portly.' He attempts a smile, as do I, just to make him feel less embarrassed. He pauses, then 'However...'

There's always a however in life. It's never, 'here it is, it's great and it's yours'. Always the caveat, the reminder that you're not that special, that life is not created for you to enjoy in any unbridled way.

'However, with this loss of blood his body has gone through serious trauma. It's going to be touch and go for a day or two but, all being well, he should pull through.'

'All being well?'

'Um, yes. We'll be keeping a close eye on him, of course.'

'Of course. Can I see him?'

He hesitates. 'You can see him but I'm afraid it's going to be through glass at this stage. We still can't risk infection. As you know, there's too much of that around in hospitals and we have to be especially careful. OK?'

I nod and he leads us through a maze of corridors, finally coming to a closed door. He motions us inside and we are in a small room with glass down one side. Beyond the glass is a bed with tubes coming out of it in all directions and in the middle of all this is David.

I sit quickly, aware that my legs are giving way. He leaves Nick and me. 'Just follow the signs to the exit when you're ready to go.'

I sit and stare. It is David and it isn't. I can see the floppy hair, the double chin but something is missing. It takes me a while to work it out. Then it comes to me. David is a fidget. He cannot sit still, always jiggling coins or scratching his ears. It's the stillness, the complete stillness. Even asleep on the sofa, as he often was after a session at the Nineteenth Hole, he was still twitching and grunting. But nothing. Just hanging there between life and death. Indecisive as ever.

I send Nick off to get another tea. He understands and goes. What do I feel? I'm really not sure. There are people sitting like this all over the country, looking at the wreckage of their partner but I can draw no strength from that. There's a deep empty feeling in my stomach. Is that pain, loss, love? Or just that I haven't eaten today? I've spent thirty-four years with that inert figure over there and, oh God, I don't know what I feel. I try to remember his voice, his laugh but, for a moment, nothing, nothing comes. Then I see him being quizzed by that policeman at Bill's yesterday; the red face, the voice rising with panic and he's back. Relief fills me and with it, at last, some tears. Not gushing, just there, almost reassuring.

'Hello, David.' I speak aloud, not caring if anyone hears. 'I'm here. And so are you. This is weird, isn't it? Me talking and you listening, for once. I want to say, just want to say I love you.'

I feel better. After so long, there must be some communication between us, some way to get through. Doesn't matter if I do or I don't, always found love a difficult word to define, covers so many different things and so little at the same time. I want to touch him, feel that little lump on the back of his hand where he got hit by a golf club. Even want to smell that slightly sour odour on his breath. Most of all, I want to get out of here, breathe some fresh air.

I say goodbye and open the door. Nick is standing outside, tea in hand. I guess he's been waiting there. I throw the tea in a bin and we head off.

Chapter 20 – December 28th 11.00 am

Barry

'Where the bloody hell do you think you're going?'

The voice seems to come from behind me as I duck under the tape. This is all I need. This day is not going according to plan. And it had started fairly well. A few rounds of Grand Theft Auto last night had buried yesterday's bloody awful experiences and, together with a good if rather short night's sleep, has cleared the brain a bit. I could see exactly how I was going to nail down our Mr David Belsworth. CCTV cameras. I'd just tell him that the whole thing had been filmed and he would crumble like a jelly. Not that jellies crumble. Not that there are any CCTV cameras in that area. But, whatever.

Up to this moment, it had been quite nice to get out of town for a while. People certainly live well round here. Nice peaceful leafy suburbs. Might even end up out here myself one day. Chief Inspector Carolson, with a house to match. Tooling along in a clapped out Fiesta from the pool doesn't quite fit the image, but a man can dream. Well, obviously not.

That's when I turned into his road. Bloody police cordons everywhere. Around his house, Holly Cottage. When is something going to be simple and straightforward for me on this case?

'Yes, you, lad, I'm talking to you.' Again with the lad. I'm twenty-eight, for God's sake. I pause, bent double, then, realising that it probably doesn't look very dignified to be crouching with my bum in the air, straighten up. Bearing down on me is a big man. Not in uniform but definitely a copper. No-one else has shoes that shiny or that big. I've often wondered whether we all became policemen because our feet were big or whether the feet just grew as we qualified.

I've had enough being browbeaten. I stand my ground.

'I'm going to interview Mr Belsworth. He's a suspect in a hit and run.' Hit and stand still actually, but now is not the time.

'No you're not.'

'I am.'

'No.' This conversation really does not seem to be getting anywhere.

'So, OK, give me one good reason why I can't see him.'

'He was stabbed, nearly died, still might. Not sure if that's one or three reasons but it looks like you've had a wasted journey, son.'

I look around now, see the forensics van, people in white coats going in and out of the front door. Then I see the Belsworths' car parked off to one side.

'Not totally wasted. Any objections to my having a good look at the Volvo over there?'

He shrugs. 'As long as you keep out of our way.'

'With pleasure. By the way, do you have any idea who did it?'

Again the shrug. 'You should know by now, son. We don't do this to catch the criminal, just to make it look as if we might.'

'No clues at all, then?'

'Clues? They don't happen in real life. No, just a lot of blood on the floor, all his, I'm guessing and graffiti all over the walls.'

'Graffiti?'

'Yes, some name. Delling. May not even be a name, may be some kind of sexual practice. Fancy a bit of delling, darling…. What?'

He's seen the expression on my face. 'You know, Inspector, I assume it is inspector, we may just have ourselves a clue. Shall we go inside?'

Chapter 21 – December 28th 12.00 noon

Jenny

It's good to be travelling along familiar roads. All those shops and turnings that I was finding so boring suddenly become very reassuring. Sainsbury's, M&S, the Indian restaurant. A whispered ordinariness; God's in his heaven and all's well with the world. Well, not quite. Our own little hiccough in the grand order may not seem too significant by cosmic standards but it's pretty damned significant to us.

I look across to Nick as he drives us carefully through the centre of the town, or rather 'the village', as the locals insist on calling it. He's doing the calm male thing but I can see that little white patch on his cheek and the throb in his neck, which I've seen before in nativity plays, school concerts, rugby matches. The classic Englishman's fear of making a twit of himself.

As we turn into the road, the ordinariness stops. Red and white tape is festooned across the entrance to the drive. It blows and flaps in the bitter December wind looking almost festive. Nick pulls in on the other side of the road, behind a rather battered Panda car. A small knot of people are gathered by the entrance.

'Looks like press,' Nick mutters.

'Yes, and busybodies. I'll bet Mrs Peterson's in there somewhere. Anyway, let's go.'

I pull my coat around me and am out of the car before I have time to think about things. A man with a camera approaches me. Nick moves quickly to put himself between the two of us but he dances round and the flash hits my eyes. A girl comes running over with a notebook.

'Are you acquainted with the family? Did you know the deceased?'

Deceased? I stop in my tracks. Turn on her.

'Do your homework, girl,' I snap. 'I know that it would be so much more exciting for you if there was a dead body but I'm afraid it's just boring old seriously injured. I'd have thought a real reporter would have checked that.'

She blushes. 'Sorry, slip of the tongue.'

I glare at her, breathe deeply to stop my heart pounding. A young uniformed policeman sees the commotion and comes out from behind the barrier. I break away from the flashing camera and move quickly towards him.

'I'm Mrs Belsworth. This is my son Nick. I live here.'

He hesitates then guides me towards the gap in the tape.

As we reach it, another figure steps forward, elderly, wrapped in a tweed coat. She has tears running down her face.

'Mrs B, I come to clean as usual but they not let me in.'

'Consuela, come with me. Let's get away from all these people.' I nod to the policeman. 'She's our cleaner. Been with us for years.' He lets all three of us through.

I look at the drive full of police cars and vans, people I don't know walking in and out of the front door, my front door. I feel like an outsider in my own garden.

'Come round the side,' the policeman pulls gently at my arm. 'We'll go in the back door.'

The garden looks orderly in its winter bareness. A few pots of pansies give off some defiant colour. A short, youngish man in a white overall is standing outside the back door dragging on a cigarette.

I give him a sharp look. 'I hope you're not going to leave that cigarette end on the terrace.'

He looks astonished at me, then dumbly shakes his head.

'She lives here,' explains the young policeman. The other man immediately stands up straight, hiding the cigarette in the palm of his hand. I feel as if I've just been saluted and walk in through the back door to my kitchen.

The washing up from two days ago sits on the draining board. On the other side of the sink, a half-empty coffee cup. The sight of it brings a lump to my throat. I never could persuade David to put his dirties into the dishwasher. On the big pine table is a pile of hamburger cartons and polystyrene coffee cups. The greasy smell of fast food hangs in the air.

Consuela tuts and bustles around, tidying up. She hasn't even taken off her coat. I sit at the table, suddenly very tired. Nick sits beside me.

'I make coffee,' announces Consuela.

'Thank you. That would be lovely.'

A tall man in plain clothes, but obviously a policeman, walks into the room and sits down with me. It feels like an invasion of my space but I say nothing.

'Mrs Belsworth, I'm Inspector Wedley. I'm in charge of the case.'

'How do you do.' I can think of nothing else to say.

Nick chimes in. 'How's it going? Any clues?'

'Potentially, plenty, sir. We need to sift everything but I think we're in with a good chance of finding the perpetrators.'

'That's good.' A silence falls. I look up at the inspector.

'So, was there anything in particular?'

'There was one thing. I'll just ask a colleague of mine to join us.' He jumps up again and disappears through the door to the hall. I catch a glimpse of white overalled activity.

Consuela places the coffee on the table as if she is presenting jewels to the queen.

'Thank you, Consuela. I suppose we had better make some for the inspector.'

She gives a dismissive Spanish jerk of the head and turns back to the sink. I'm not sure if this means that the inspector will get his coffee, albeit begrudgingly, or not.

He reappears and in his wake is the policeman from Bill's yesterday. He does keep turning up, that boy. I feel my heartbeat quicken.

'Hello again, Mrs Belsworth.' He reaches out a hand, which I take.

'Sergeant Carolson, isn't it?' He's pleased that I've remembered. Good. I need to keep him under control. 'My son, Nick, Sergeant. He is kindly acting as chauffeur and shoulder to lean on.'

'How is your husband, Mrs Belsworth?'

'Thank you. He's, well, he's as you would expect after a knife wound.' I find it hard to get the word 'knife' out. 'Not out of danger but heading, we hope, in the right direction.'

'I'm glad. I hope it continues that way.'

Must be careful, I'm starting to warm to this man.

'So, Sergeant, what brings you all the way out here?'

'Well, you do, you and your husband. I actually came out to see him but, obviously…'

'Yes, as you say, obviously.'

'Mrs Belsworth, let me get to the point.'

'That would be nice.'

'I came out here today to check your car. I believed, still believe, that it was the car that struck Sean Delling.'

'You're persistent, I'll give you that. And single-minded.' I sigh. 'And yes, you're right, it was.'

'Mum.' Nick's warning voice.

I shrug. 'Look, your father is lying in intensive care, I'm homeless. It really isn't the time to shadow box any more. Sergeant, it was a complete accident, the boy ran in front of the car as David, my husband, was driving across the square to rescue me.'

'Rescue you?'

'I'd rather foolhardily gone to help Bill Johnson, while all the youths were still kicking him. David saw I was in danger and drove across to whisk me away. As it turned out, that wasn't necessary.'

Consuela walks across, slams down two more coffees, sniffs and withdraws to the sink. From there she watches, arms folded.

'I think those are for you,' I murmur. Carolson picks his up and cups it in his hands. His fingernails are bitten.

'Thank you.' He turns to the inspector. 'There's your link. Now we know where to look for the guys who did this.' He sounds triumphant, far from the beaten down style that I've seen up to now.

The inspector leans in. 'Mrs Belsworth,' he speaks with that condescending voice that shows a certainty in the superiority of male logic over female silliness, 'We believe that the attack on your home and your husband was a revenge attack because of the death of Sean Delling.'

'Well, of course it bloody was,' I glare back at him. 'That much was obvious within five seconds of walking into the house. Is that it? I mean, is that the sum total of your brilliant deduction processes over the last eighteen hours? So what are you going to do about it?' I'm shouting at him and it feels good. 'You know at least who's behind this and probably who did it. So get on with it, for God's sake.'

I expect Nick's restraining hand on my arm but there's nothing. I glance at him and he's nodding vigorously.

The inspector looks queasy. 'I assure you that we have the case in hand. We do have to go through the proper procedures.'

'May I suggest, Inspector,' Nick's quiet voice responds, 'that the proper procedures move rather faster. I have close connections to our MP, which I would be loath to have to use but will, if necessary. So perhaps this would be a time for taking your finger out of your arse.'

Good for you, Nick. Your mother's son, definitely.

'And,' I add, 'when am I going to get my home back?'

The inspector rallies. 'I'm sure you would want us to do our job thoroughly. We will move with all due haste both to clear up here and to investigate further. It will be quicker if we are able to get on with our work without interference.'

'When?' I persist.

'We will finish here by tonight. You may return tomorrow. We will leave a police guard tonight but after that, unless you put in a special request, you will be on your own.'

'Fine,' I reply with more confidence than I feel. 'Is the alarm system reinstated?'

'You will have to deal with your supplier on that.'

'I'll give him a call today, Mum, get him to come round in morning.'

'Thanks, Nick.' I get up. 'Well, we'd better not keep these gentlemen from their important work.'

The inspector rises to his full height. 'I would like you to look round the house, check if anything has been stolen.'

'No. I think I need another day before I can face that.'

'It would be much better if you could do it today.'

'No, I'm sorry, can we do it tomorrow morning?'

The inspector nods condescendingly, clearly feels that he now has the upper hand again. 'Of course. I'll arrange for a constable to be here to meet you.'

A constable? Is that all I'm worth?

'Thank you. Consuela, would you be able to help tomorrow, to tidy up?'

She nods rapidly. 'Of course, Mrs B. What time I come?'

'Let's say ten thirty.' I raise my eyebrows to the inspector, who nods.

I leave the kitchen thankfully and stand in the chill outside, breathing deeply. I am pleased to see that a Starbucks coffee carton has been wedged against a brick for the cigarette butts. The garden smells so sweet in the summer. All I can smell now is wet mud.

As we walk back to the car, I turn to Nick.

'So, now you know. Not the ideal parents for a budding lawyer, are we?'

He puts his arm through mine.

'No, total disaster, but I wouldn't swap you.'

'Thank you.'

I hear my name being called. Carolson is running after us. He doesn't look as if running is a natural behaviour for him. He reaches us, slightly breathless.

'Mrs Belsworth, may I talk to you confidentially?'

'Yes, of course, though nothing is a secret from my son.'

'No, no. I meant confidential as in not in front of the other policemen.'

'Oh. OK.'

'It's just that, well, you see,' his eyes slide off mine and he gazes across the road.

'Yes.'

'Well, the fact is, I don't think that this case, I mean, what happened to your husband, will be investigated very thoroughly.'

'What do you mean?'

'Look, I won't go into detail too much, if you don't mind, but I'd like to check a few things out myself. It's on my patch and I think I know where to go to find out more about the gang that attacked Mr Johnson.'

'Why are you telling me this?'

'I could see in there that you weren't happy with Inspector Wedley's answers. I don't want you to think that the police are not doing anything. I mean, that's not why I became a policeman.'

'And?'

'Sorry?'

'Sergeant Carolson, there's something else here. I mean, it's great that you are taking an interest and all that and I certainly don't want to discourage you, but this doesn't feel like the whole story.'

He hesitates. Then a rueful grin spreads on his round face.

'You should have been a policeman, I mean policewoman, Mrs Belsworth. Well, yes, there is one more thing. I mean, look, you've been straight with me about the car and, well, I feel that I owe you this. I think you probably know that I hung back that night, when the old chap was attacked. I don't feel very proud of myself, to be honest and I'd like to do this to sort of make up.'

'OK, it's a deal.' I take a piece of paper and a pen out of my bag. 'Here's my number. Call me if there's anything we should discuss.'

'Thanks, Mrs Belsworth, I will.'

'It's Jenny. Call me Jenny.'

'Barry.'

We shake hands.

'Right.' I pull my coat around me. 'Before we all freeze to death, we'd better get on.'

Nick and I walk towards the car. The newspaper reporter rushes forward but I manage to freeze her to the spot with a glare. She'll never make it to the nationals if she wimps out that easily.

'Interesting conversation,' comments Nick.

'Yes.' I swing myself into the passenger seat. 'I still don't think we've got the whole story.'

Chapter 22 – Dec 28th 4.30pm

Cressida

'OK, darling, I'll see you when I see you. Sorry I can't be any earlier but you know how Dominic is. When he's got the bit between his teeth it's all hands to the pump, if that's not too mixed a metaphor.'

I hear Nick's chuckle at the end of the phone. He is such a sweet one, I hate to do this to him. Still, what the eye doesn't see and all that.

'Cress, I'd better get back to Mum. I'm trying to persuade her to come out and eat at the Italian opposite. She seems to have been living off coffee since the attack. Look, I'll see you later. Give Dominic my best.'

'Of course, bye sweety.'

I hang up and go through to Dominic's office to report on progress. He's just finishing working on the speech with Little Fat Andy.

'OK, Andy, just those final tweaks to the ending so we hit a rousing finale and I think we're there. Have them dancing in the aisles. You can bugger off now. We can sort it in the morning.'

'Oh, OK. I'll, er, see you then. Night.'

'Night,' we chorus.

The door closes behind him. Dominic turns to me. 'OK, Cressida, what have you got for me?'

I put my papers carefully on the table, reach behind me and pull down the zip of my dress, letting it drop to the floor.

'Well, there's this.'

Chapter 23 – December 28th 7.30pm

Bill

I look around the dingy room. Chas has found us a nice anonymous flat above a dry cleaners. I don't ask how he finds them; Chas has many different businesses, some straighter than others. That's how we know each other, after all. He's here, of course, on my right, dapper as ever, then John, Alan and Michael, the accountant, the dentist and the advertising man. All ex, of course, none of them young enough to cut it in their chosen professions any more. At least, that's what the next generation down say. John pushes his glasses up his nose every ten seconds, Alan looks as if a puff of wind would blow him away and Michael's forever running his hands through his thinning hair and trying to catch a glimpse of himself in the mirror. Not the most effective guerrilla army in the world but one has to play the cards one is given.

I call them to order. 'OK, now that we have dealt with the critical decision of who wants tea and who wants coffee, I suggest we get stuck in. There's a lot to cover tonight. There's only two days to go. Michael, let's start with you. Have you got the equipment?'

'Absolutely. No probs. An old buddy of mine in the biz came up trumps. He doesn't know what it's for, of course, spun him a yarn about children's parties at the orphanage, got them for next to nothing.'

'OK, excellent. Well done.' Michael preens, grinning round the room at the others. I suppress a sigh and move on.

'And John, did you manage to get passes for everyone?'

'Yes, ten in total. All sent to an untraceable email address. They're free, so no charge to the undertaking.'

'OK, good and Alan, did you get the gas?'

Alan clears his throat nervously, as he does every time he speaks. 'Yes, the cylinders are in my garage at the moment. I have to say I'll be glad to see the back of them.

'Not long now,' I reassure him. 'We'll send someone round with a white van at ten tomorrow morning to pick them up.'

'Bill,' John interjects, 'there's something I don't get here. This is going to be a youth rally. There's none of us can qualify as youth by any stretch of the imagination. Who are the passes for?'

'Oh, they're for us. But we're not going to watch the show. Don't worry about it. In these envelopes here are instructions for each of you. I want you to take them away and memorise every detail. Don't discuss it with each other and don't, under any circumstances, bring the instructions with you on the thirtieth. Learn them and burn them, OK?' I look around. John is running a finger round his collar, Alan is staring at the floor and Michael is jigging his leg up and down like a boy on a first date.

'Now Chas,' I continue, suppressing another sigh, 'Have you got the drivers lined up?'

'Yup. Best in the business.'

They'll need to be. We'll want to get out of there in a hurry once the deed is done. Now, gentlemen, any questions?'

Alan's hand goes up. I think I know what's coming. 'Not exactly a question, Bill, but I'm afraid I'm not going to be able to be there on the night.'

'Why's that, pray?'

'Well, Amanda has arranged a soirée, it being the evening before New Year's Eve.'

'Sorry, I don't get the connection.'

A hefty clearing of throat. 'Well, you see, we always go to some neighbours on New Year's Eve and Amanda was feeling that people might not think that we'd done our bit, entertaining-wise, you know, during the festive season. So, she has decided to hold an event that night and, naturally, my presence is required.'

'I see. Well, we'll have to get by without you then. I'm sure we'll manage, somehow.'

'Yes. Sorry.' He hands his envelope back and wipes his hands on his trousers.

'Right, if that's it, I'll let you all get back to your loved ones. Chas and I just need to think through the logistics one more time. Those of you who are still coming, you know where to meet for the final briefing.'

A muttering of good nights and we are on our own.

'Scotch?' I offer Chas.

'Don't mind if I do.'

I pull a hip flask and some plastic tumblers out of my hold-all and pour good measures.

'Now, we're one down,' I say. 'Bloody nuisance, what a wimp. I could bloody strangle him. Who else have we got?'

Chas takes a deep breath. 'No-one. You know that. We were already stretched because of Gerry. What was Alan going to do?'

'Release one of the key cylinders, in the auditorium. He is supposed to be the expert, after all.'

'We could shuffle everyone round one and lose a minor one.'

'No, that would just confuse them all.'

'What about Jenny?'

I stare at Chas. 'Optimistic, I'd say. She's up for something but right now, she's got a husband in hospital and a vandalised house.'

Chas shrugs. 'All the more reason to get out and do something. She must be wanting to beat up the whole world right now. Ask her. What can you lose?'

I consider my options. There are none and, if I'm honest with myself, the prospect of having her involved is attractive. 'OK, I'll call her in the morning. Now, let's go over everything in detail one more time. Oh, and I'd be grateful if, some time after the new year, Alan met with a little accident. Nothing serious, you know.'

'He may get beaten up,' Chas grins. 'It's dangerous out there on the streets, you know.'

Chapter 24 – December 28th 9.45pm

Cressida

I'm still tingling. That was just amazing. I think it was the sheer naughtiness of it, I mean, in his office. Anyone could have walked in. Not that there was anyone about, I suppose. All sitting at home, watching telly. But there's that thing about risking being caught, makes it all that much more exciting.

I suppress a giggle as my taxi pulls up to the door of the flats. The look on Dominic's face as I dropped my dress. Talk about the cat that got the cream. Didn't seem in the least surprised, cocky sod.

'Yes,' he said, 'That'll do nicely,' as if I'd just offered him tea and a bun. And me in my best Agent Provocateur. Still, that's Dominic. I've always found in life that you get what you expect, and he expects everything. Well, he got me, with a vengeance. Two hours' worth. Even Nicky can usually only manage an hour and I thought he was pretty good. Granted, it was a bit unsubtle and not a lot of the caring, sharing stuff but what the hell. I'll train him later.

I really think Dominic believes he was doing me a favour, screwing the little star-struck secretary. Well, he'll find out.

Now, I need to let myself in quietly. Damn, the sitting room light's on. I was rather hoping they'd decided on an early night. I put my head round the door. 'Hi, I'm back.' 'Hi, Cress, get everything done?' Nicky asks.

'Just about. I'll have to do a bit more tomorrow, I'm afraid.'

'Oh, shame. I was hoping you could help at Mum's house, tidying up.'

'Maybe later in the day. Right now, I need a shower.'

'Did you eat?'

'Yes, we got pizzas sent in.'

I turn to Jenny, who's sitting across from Nicky. 'How are you today, Jenny?'

'Oh, you know. Still alive and still here, I'm afraid. Be gone tomorrow, though, all being well.'

'Oh, stay as long as you want.'

Jenny's looking at me in an inquisitive way. Makes me feel awkward. Going to have to watch her.

'Well, I'm going to get into that shower while I can still stand.'

Nicky gives me a wave. 'OK, see you in a little while.'

I go to wash off the smell of Dominic. Shame, really, but there's more where that came from.

Jenny

OK, girl. Deep breath. It's your home, after all, time to claim it back.

Nick and Consuela hover behind me as I reach forward and unlock the kitchen door. The young policeman who was on duty yesterday is here too, hanging back, embarrassed, I guess, at having to be present at such a personal moment.

'I have to accompany you, madam, to ascertain whether any of your property is missing.'

Yes, my husband, but he's going to have to find his own way back. A brief visit to the hospital this morning had me gritting my teeth in the face of a barrage of platitudes, 'as good as can be expected, some progress but not yet out of danger, of course, slow and steady,' blah, blah.

So, here I am. I thought about braving it and going straight in through the front door but wimped out at the last minute. This feels brave enough, frankly.

I'm glad to see that the cup with the cigarette butts has been removed. The kitchen's fairly tidy, just a couple more polystyrene coffee cups, which Consuela quickly gathers up with a sniff and dumps in the bin. In front of us is the door through to the hall. We all stop and stare at it.

'OK.' I break the silence. 'We can't spend the whole day looking at a door. Come on.'

With more determination than I feel, I stride over and throw it open. We are hit by a chemical smell, like a laboratory. The usual smell of flowers and wood polish is so completely overwhelmed that for a moment I wonder whether I'm in the right place. I walk through, followed by the others.

'Dios mio,' I hear Consuela gasp as she sees the walls. I put my hand on her arm and she grabs my fingers. The red paint, which I'd only glimpsed on the night, drips down the walls all the way up the stairs. Again and again the word Delling, sometimes barely legible, sometimes unfinished, but repeated and repeated. Beneath it and around it, the neat Osborne and Little paper with its swirls and textures now looks absurd, like some tweedy Conservative lady at a rave.

I force myself to look at the floor. At first, I'm surprised to see that the blood has dried; there had seemed to be so much of it that I had expected it still to be lying there in a pool. Now just a dark stain on the parquet.

'Right, I'll check the rest of the house with the constable here. Consuela, would you please start to clean in here and Nick, we are going to have to get this wallpaper off today. There's a steamer, wallpaper-stripping thing, that your father bought but never used, out in the garage and the scrapers should be there too, with the tools. The step ladder is at the back, you'll see it.'

They scurry off, glad to be occupied. I take a deep breath and head up the stairs, careful not to touch anything. There's powder all the way up the banister, I guess from the police fingerprinting.

I slowly push open the door to our bedroom. I don't know what I'm expecting to find but am confused to see it looking completely normal. I had hurriedly thrown the duvet over the bed before we headed off to see Bill that morning and it still lies exactly as I left it. David's golfing shirt that I'd made him change hangs over the chair by the window. Seeing it makes me start to shake.

'Would you like to sit for a minute, madam?' asks the constable nervously.

'No, it's OK. Thank you. Just all a bit weird, you know.' I look away, go to the dressing table to check the drawers. Everything seems to be in place. Jewellery is in its usual hiding place, under the towels in the linen cupboard.

We work through the other rooms and, as far as I can see, everything is as it should be.

'Strange,' mutters the constable, 'That they should go to all the trouble of disabling quite a sophisticated alarm system and then not nick stuff. Have they moved anything?'

I look around again. 'No, not as far as I can see. Maybe we came back too early, disturbed them.'

'Possible, I suppose. Question is, how did they know that you were out in the first place?'

'It was already dark when we got back and we hadn't left any lights on in the house. Perhaps they just watched the house, waited for us to go.' I glance involuntarily out through the window to the front garden. Although the road is not visible from here, I have the sense of someone watching. If I'm going to stay here, I'll need to get rid of this paranoia.

'How long were you out?' The constable's voice is calmly reassuring.

'I suppose about, oh, six hours. So, no, with that logic they would have had time to steal everything they wanted. I suppose they probably waited until dark and just took pot luck.'

'In my experience, these things are rarely that carefully planned.'

In his experience? I take a look at him. He's younger than Nick. Still, it's good to talk to someone who seems to be thinking about this case.

After we have checked the other rooms, I send him on his way, assuring him that I would be in touch if I found anything missing. Consuela is busy scrubbing and Nick has brought everything in from the garage and is preparing the steamer. I go to my room to change into some old clothes. Not being able to get upstairs yesterday had meant a trip to the shops for an emergency outfit; it's good to get back into something familiar.

As I'm changing, the phone rings. I pick up the bedroom extension.

'Jenny, it's Bill. How are you?'

His deep voice seems to calm me immediately. Maybe it's his years as a policeman, maybe it's just him. Whatever it is, it's very welcome.

'Oh, hi, Bill. I'm OK, what's the expression, as well as can be expected in the circumstances.'

He laughs gently. Nice sound.

'How's David?' he asks.

'Slow and steady progress, according to the hospital, whatever that means. Not yet out of danger but, well, who knows.'

'Wish him well from me when you see him.'

'Certainly will.'

'And what about you?'

'Well, as you'll gather, I'm at the house. The police have cleared off now and I'm here with my son Nick and our cleaner, trying to get the place back into something I'd want to live in.'

'Jenny, I suppose you haven't really had a chance to think about what we discussed the other day.'

'To be honest, I have. It was good to have something else to think about during the long hours of waiting.'

'And?'

'And, as you'd expect, especially now, I think you're right. To be honest, if there was anything I could do right now to get my own back, I'd jump at the chance.'

There's a pause at the other end of the phone.

'Actually, there may be. Listen, and you can say no to this if you want, we've got something coming up tomorrow, the thirtieth. Someone has dropped out and we need one more person to help.'

'Sounds interesting. What's it all about?'

'Look. I don't want to talk on the phone about it. Why don't you come over and we can discuss it?'

'I wouldn't be able to get to you until tomorrow morning.'

'That's OK. What time?'

'I'll have to go and see David first. Shall we say about ten thirty?'

'Sounds good. Would you then be free for the whole day?'

'Well, I had planned tea with the Queen but I'll just put her off.'

He laughs again. 'I'm sure she won't mind. I'll see you then.'

'Great, sounds intriguing. Bye.'

I head downstairs, feeling as if the balance between me and the world has been tipped back a little in my favour.

Nick looks up.

'Who was that?'

'Oh, a well-wisher. Wanted to know if I needed anything. Wasn't that nice?' I ignore the quizzical look from Nick. 'Now, let's get on.'

By two o'clock, the hall and part of the stairs are stripped. The man from the alarm company has been in and all is working again. We call a halt and the three of us head off to the Italian restaurant in the centre of Pinner for a reviving plate of pasta and a bottle of good red wine. When we return, I am able to go in through the front door. I feel an elating sense of victory as I walk into the transformed hall. We have eliminated the intruders. We set to work with a will to finish the job and by six I call a halt.

'Thank you both. Thank you so much.' I pay Consuela double her usual rate. She protests briefly but I insist. Nick hangs back a bit longer after she's gone.

'Now, mum, are you sure you're OK? You could come back to the flat tonight if you want. Or I could stay.'

'No, you get back to Cressida. She'll be tired and in need of some TLC. I'll be OK, really. I have to get back on the horse, so to speak, now, or I may never do it.'

And, judging by the way she looked last night, young man, you're going to have to put in some work there if you want to keep her. Back in my banking days, there was a girl, don't remember her name now, who used to talk about some of the others in the morning having 'that just fucked look'. And that's what I saw last night, without a doubt. I feel my Mother Protector instincts soaring up but resist the urge to tell Nick. He'll have to work this one out for himself, I'm afraid. I really have enough for now.

I wave Nick off and go back in. I look around at the denuded hall and whisper an apology. Time to change before my evening visit to the hospital. And then it strikes me. With all the discussion about when and how these men got in, one question has not been asked. How the hell did they know where we lived in the first place?

Chapter 26 – December 29th 7.30pm

Barry

The games shop is dimly lit. It's like walking into a cave, black walls and spotlights on the tables. Each table is laid out like a battleground, with pieces of wrecked houses and giant beasts crawling across the countryside. There is a quiet buzz of conversation. The showcases around the walls glitter with models of twisted, contorted trolls, golems and goblins. I feel at home.

I go to my usual place at Table Four. Three figures are already hunched over it. One – long, straggly hair falling over a thin face and thick, black-rimmed specs – turns to me.

'Ah, Mogalev the Magnificent, I presume.'

'That's Mangoladrev the Magnificent, actually,' I respond, deepening my voice as far as it will go.

'Sorry, Barry.'

'You are forgiven. Now, where are we?' I take my seat.

'The evil hordes of Ravenbeard have conquered Busli and the Orks of Gethywyn are coming from the North.'

'Right. Better get stuck in then. Have you summoned the Kalihar Shapechangers?'

'Of course. And we have built up the superpowers of the White Warriors Command.'

'Naturally. Right, I'll just get myself a coffee. Anyone else?'

I know that this round of the game will take a good three hours. No hurry. About an hour into it, I raise the reason I've come there, besides the pleasure of gaming.

'Anyone hear anything about this youth rally on Thursday, the one at the O2?'

Blank stares all round, except from Jake, aka Peverel the Destroyer. 'Yeah, I hear it's going to be quite a bash. There's a big poster about it at the Albion Café. Down on Albion Street,' he adds superfluously.

'Anyone thinking of going?'

They look at me in astonishment. I can understand that; it is rare that anything to do with this century impinges on their lives.

'I thought I might take a look.'

'I do remind you, actually,' the squeaky voice of Demonthrust comes back at me, 'that Thursday evenings are, by tradition, the night when we take on Abysmo Theodread on Table Two. I mean, throw these traditions out of the window if you wish.'

'I know, I appreciate that, but I'm going to be on duty that night anyway.'

'Again?'

'Yeah, sorry. Anyway, look at it this way, old Abysmo is immortal so I'm sure he wouldn't mind waiting for an extra week.'

The frowns round the table show I have gone too far with this bit of lesé majesté. Not for the first time, I find myself wondering if I have actually outgrown this group.

Jake looks at me with that disappointed look usually perfected by schoolteachers, of which noble clan he is a member. 'I'm surprised you need reminding that Abysmo Theodread is not actually immortal but is, in fact, vulnerable to the simultaneous attack of Dragnid Orks and Formorian Goblins.'

'Yes, but how likely is that?'

'Stranger things have happened.'

'Shall we get back to the game?'

The next two hours pass in concentration as we manoeuvre our way round this small part of Middle Earth. Eventually, with foes vanquished, or at least repulsed for the time being, we sit back and exchange high fives.

'Anyone up for the next chapter?'

I shake my head, feigning sadness. 'Not for me. Duty calls, I'm afraid.'

'They're working you too hard, Barry. You should complain.'

I shrug. 'Maybe I'll set some Gartharkian Elves onto them.'

Amid sympathetic laughter, I take my leave and head for the Albion Café.

Albion Street has seen better days. In the time before the crash, it boasted quite a few little shops where you could buy antique pictures, modern lamps or state of the art music equipment. Now there are more shops boarded up than open. The Albion Café sits half way along the road. The interior is a hybrid of the formica-topped tables and dull grey cutlery of the traditional egg and chips caff and the neon-lit menu over the counter that someone clearly thought would make it look trendy and a true competitor to McDonalds. Truth be told, I suspect the only reason anyone went in was that it was cheaper than all the others. Even that hadn't enticed me in before, not that I was in this part of town very often.

Today, there are just three people, sitting hugging big white tea mugs at a table in the corner. I walk up to the counter, pausing on the way to read the poster on the wall. It shouts at me in dayglo colours.

Justice for All
Come and hear Dominic Evans,
the voice of the younger generation.

The only man who knows what's going on and knows what to do about it.
Let's do it!!!

Below are the details of place and time. I have vague memories of an English teacher saying 'If you have to use an exclamation mark, it means you have not expressed yourself clearly. Save them for your letters home.' I don't know what he would have made of three in a row.

I order a tea. 'Do you know anything about that rally?' I jerk my head towards the poster.

The man behind the counter, tired, middle aged, probably Arab, shrugs. 'What's to know? It's happening there and then. Is all.'

'No, I just wondered what they were going to talk about.'

Another shrug. 'Ask him,' pointing to one of the three. 'He put it up.'

I pay for my tea and carry it over to where the three are sitting in silence. None of them seem familiar from Boxing Day night but it was dark and they all had hoodies, so it could have been them. I'll find out eventually.

'Any of you know a bit more about that rally thing?' I ask as casually as possible.

'What do you want to know?' The speaker looks up at me with little interest.

'Well, it sounds like something I'd be interested in. Just want to know what he might be talking about.'

'You heard of Dominic Evans?'

'Of course. Talks a lot of sense, if you ask me.'

'Yeah, you can say that again. He's like the only one who speaks for us, you know, the one who didn't make his money by fucking things up for the rest of the world. I've heard tomorrow's thing is about taking that to the next stage.'

'Taking it to the next stage; what does that mean?'

'Well, nothing's going to happen unless we make a noise about it, is it? I mean, if we wait for parliament, those bastards will just talk forever and deliver fuck all. No, brother, we have to make things happen.'

I nod slowly. 'Yeah, you're right. Question is, how?'

'Let's see what Dominic has to say. If anyone has an answer, it'll be him.'

'Sounds good. I'll definitely be there, then.'

'Good for you, mate. May see you there.'

I drain my tea and head off. This'll show bloody Williamson and Taff sodding Jones. I'll be in CID before any of them know what's happened.

Chapter 27 – December 29th 10.30pm

David

I'm floating.

I'm sitting on my chair, the one I always used in the corner of Granny's drawing room and I'm floating around, looking down on them. They can't see me. They don't know I'm there.

I'm outside, on the beach, sandcastles changing shapes, sea monsters, jellies, singing to me. 'Michelle, ma belle…' Always hated that song but I'm singing along.

Hard school desk. Writing colours. Colours everywhere, big swirls. Like rainbows. Yellow Submarine. Mother waving at me from between the orange and the yellow. Out of my French exercise book.

Swooping, diving, falling.

Chapter 28 – December 30th 4.00pm

Bill

'OK, everyone, do any of you have any questions?' This is your last chance to ask. After this we're on our way and nothing can change the plan.

I look around the room. Heads shake.

'Good. Right, you all know how you're getting there. Those of you going on the tube, I repeat, you don't know each other, you do not, under any circumstances talk or discuss anything to do with this evening.' I look around the room as fiercely as I can, rekindling a technique that I used to scare young coppers. 'Right, off you go. Good luck and we'll be in touch about Birmingham next week, once we see how this one goes.'

Everyone gathers up their things and shuffles towards the door. A motley crew by any measure but if they all stick to their simple instructions, we'll get there. I call Jenny back.

'Jenny, wait a minute.' We wait until everyone else has gone. 'Are you still OK with this?'

She looks at me very steadily, a look that reminds me strongly and painfully of Mary. The last three days are etched into the lines on her face but the eyes are alive.

'Yes, I'm OK.'

'Good. Now then, let's go over it one more time.'

She shakes her head. 'Bill, I'm fine. We covered it six times earlier on. I walk down the middle aisle, put it down, go on to the top and press the remote. Then I get out. It's not that complicated.'

'And you remember where to find it?'

'Cupboard, Level 6, combination 2619.'

I smile. 'Sorry, I'm fussing. It's just that you've been through the wars this week and I don't want to put any more pressure on you than is absolutely necessary.'

'Don't worry.' She puts her hand on my arm. 'You've got bigger things to think about. I'll be fine. I'm looking forward to it.'

I can see this is true; her eyes are shining and there is a determined set to her mouth that says that she will not be crossed. It makes me want to kiss her, but now is not the time.

'Good. Now, we'd better go. You come with Chas and me. We'll take one of the cars to within half a mile, then walk. That way we'll be in before the crowds.'

As we're walking to the car, she turns to me.

'You know, there is one thing that's still bothering me.'

'What's that?'

'How did they know where we lived?'

'Yes, I've wondered about that. Obviously, someone got the number of your car.'

'Sure, but that's just a number.'

'Well, there are ways that you can trace a number back to the address. They're all strictly controlled, either through the DVLA or the police, but there's always someone you can buy. My guess would be the police. Notoriously leaky and there's bound to be people who agree with this bunch.'

'That's what I thought.'

'They're well organised, we know that. Look, Jenny, it's quite probable that all they wanted to do was frighten you. You just turned up at the wrong time.'

'Maybe. Or maybe not. Maybe what happened was exactly what was intended.'

Chapter 29 – December 30th 6.00pm

Cressida

Big night tonight. In more ways than one if I have my way. Dominic is keyed up, been pacing the office all afternoon, snapping at everyone. He's tucked away in his dressing room now. I'll stay clear. He's not going to want any nooky before the speech, he'll want to be absolutely at his best. Afterwards, that may be a different matter.

This is just such a rush. Everyone is really wired, it feels like the last day of term and a rock concert all rolled into one. We all know that things are going to happen tonight. It will never be the same again.

I can hear people coming in. There's a buzz coming up from the auditorium. It's really happening at last.

Little Fat Andy rolls into view.

'Hey, Cress.'

'Cressida.'

'Whatever. Going to be a great night. I've given him a really kick-arse speech. Be some celebrating afterwards.'

'No doubt.'

'Maybe you and I could slip away and celebrate somewhere, after it all dies down.'

I give him my beaming smile, raising the poor slob's hopes for a brief moment before putting the boot in. 'I'm going to be busy here until at least midnight and to be quite honest, if I was free, I would rather eat slugs that be anywhere alone with you. So, in case I'm not making myself clear, that's a no.'

'Bitch.'

'Pardon?'

'You are such a bitch. Think you're God's gift, don't you? I've seen the way you've been gazing at Dominic, fluttering the lashes. I've been with him for a long time, a lot longer than you, and believe me, Miss Public School Barbie Doll, you're not the first to get spread-eagled across his desk and you certainly won't be the last.'

'I don't know what you're talking about. Dominic and I have a perfectly professional relationship. You can admire someone without wanting to get into their pants, you know. Just as you can loathe someone without, without whatever.'

'Yeah, leave the fine phrases to me, girl. It's what I do. You just stick to the filing.'

The little toad waddled off before I could think of a good reply, damn it. And damn him. Has he been at the keyhole? What does he know? I think it's time Dominic got himself another speechwriter.

'Cressida, Dominic wants to see you.' One of the security team looms into view, a big black guy, Ramon, I think his name is, who rarely leaves Dominic's side in public. Pretty useless as a guard, Dominic says, but great for the street cred.

'I'm on my way.' Pull yourself together, girl. The last thing Dominic wants to see is a wobbly team member at this moment. I climb the metal stairs to the dressing rooms, fix a big smile and walk in.

'Dominic, you look great.' He does: immaculate black suit, open-necked white shirt, touch of sun tan making his pale blue eyes shine out.

'I know. Now, I need you to double check the placard wavers.'

'I did about ten minutes ago. They're all in place.'

'Good girl. Is there anything we've forgotten?'

'No, I've been through my checklists ten times. It's all ready for you to blow them out of their seats.'

In the background, we hear the rock band doing their sound check. The first chords blast out across the auditorium. I had a hand in booking them, carefully chosen to build the excitement. He grins at me.

'Right. Good. Now, off you go. I need to focus. I'm sure I'll have something for you to do after we're done.'

'Your wish is my command, oh master.' I give a deep curtsey and undulate out.

Just time to check whether the placard wavers actually are in place.

Chapter 30 – December 30th 6.00pm

Barry

It's good when your hunch turns out to be right. Doesn't happen to me very often. So, I'm down at the Albion at about three. I reckon a crowd will be going from there, given the poster and some kind of local leader. And I'm right! A good twenty-five, I'd guess. There'd been a fair amount of drinking beforehand, by the looks of it, too. I'd had a quick half myself, just to make sure there was a smell of beer on my breath. Another good idea.

I found out that the guy I'd met in the café was called Jeff and he was clearly the organiser. He was checking off people against a list and giving instructions about where everyone was to meet once we got there, in case they got split up on the way. Finally, by three fifteen, he was satisfied and they all headed off for the tube, and I just tagged along.

The Jubilee Line was full of people all about our age. It was like going to a football match, not that I've done a lot of that but I've seen it. At one end of the carriage, a chant of 'Engerland, Engerland, Engerland' started up. Down the other end, chants of 'What do we want', 'Justice', 'Who do we want it from', 'The Oldies' echoed back. I felt sorry for a couple of older people who had made the mistake of getting on the train at the same time. They scurried off at the first opportunity, chased out by jeers and whistles, and stood on the platform, shocked and bewildered, as the train pulled out.

I'm surprised, don't know why, that there are some girls in our group. I find myself squeezed up against one of them. She has a stud in her nose, two rings through her lower lip and her hair is in Rasta ringlets. Not my usual thing, talking to girls, but I am on a case here and I've got to make the effort.

'So, how do you know Jeff?' I ventured.

She looked up at me, chewing vigorously.

'Known him a long time, since school. You?'

'Just this week. I saw the ad in the café and he was there too. We got talking.'

'You not from round our way then?'

'Yeah, well, couple of miles away, towards the park.'

'So how come you were in the café, then?'

Shit, didn't think of that. Mind racing, nothing coming.

'Sorry? How do you mean?'

'Simple question. What brought you to the Albion?'

'Oh, sorry, misunderstood. No, you see, I was visiting a friend but he, er, he wasn't in, which was a pity, because I'd come over especially and I'd called to say I was coming and everything but he wasn't there and so, well, so I just needed a hot drink and there it was, the Albion. I went in, saw the poster and then…'

'Yeah, like you said.' She's staring over my shoulder. Girls seem to do a lot of that with me. 'It's OK, I don't need your whole life story.'

'Sorry. So, you looking forward to this afternoon?'

She shrugs. 'It's something to do. It's always, like, so boring, this week after Christmas. I mean, Christmas Day is bad enough, being cooped up with the family and the aunts and all that but at least something occasionally happens, even if it's just more food. Then it's just, like, nothing, you know what I mean? I'd be looking forward to going back to work, if I had a job.'

I want to tell her how lucky she is, having people to share Christmas with, but that would be telling too much about me, could lead to some awkward questions.

'You been without a job for a while?'

'Yeah, me and half the country. I've retrained to be a care assistant, thought I'd get in on looking after the rich oldies, but like all these government schemes, it was just another con, a way of making the numbers look better for a month or two. I mean, who do they think they're fooling?' This last bit is delivered down the carriage and evokes some slightly confused cheers.

Awkward silence, well, awkward to me, anyway.

'Well, I think it's going to be a really interesting evening,' I venture.

Another shrug. 'Yea, maybe.' She brightens. 'Hey, I hear they've got Janey Jamira playing, you know, before the speech thing.'

'Oh, right. Great.'

She looks at me and grins, the rings in her lip sparkling. 'You've no idea who that is, have you?'

'Well, no, not really. Pop's, you know, not my thing.'

'You're a bit of a nerd, aren't you?'

My turn to shrug. 'Yeah, probably.'

'That's OK, I quite like nerds. Had a bellyful of the big macho, fuck-em and forget-em types, to be honest. So, tell me, you into computer games and take-away Chinese then?'

'Well, yes, actually.'

'And you have an office job where you fill up forms all day.'

'Uh, huh.'

She laughs, but not unkindly, or that may be wishful thinking on my part.

'And you live on your own in a bedsit that smells of old clothes and packet soup.'

This is getting too accurate. Time to fight back. 'Well, yes, I do live on my own but that's because my parents are dead and I was an only child.'

'Oh, right. Sorry. I mean, I didn't mean to take the piss or anything. Just a joke.'

'It's OK. I deserved it. I must do something about de-nerding myself.'

'De-nerding. That's such a nerdy thing to say.'

'Looks like I can't win, then, nerded for life.'

'Oh, I don't know. Maybe I should take you on as a project. What's your name, by the way?'

'Oh, sorry, Barry. It's Barry.'

'Yea, thought it might be something like that. I'm Salita.'

'Salita, that's a great name. I've always wondered if your name kind of defines what you end up doing.'

'Nah, that's a cop out. I mean, I wasn't born Salita, and don't ask what name I was born with, I just made it up when I was about twelve and insisted on everyone calling me that.'

'Oh, right. So, you think if I called myself Rock or Titan or something, my world would change?'

She looks me up and down. 'Yeah, well, there are limits.'

She must see my shoulders slump because she pats my arm.

'Never mind, Barry Nerd, all is not yet lost. Stick to your Auntie Salita and we'll see what we can do for you.'

Through this conversation the tube has been trundling under the respectable part of London. Bond Street, Green Park, Westminster come and go, then we are South of the river where real people live and it starts to really fill up. Salita and I are squashed together. She puts an arm round my waist to steady herself. It feels good; I have to keep telling myself that it's meaningless, it's just what ordinary people do all the time. It's not an invitation to anything. But it does feel good. And she did say I should stick with her.

Best not to mention the Dungeons and Dragons.

Chapter 31 – December 30th 7.45pm

Jenny

Right, girl, you're on your own. Now, along the gantry, down the zigzag metal stairs on the back wall of the stage. No one told me how steep the steps would be. Got to be careful, lose your footing on these and it would definitely hurt. Thank God I don't have to carry the bag down here. Now, off to the right.

I couldn't believe how easy it was to get in. The overalls helped, mind. Nothing like an official badge to get past people. Dad used to be amazed when people would let him into their house. Just a badge saying Gas Board and he was in. He used to explain that they should be more careful but I don't think many listened. Obviously still don't, despite everything.

Baseball cap's quite cool. And it keeps the CCTV cameras off your face. I tried to wear one once, on that holiday to Miami but David was having none of it.

'I'm not going to be seen on the streets with you dressed like a McDonald's check-out girl.'

I'd given in, just to preserve the peace. There are things worth taking a stand for and a baseball cap's not one of them. Went out for the rest of the trip in some big floppy number, as I recall. And insisted on stopping for drinks every hour, in very expensive cafés. Poor old David. He really was the proverbial fish in the barrel when it came to getting my own back.

Must stop talking about him in the past tense.

How's it going to be now? Will I be dancing attendance on him? I wonder. No, concentrate, save that for later.

I feel proud to have survived last night at home alone. I used to be home a lot on my own when David was travelling but that was easy. For one thing, it was finite; I knew when he was coming back. And it never occurred to me that I might be attacked, safe in my castle. Just set the alarm and went to bed. Mind you, we had dear old Max in those days, curled up at the end of the bed, though he was such a softy he would have been no protection at all. Unless he'd licked the intruders to death.

I hardly slept last night, propped up in bed reading trashy magazines through the small hours, just dozing a bit, getting up to make cups of tea. It was good that I had Bill to look forward to, give some shape to the coming day, something different and the sense of actually doing something. That's the problem with someone in hospital, you're just treading water, as trapped as they are.

God, that band's dreadful. I can see why they were chosen though; they're whipping the audience up with their chants and their leaping about. Very clever. This man's been watching the American election rallies.

Oh, thank God, they're finishing. Right. Off I go, Level 6, combination 2619.

Chapter 32 – December 30th 7.55pm

Cressida

Right, here we go. Everyone's in place and the team's clearing the band's kit. It's so exciting. Five minutes to go. I'm sure Dominic knows but I'll just go up and see.

Ramon's on the door, classic stance, legs apart, hands folded in front of him. Why do they all do that, like they're protecting their genitals? Must have seen it in some film. The door opens and there he is. The light from the room kind of silhouettes him. He looks fantastic and I tell him so. He raises an arm to acknowledge me but I can tell he's somewhere else in his mind. He sets off towards the wings, Ramon on his heels and I go back to my vantage point at the other side of the wide stage. A large podium has risen up, though I know, from past performances, that he will hardly use it, preferring to prowl around the stage. He has that technique of making everyone in the audience think he is talking directly to them.

There's a real buzz from the crowd. Our people reckon there's nearly two thousand here this evening, that's full house for this auditorium. Maybe next time we'll use the bigger one. That takes about ten thou. That would probably make it the biggest political rally ever in this country. Even this one's up there with the most famous, and I'm here, right at the centre of it. Nicky's out there somewhere too. Managed to drag him away from his mother for one day. Apparently, she had something to do anyway.

They're putting the lights down, the crowd's falling silent in expectation. The fanfare's starting and I can see Dominic poised, bouncing on the balls of his feet on the far side of the stage.

The fanfare rises to a crescendo. The voice echoes over the speakers.

'Ladies and gentlemen, please put your hands together, raise the roof for the one person in this country who knows what's happening, the one voice speaking up for justice for all, the one man who's there, making it happen for you, Dominic Evans.'

He strides out into the spotlight, hand raised, and stands like a rock in the centre of the stage. No silly jigging about, just stands there and accepts the applause. Waits for it to die down slightly, not completely. It takes a long time.

He steps forward, right to the edge of the stage and looks around. I can feel the expectation.

He starts to speak.

'Is there anyone in this room tonight who feels that they are getting a fair deal?'

The crowd roars back 'No'.

'Is there anyone in this room tonight who feels that this country is heading in the right direction?'

'No.' I find I'm shouting too.

'Is there anyone in this room tonight who feels that we have anything to be grateful to the older generation for?'

'No!' This time the walls seem to vibrate with the sheer noise.

He waits for it to die down. His voice drops to a confidential tone.

'OK, let me tell you what we, you and I, are going to do about it.'

I find I'm bouncing up and down like a teenager at her first pop concert. I see Little Fat Andy in the wings opposite and give him a conciliatory wave; we are, after all, supposed to be working together for this cause and I should keep him sweet. I get two fingers back and he turns away. Right, at least I know where we stand. And what needs to be done.

Some minion pushes past me with a heavy bag, sending me staggering forward.

'Careful, you idiot!' I shout after him but just see some guy in overalls and a baseball cap disappearing down the stairs towards the auditorium.

No reply. Stuff him. I turn back to give Dominic my full attention.

Chapter 33 – December 30th 7.45pm

Barry

Well, Salita said I should stick with her, so I did. She didn't seem to mind. I was quite disappointed in a way when we got to North Greenwich and we all piled out. I'd enjoyed the forced intimacy of the crowded tube.

We ran across the windswept open space to the great flying saucer shape of the O2. I remember being brought here as a teenager when it was the Millennium Dome. One of the most boring days of my life, as I recall, and I don't think I've been back since.

Anyway, we get ourselves seated in the right area and I head off to get Cokes and hot dogs, vegetarian for Salita, meat for me. When I get back, she's chatting to some friends. My heart sinks. This is usually the point where I fade away. But she waves me over.

'Everybody, this is Fernando.' I look around, confused. She grins at me again. I'm getting to like that grin, in spite of all the face furniture hanging off it. 'That's you,' she whispers, 'I thought you needed a bit of re-inventing.'

'Oh, right. Do you want the Spanish accent too?'

'Don't push your luck. It's more mysterious, anyway, having a name like that and coming from Brent.'

'Right.' I like the idea of being mysterious, especially in the circumstances. As it turns out, no one really asks me much about myself but I'm quite happy to listen as they gossip about friends and music.

Then the volume of the band, Janey Whatsit, drowns out any conversation. Everyone's jumping up and down. I do my best to copy them. Not the time to admit that my favourite music is

Elgar's Dream of Gerontius. When both your parents are classical musicians, it's hard to escape, even if I didn't inherit their skill.

I take time to look around. It makes me, at twenty-eight, feel quite old. There's a real mixture of men and girls in the latest fashions, through to thousands in jeans and loose shirts, parkas thrown down on their seats as they dance around. The jeans and loose shirts dominate, by far. An easy constituency to build up, I'd think. Hard up, not much work and no great optimism for the future. I really can't blame them latching onto this man; no one else is offering them anything or even showing signs of taking any notice of them.

At last, just as my head is really starting to hurt, the set finishes, the band take their bows and flounce off. Everyone settles back into their seats. I see Salita's face is flushed and her eyes are bright. I wonder if it's just from the music or whether there's been some chemical help. That's not for today anyway. I'm sure she's not the only one here to have popped something. I need to stay focused on the big one, getting inside this network. I spot Jeff, the organiser, in the row behind and lean across.

'I'm really glad I came,' I yell over to him. He looks at me blankly for a moment. I try not to be offended; they do say that one of the attributes of a great detective is to have a very forgettable face. Clearly, I qualify.

'Barry, we met earlier this week at the Albion,' I prompt.

He nods. 'Right. Glad you're enjoying it.'

I search for a way of continuing the conversation. 'I'll give you my mobile number. It'd be great if you could let me know if there's any other events. I'd be really interested in helping the cause.'

He looks at me, quizzically. After a pause, he answers.

'OK, Barry, you do that. Here, put it into my phone,' and he hands it over. No chance to scroll through, with him watching, so I pass mine over to him.

'Can you do the same?'

He passes it straight back. 'Don't worry about that, Barry. I'll call you.'

'Oh, OK.'

Damn.

Salita leans across. 'Hey, this is better than I expected.'

I grin back. Perhaps she's my pathway in.

'Told you. And the best is still to come. This guy's dynamite.' I say it loud enough for Jeff to hear.

A fanfare starts playing and everyone turns back towards the stage. It's now clear, except for a large rostrum in the centre. The fanfare gets louder, a kind of vibration build up. Everyone feels it. They're all leaning forward, eyes fixed on the empty stage. The fanfare hits its crescendo, a voice comes echoing over the speakers, spotlights flash on, creating a dazzling pool of light. And suddenly, there he is. Everyone's on their feet. Placards appear from nowhere. The yelling and screaming is louder than anything the band whipped up. I'm up too and I'm not acting. It's impossible to ignore.

He comes forward, fires questions at us and we yell back the answers he wants. Giant screens either side of the stage help us to see each nuance. Every eye is pinned on him, except a couple of attendants wandering up the aisles with bags of something. Like us at football matches, having to face away from the game.

'Right, let me tell you what we, you and I, are going to do about it.'

This is the bit I want to hear. What's the plan?

'I have the greatest respect for parliament,' whistles from the crowd, 'as an institution.' The giant images grin down on us, sharing the joke, though we're not sure what the joke is just yet. 'But not for this parliament.' The cheers rise up, he talks on through them. 'Not for this ragged, half-arsed, scared, grey-whiskered,' he punches out each word, waiting for the 'Yeah' to fly back at him, 'fat-bellied do-nothings with their free lunches and free houses. What do they know? What do they know about us, sitting there in their cosy clubs, double-glazed against the dissatisfaction that beats against their door?

Well, my friends, they're going to know. They're going to know whether they like it or not. And who's going to tell them? Who's going to tell them?'

'We are,' echoes around the auditorium.

He waits for it to die down, standing, legs wide, hands on hips. Then he talks, this time more softly.

'The only way to create change in this sludged-up country is on the streets. We own the streets, we have the right, we are fighting for justice.'

On that word, everyone is applauding, jumping up and down. Placards are waving from side to side. The sheer energy of it scares me. I drop out of the trance that he has created and look around. There're all gazing at him; it's like a revivalist meeting. He could do anything he wants with this crowd. What does he want?

Then suddenly, behind the cheers, as they die down, we hear a loud whistle. A confused silence. Everyone looks round. Then we hear a series of small explosions, five, maybe six, not bangs exactly, more like pops. People start to crouch down then stop, amazed, as, either side of the stage, in front of the big screens, something starts to move. Two weird, brightly coloured shapes wobble upwards and outwards from behind the footlights. They're somehow fixed to the floor but they reach up and up until they must be fifteen feet in height. And all round the auditorium, in about six or seven different places, smaller versions of the same thing are appearing, in aisles, in boxes.

Within five seconds, maybe less, it's clear what they are. All around us are giant wobbling figures of clowns, bulbous, grinning, with pointy hats and big red buttons down their fronts. Through the silence we start to hear, quietly then louder, laughter, an unreal sound like a hundred Santa Claus going 'ho, ho, ho' very slowly. It fills the space. And it's catching. People are starting to laugh. In no time, the laughter of the crowd has drowned the recorded sounds.

I look at the stage. Evans is still standing there, flatfooted, as if he has been deflated as the giant clowns inflated. He holds up his hands to quieten us down but he's lost us. Totally. A big black guy comes awkwardly onto the stage and stands hesitantly behind him. Then a smaller, rather dumpy man comes over and whispers into his ear. Evans allows himself to be dragged off.

And all this time, the clowns are bouncing, happily grinning down at us.

An announcement comes over the speakers. 'Ladies and gentleman, we have a security alert. Please stay in your seats. The stewards will give you instructions on what to do very shortly.'

The laughter dies quickly. All around me, people ignore the instruction and start heading for the doors. Next to me, Salita starts to climb over the back of the seat. I grab her.

'What the hell are you doing? Let go of me.'

'Salita, listen. I know about these things. You must stay seated. It's too dangerous to try to get out. You'll be crushed.'

'Bollocks. You heard. Security alert. That means bombs. Now let me go.' She struggles to free herself.

'No, it doesn't. And I'm not going to let you go. Listen to me. Something weird just happened but that doesn't mean we're in any danger. That's the danger, over there.' I point to the crowds trying to force their way through the doors. Already we can hear screams coming from inside the mass of people. The voice comes over the speakers again, urging everyone to sit and wait.

Salita slumps back in her chair. 'Well, it's too late now anyway. We can't get out, even if we wanted to.' She looks closely at me. 'How come you know so much about all this stuff, Barry?'

I shrug. 'I'm a nerd. Nerds know. We're useful people to have around in an emergency.'

'What the hell just happened here?'

I look around. The clowns are starting to slowly subside bowing forward as if taking applause.

'Either they ordered the wrong kit or someone just sabotaged this whole event.'

More people, realising the exits are impassable, are moving hesitantly back to their seats. There's still a mass of people by the exits. I wonder if I should go and help. But who's going to listen to me, out of uniform? Hard enough in uniform. I decide to stick with Salita. She's staring around her, swivelling in her chair, trying to see as much as possible.

'But why, why would they sabotage us? And who?'

'Evans is trying to change things. There's always people who don't want change.'

'Old people, you mean?'

I think of Bill and the two, David and Jenny, who rescued him. Hardly your typical urban terrorists. Mind you, this was hardly the typical terrorist attack. But it could have been. I realise how easy it would have been to plant bombs instead of clowns.

I shudder. Salita notices. 'What's up?'

'Oh, I don't know. It's just that, when you think about it, nowhere's really safe nowadays. I mean, look at us here. You'd have thought a great evening out, bit of fun, be part of something and now we've got people jumping over each other to escape.' I glance over to the exits again. The crush has eased. A few people, mainly girls, are sitting on the floor with attendants bending over them. I don't see any bodies; I hope that means there aren't any. I turn back to Salita.

'Right. I think we can get out of here.'

'What about obeying orders and doing what we're told?'

'The stewards all seem to be otherwise engaged, to be honest.'

We look around for the others and find we're on our own. 'They must all have got away,' observes Salita. 'Come on, maybe we'll find them outside.' And she takes my hand and leads me towards the exit.

Chapter 34 – December 30th 8.15pm

Cressida

I had to run to get to Dominic's dressing room before him, up those stairs so fast I didn't have time to be breathless. Catching up on me now, though. God, here he comes. He's white as a sheet.

'You, Cressida, what the hell happened out there? Don't we have fucking security people? What do they think their job is, stopping the trolls dropping fucking gum on the floor and screwing in the toilets? Jesus Christ, didn't you brief them? Didn't they know something might happen?'

I decide it's best to say nothing, still gasping for breath. He glares at me.

'Well?'

Wrong tactic. Deep breath. 'Dominic, of course I briefed them. I told them, you can see it in the notes, that certain parties might try to disrupt us.'

'Well, certain parties sodding well did disrupt us.' He picks up a folding chair and flings it along the corridor, away from me, luckily. I stand my ground. 'Whatever you did, you didn't do it well enough.'

'Oh. That's not fair.'

'Fair? Fair? I've just been made to look like the biggest bloody fool in Britain and you're telling me what's fair. You've really let me down here, Cressida. Now just fuck off out of my sight.'

Now is not the time to argue. I'm sure he'll see when he calms down that it wasn't my fault. Anyway, I'm not sure I can trust my voice. I walk away, find a corner and get my breath back. I fumble for my phone. I need to find Nicky.

Ramon appears, looking at me wide eyed, more shocked that I consider necessary. I make to go past him but he grabs my arm.

'What?'

'Something's happened.'

'Yeah, right. I think we've all noticed that.'

'No, I mean something else.'

His voice is wobbly. I turn towards him.

'What?'

'Andy. You know, Andy Woodham.'

'Yes, of course I know. What about him?'

'He's dead.'

Chapter 35 – December 30th 10.00pm

Bill

'This evening's rally for Dominic Evans' Justice for All movement ended in farce when six giant inflatable clowns suddenly appeared in the auditorium at the O2 Centre. For a packed crowd of twenty thousand, however, amusement quickly turned to panic. Twenty six people were injured in the rush for the exits, five seriously. Over to our correspondent, Richard Wallace, at the scene.'

A cold and windswept reporter appears on screen, the O2 rising behind him. 'Yes, John, things certainly did not turn out the way they were planned today. Just as Dominic Evans was getting into his stride, with the audience cheering him on, these giant inflatables suddenly loomed up either side of the stage and at strategic points around the auditorium. Although television cameras were not allowed into the meeting today, there is plenty of mobile phone footage such as this.'

The screen fills with rather grainy film of two of the inflatables. I chuckle with satisfaction.

The newsreader comes back on. 'An extraordinary turn of events. Looks like YouTube will be busy tonight. Is there any news on who might be responsible for this?'

'None at all at this stage, John. Mr Evans himself was not available for interview but has issued this statement. *There are clearly people in this country who do not want the truth to be told. Be certain, however, that their attempts to shut us up will not succeed. We will be heard.*

I understand that another event is planned for Birmingham next week. I'm certain that Mr Evans' security will be a lot tighter by then. John.'

'Richard, thank you. Now, other news and in the United States today…'

I press the off button on the remote control and pour Chas and me large whiskies.

'A good day's work, I think. Now, are we sure that nothing can be traced back to us?'

'I think we're OK. Everyone kept their baseball hats on, so there shouldn't be any CCTV footage, and we know there were no cameras working where the cars were waiting, 'cos we fixed them ourselves.'

'What about the clowns? Someone's going to see that footage and know where they came from.'

'Yeah, I've been wondering about that. Michael said he got them from a friend, didn't he? And that friend is going to be fairly pissed off when he realises he's not going to get them back.'

'I think Michael would enjoy a good holiday just about now. I'm sure you can persuade him. And find out who the friend is who supplied them. We'll need to get to him and pay him off, so he keeps quiet.'

'Already done. The name was on the boxes, before I scratched it off. One of my lads was round there this afternoon.'

Not for the first time, I'm glad that Chas is in the frame. Considering we started on opposite sides of the table all those years ago, we seem to make a good team. Not that I'd ever drop my guard completely. He has an expensive lifestyle and a greedy family to maintain. There's stuff he doesn't know and never will. That way, he stays a good lieutenant, rather than a rival leader.

Chapter 36 – December 30th 10.30pm

Jenny

The bath water's hot and right up to my neck. It's good. I can feel all the tension ease out of my limbs. And there was certainly tension. I was so scared, my legs just wobbled under me.

Just as I got to that locker some great big security guard comes wandering along, wants to know the time, starts talking about what an idiot Dominic Evans is. Luckily he gets a call on his walkie talkie thing, telling him his tea's ready, so he's off just in time for me to get the bag out and head round the side of the stage.

Then, I really thought I was sunk. I round the corner and see the elegant bow in the hair of the person standing just ten feet away from me. Only bloody Cressida. Fortunately she's so wrapped up in watching her hero on stage that she doesn't see me coming. Then I nearly blow the whole thing. I guess I must have misjudged the gap, under-estimated the size of the bag or something, but whatever it was I cannon into her as I'm sneaking round behind her. I was off down those stairs like a meerkat down a burrow, her abuse chasing me down. I wonder what she would say if she realised she had been swearing at her future mother-in-law. Not that I am, probably, not now that she's got the hots for Evans.

Quite relieved, really, apart from the pain it's going to give Nick, which I can't forgive. Must be hard, giving up your son, becoming just a walk-on, supporting actress in your own child's life, always treading on egg shells. It'll happen one day but not, I think, with that one.

Anyway, the rest was easy after that. Dropped the bag in the aisle, headed to the top, pressed the remote and got out of there. The van was waiting exactly where it was planned and dropped me near Wembley Park tube. I got into the van as a worker in overalls and got out as a middle class lady on her way back from some shopping. I was home in time for the ten o'clock news headlines, then straight into this bath.

Good to see the coverage. I got a real buzz in my stomach, knowing I'd been there, that I had made this happen. Not that I can tell anyone. That doesn't bother me, I've never been a gossip. I've always found that men are much worse gossips than women, actually.

Talking of which, I must go to see David first thing tomorrow. What with everything today, I didn't get the chance to do my evening visit. I wonder if he noticed.

Cressida

'God, Nicky, where have you been?' I march into the living room and stare at him indignantly.

'Here. I hung around at the O2 for a while then, when you didn't answer my calls, I came home. Didn't you pick up my messages?'

'I've had more than enough to deal with tonight without picking up messages, thank you. You could have waited.'

'I did. Look, let me pour you a drink. I mean, I can imagine the atmosphere back there…'

'You don't know the half of it, sitting here with your bloody telly and your glass of wine.'

'Hey, hold on a minute. What did you expect? That I should hang around like some manservant till you deigned to appear.'

'Nicky. I've had a dreadful night. The least you can do is be a little sympathetic.'

'Well, the least you can do is not take it out on me.'

'Right. I'm going to have a shower, then I'm going to bed. The duvet for the sofa's still out from your mum's stay. I suggest you make yourself comfortable.'

I stalk out before he has the chance to reply. Of course I didn't answer his stupid messages. 'Hi, Cress, I'm at Gate 12. Come and get me.' 'Hi, it's me. Again. Still at Gate 12. They're starting to look at me in a funny way.' 'Hi, my feet hurt. I'm heading for home.'

Really, given the fact that I was looking at a dead body, I was hardly going to reply. After Ramon told me his news, I rushed round with him to see what he was talking about. And there was Andy, lying in a sort of plump heap at the bottom of the big metal staircase behind the stage.

He wasn't the first dead body I've seen. A couple of years ago we passed a crash where someone had gone through the windscreen and was lying across the bonnet of the car, obviously dead. But it was the first time I'd seen someone I knew, someone I'd been talking to just a few minutes before. It seemed impossible that all that brainpower could have been just stopped dead like that. But I suppose that's what stopped dead means. Just that.

I thought back to my conversation with him and wished for a moment that I'd been a little kinder. But it soon passed. People were just standing round staring; someone needed to take charge. I turn to Ramon.

'Go and tell Dominic what's happened. Tell him I've got it all under control. You,' I point to one of the backstage minions, 'Go and get the police and the ambulance people from out front. Now, did anyone see what happened?' Heads shake all round. 'Right, get on with whatever it is you all do but don't leave until the police say you can.'

Within a minute, a group of policemen appear, a couple of young uniformed constables with an older man in a suit and raincoat.

The two younger ones stand back as the older man approaches Andy's body. He kneels, peers carefully, as if he were examining a plant at the garden centre but does not touch. He glares around at the other crew members, who have reappeared, and then stands up.

'Did any of you see anything?'

Again heads shake. Silence.

I feel I should be the one to speak up. 'We were all out front watching the speech, then dealing with the, um, incident.'

'I see, and you are..?'

'Cressida Huntley-Jones.'

He signals to one of the constables to start taking notes.

'That would be Huntley hyphen Jones, I assume.'

I detect the usual slight sarcasm of the lower orders whenever confronted by a double-barrelled name.

'That's right.'

'And this is…?

'Andy Woodham. He's… *was* the speechwriter for Dominic Evans.'

'And you were colleagues?'

'That's right. I'm Mr Evans' PA.'

'Are you indeed?' The others are starting to inch away, leaving me to deal with the police. He notices, even though he's looking at me. 'Everyone stay where you are, please, I haven't finished with you.' He focuses on me again. 'And where is Mr Evans just now? I feel we should have a little chat.'

I'm about to reply when a voice comes from behind me. 'Mr Evans has left the building.'

I turn to see Ramon. Why isn't he with Dominic?

The policeman's eyes widen. 'And you are..?'

'Ramon.'

'And do you have another name?'

Ramon replies hesitantly, 'Rodrigues.'

'And don't tell me, you work for Mr Evans as well.'

'That's right.'

'Well, goodness me, he does have a lot of people around him, doesn't he? And where is Mr Evans off to, pray?'

'I don't know.'

'Constable, take Mr Rodrigues' details, as well as those of the others here.' He stares back at me. 'I assume you will be able to contact Mr Evans should we need to talk to him, being his PA and all.'

I nod.

'Well, Miss Huntley hyphen Jones, it looks as if it's just you and me then. Shall we find somewhere to sit down and you can tell me everything you know?'

We go up to Dominic's dressing room. Although he's gone, the scent of his cologne still hangs in the air. I hope it will be comforting but I doubt it. He notices it too but says nothing.

I sit on one of the hard-backed chairs. He pulls another over so he is opposite me, and a little closer than I would have liked.

'So, take me through the evening. When did you last see Mr Woodham? And, for that matter, when did you last see Mr Evans?'

I tell him about seeing Andy standing in the wings, about the start of the speech and the chaos that followed. Andy had gone on stage with Ramon at that moment, after the clowns appeared. I assumed at the time he was trying to rescue the situation somehow. I was too busy getting the stage lights off and curtains closed.

'And when did you last talk to him?'

'Just before the speech.'

'Tell me about Mr Woodham's state of mind when you spoke.'

'What do you mean?'

'Don't worry about what I mean, Miss, just tell me.'

'Look, Inspector… I assume it is inspector.'

'I'm sorry, I didn't introduce myself, did I? Inspector Williamson.'

'And you're part of the team here at the O2, I assume.'

He shakes his head slowly. 'Usually based in Brent but called in here to provide Christmas break cover tonight. Aren't I the lucky one? And tell me, Miss Huntley hyphen Jones, why don't you want to tell me about Mr Woodham's state of mind?'

'There's nothing not to tell. He was fine. We chatted for a while before the speech, then we both had to get things done.'

There's a soft knock at the door. I'm about to answer when he calls 'Come'. One of the constables comes in.

'What?'

'May I have a word, Inspector?'

'Is it important?'

'I think so.'

'It had better be.'

He rises with a sigh and goes out, closing the door after him. I go to get a drink of water and see that my hand is shaking. I take several deep breaths to calm down and wonder where Dominic is. I can't blame him for disappearing; he has to stay clean, free of scandal. But I wish he were here. He'd know how to deal with this man. The door opens. Williamson crosses the room and sits. I drink down the water and take my place again.

'Tell me, Miss, did you get on well with the deceased?'

Hearing Andy called 'the deceased' pulls me up short.

'How do you mean?'

'I mean just that. Did you get on well?'

'OK, really. We were both working for the same cause, after all.'

He nods slowly. I try to breathe normally. He scratches his head.

'No, it's just that one of the people out there says that, just before the speech, which was, of course, just before the death of Mr Woodham, you and he had a blazing row during which he called you,' he glances at his notebook, 'A bitch.'

He stares straight at me, a lion about to bite the head off his prey. And waits.

'Well, yes, there were a few words. But heat of the moment, you know, everyone was a bit edgy.'

'And what were these few words about?'

'Oh, just some detail of the arrangements.'

'What detail?'

'I don't really remember.'

He leans even closer. 'Do try.'

'I think it was about, yes, it was about which tie Dominic, Mr Evans, was to wear.'

'I see. And that's why he called you a bitch. Feel strongly about neckwear, did he?'

'Like I say, we were all overwrought.'

Again the slow nod.

'Anything else you'd like to tell me?'

I give a bright smile, or at least my best attempt. 'No, no, I don't think so.'

'Miss Huntley-Jones, I'd like you to come and see me at the police station in Brent, Lancaster Road tomorrow morning. I think we have more to discuss.'

'But I have to work.'

'This is a possible murder inquiry. I think you can justify taking the morning off. Shall we say ten thirty?'

I nod.

'And feel free to bring a legal advisor if you wish.'

My heart jumps. 'Why would I need one?'

He shrugs. 'You never know, do you? Oh, and I'll need a contact number for your Mr Evans.'

'Now?'

'Now.'

I give him the office number.

'I don't think he'll be at the office just now. A mobile will do fine.'

'I'm not allowed to give out his mobile number.'

He leans in even closer. 'I'm the police, Miss Huntley-Jones. I decide what's allowed.'

He gets the number.

'Thank you. Goodnight, Miss Huntley-Jones.'

I leave the room, fighting down the urge to run. Outside, our cars have all gone. I walk past a group of shouting drunks to the tube. It's raining.

Now, showered and lying in bed, I would really like Nicky beside me to cuddle up to. But I'm damned if I'll be the first to apologise.

Chapter 38 – December 31st 3.30am

Barry

I open my eyes and stare at the ceiling. The windows are covered by a sort of gauze, no curtains, and let in a soft, filtered version of the street lights outside. I can make out the lampshade with all its tassels. From Thailand, I think she said. Over on the opposite wall, there's a big poster of some rap artist that I've not heard of. The room smells strongly of that perfume you get when you burn joss sticks. It's silent, unusual for the middle of the city. I look at my watch. Half past three. That will be why.

Beside me, Salita stirs, rolls over towards me and lays her bare arm across my chest. I turn towards her. She half opens one eye, which makes her look like a sort of pirate.

'Hi,' she whispers.

'Hi, yourself.'

How did this happen? The journey back was easy enough. We chatted all the way. I deliberately went past my stop so I could see her home. Not hoping for anything, just being polite, gentlemanly. Well, OK, maybe hoping, but hopes don't usually come to much with me. Normally, a cup of coffee and a peck on the cheek is a triumph.

It seemed quite natural to hold hands on the way from the tube. Suddenly she stops.

'I thought you lived the other way.'

'I do. I'm walking you home first. It's been an exciting evening and it's getting late. But look, if you don't want…'

'No, it's sweet. Thanks. Just not what I'm used to, you know.'

We walked on, got to a narrow alley.

'I'm just down there.'

'Looks scary.'

'Not really. You get used to it. That and having mace in your pocket.'

'Is that legal?'

'Who cares?'

Shut up, Barry, you're an office worker, not a cop.

'So…'

'So…' She grins that grin. 'Would you like to come up?'

'Sure. OK. If it's not inconveniencing you.'

'No, Barry, you're not inconveniencing me.'

Half way down the alley is a scuffed and dented door. We go in and up a narrow, carpetless staircase to the top floor.

The room is not like any I've ever been in. It's the sort of place that would have made my mother reach instantly for the J cloth. Coffee mugs form a haphazard queue for the sink; some have clearly been waiting a long time. A brass lamp in the shape of a very naked lady emerges on a side table from piles of old newspapers. Salita sits me down on a beaten up sofa, it's multi-coloured stripes faded and stained.

'So, do you live here alone?'

She raises an eyebrow. 'Sometimes, why? You going to jump me?'

'No, no. I just… I mean, I wouldn't, you know…'

'Looks like I'll have to do all the hard work, then.'

She sits astride my legs. I open my mouth to speak but she shuts it with a kiss. She tastes of chewing gum and Coke. It's nice.

After a long pause, I break away.

'Listen, you don't have to ….'

She puts a finger on my lips. 'Barry, listen. This is not a thank you present. This is not because I feel sorry for you. It's not Fuck a Nerd Week. I fancy you. OK?'

'You have weird taste.'

'Don't do yourself down. You may not be Clooney but you're a nice guy and I don't get to see many of those. Now shut up before I change my mind.'

And now it's half past three and I have to be on duty at eight.

'Salita.'

'Yeah?' The eye half opens again.

'I have to go soon.'

She snuggles in closer. 'Well, we'd better make the most of the time we have left, hadn't we?'

Chapter 39 – December 31st 5.00am

David

I wonder where everyone is. There's lights around but I don't see anyone. I mean, where's, um, oh, I know her, the lady, been in to see me. J, begins with a J.

Someone's coming. What should I do? I don't know if I'm supposed to be here or not. Can't hide. She's coming straight for me. Looks like a uniform. A nurse, must be, or a fireman. She leans over me. Help.

'Hello, David, you're awake.'

So, I'm called David, or Awake. I try a reply but nothing comes out. I try again and force a whisper.

'Hello.'

'Well done. It's good to see you coming back to us. Doctor will be very pleased.'

I feel incredibly proud at the compliment and grin. But what did she mean, coming back? Where have I been? I want to ask her but she leans away to look at the machines beside me.

'Now, you settle down again David. Doctor will be round to see you in the morning.'

'What happened to me?' I manage.

'You've had a nasty accident but it seems you're on the mend now.'

'Oh.' I don't know what to say.

She pats my shoulder. 'Night, night, David.'

I lie back, look at the bare white ceiling and try to remember.

Chapter 40 – December 31st 9.30am

Bill

New Year's Eve. My least favourite day of the year. Used to hate it even when Mary was alive. Never could see the point in celebrating the fact that time had passed and would never return.

And, of course, if you were on duty, and I usually tried to be, you spent the whole night dealing with people who had celebrated themselves into an early grave. Seen too many of those. When I was younger, I used to wonder if they'd had any idea, earlier in the evening, as they put on their best knickers and dressed up for the parties, that they would end up on a slab. Of course not. That's not how life works.

Hard to believe in God when you see those pretty things laid out, have to deal with the parents. I found with most of us, you go to one extreme or another, either staring-eyed born again Methodist lay preachers or total cynics about the whole thing. I managed to hang in middle somehow, probably the influence of Mary and her good Irish Catholic upbringing.

Come on, Bill, snap out of it. I know what's happening to you. Morning after tristesse, as the French say. Big anti-climax after last night. No one to tell, no one to share it with. I'll pop down to the pub later and talk about football and the weather. That'll pass the time. Then it's back to business. Need to check on the money flow.

Doorbell rings. Can't be Chas, he's got family commitments. Maybe the Patels, asking me back for another curry.

I open the door to a very welcome surprise. 'Jenny, how lovely. Do come in out of the cold.'

'Bill, I hope this is OK. I was just passing and thought you might like some company.'

Just passing? I doubt it; we're nowhere near the hospital. Still, no need to probe, I'm sure it will all come out.

'Do come in. I was just going to put the kettle on.'

We chat about the weather and the news as I busy myself getting coffee. She seems hesitant to talk about last night.

I give her permission.

'So, you got home OK?'

'Oh, yes. It was rather thrilling, actually, sitting there on the tube like a typical suburban lady coming back from a day in town, looking round and thinking 'I know something you don't know.''

'But not tempted to share that knowledge?'

'God, no. As I've told you, it's the men who are the blabbermouths, not the women. No, I just hug the knowledge to me. It keeps me warm.'

We sit at the kitchen table with our coffees. I open the biscuit tin.

'And it's OK being at home on your own?'

'Yes. I put the alarm on downstairs when I go up at night. We never really bother with that when it's the two of us.' She hesitates for a moment, the smile wobbles, then deep breath and she's off again. 'But, no, I feel safe. Probably a complete illusion but it's good enough for me.'

'Good. Now, tell me more about David. Is there a date for coming home?'

Her brow furrows rather sweetly. 'They seem to think he could come out in about a week's time, maybe less, as long as there are no setbacks, of course.'

I lean forward. 'How do you feel about that?'

She looks startled. 'Well, I, it's good news. Of course.'

'But you'll be stuck at home looking after him, is that what you're thinking, back to being the dutiful wife?'

She nods. Tears start to form. 'He could go to a nursing home for a while, of course, we have good insurance, but I know he'll want to be at home.'

I put my hand on hers. It's small and warm.

'It's OK to feel that, you know,' I say, as gently as I can.

'No it's not.' She sits up straight but leaves her hand under mine. 'It's selfish and unfair. It's not David's fault that he was stabbed. For better or for worse. That's what I signed up for.'

'Are there people who can help you?'

'Yes, I'm sure there are and the insurance covers some home nursing. But most of it's going to be me. David's not good on his own, never has been. I think I'm stuck for a while. Actually, something I was going to ask you. You know that David was a banker? Actually, we both were.'

'Oh, now you're telling me something I didn't know. You were a banker too?'

'Yes, before the kids arrived. We, David and I, we met at the bank.' She giggles. Nice sound. 'In fact, and I don't usually tell anyone this, I was his boss.'

'Now, why does that not surprise me?'

'Yes, nearly fired him at one point! Anyway, I was wondering, once he's well enough, whether he could do your accounts, you know, for the, what shall I call them, the little expeditions? It would give him something to think about, other than himself.'

'Well, there's not much to do at the moment, all back of a fag packet stuff, but, who knows?'

'Actually, I was meaning to ask about where the money came from for all that stuff yesterday.'

I work on keeping my voice as level as possible – need to get off the subject.

'Oh, we have one or two people who support us and we chip in a bit ourselves, where we can.'

She leans back. 'In other words, mind your own business, Jenny.'

'No, no state secrets, it's just better if things are kept compartmentalised.'

'You mean, if someone gets picked up, it's best that they know as little as possible.'

'I suppose so, yes.'

'Is there much chance of anyone being picked up?'

The phone rings. I excuse myself, hiding my relief, and go to answer it. Chas's voice comes on the line.

'Hi, Bill.'

'Oh, hello, Chas, I'm just sitting here having a cup of coffee with Jenny. She just dropped in. Isn't that nice?'

'OK. I'll be brief. Andrew's sorted. And I've made arrangements for Alan to be, how can I put it, a little re-arranged, given that he stuffed us up at the last minute?'

'I'll have to get back to you about that.'

'OK, I'm tied up with the family for the rest of the day but we can talk tomorrow.'

'Fine.'

I ring off and return to Jenny. Don't have the nerve to take her hand again.

'Sorry about that. You were asking about risk. Well, we're pretty watertight but there's always the random factor. Most of my breakthroughs in the force came by stumbling across something by chance. It happens.' She's nodding, thoughtfully. 'Does that worry you?'

'No.' She smiles. 'I was just thinking of the reaction of the neighbours, knowing that this pillar of the community was an urban terrorist, albeit with clowns rather than bombs. Or my kids.' She laughs. 'Boring old Mum getting up to tricks like that.'

'Talking of kids, how are Nick and, er, Cressida, wasn't it?'

'Nick's been a tremendous support over the last few days. He'll be going back to work, of course, the day after tomorrow, but by then things should be well sorted. As for Cressida, well, between you and me, I have very strong suspicions about that girl.'

'How do you mean?'

'I think she's having an affair with Dominic Evans.'

I grip my hands together under the table, and stay quiet and casual as a whole list of possibilities writes itself. 'What makes you think so?'

She shrugs. 'Not the sort of thing that you would call evidence. Just good old feminine intuition.'

'I've learnt over the years not to undervalue that.'

'You know I stayed at their flat for two nights after the attack? Well, she's been working all week for Evans, no doubt planning the rally.'

'Not convincing so far.'

She slaps my hand. 'I haven't come to the meaty bit yet. On the second night, so that would have been the twenty-eighth, she came back very late looking decidedly, let's say, satisfied. Wouldn't look me in the eye at all, unusual for a forthright madam like her.'

'And you think...?'

'Bill, I don't think, I know.'

'Are you going to tell Nick?'

'I don't think so. I'm unsure. What would you do?'

'Not blessed with children, I'm afraid, so I'm not a good guide. I'd suggest that you hold back for now, though.'

'That's what I thought.' She takes a deep breath. 'Bill, I have to tell you, yesterday was just fantastic for me. I don't remember when I ever felt so alive before. I just want to say thank you for inviting me along.'

Her eyes are shining again. I smile; she makes it sound like we've been to a party.

'Plenty more, all being well. Birmingham next week.'

'Great. Count me in.'

'With pleasure. I think you'll be a very valuable member of our little band.'

'Gosh, Bill, here's me wittering on; I haven't even asked you about your injuries. How are you?'

'Oh, you know, tough old hide. I'll mend.'

Her hand comes up and touches my face where the bruises are. Her focus is totally on me. '*From thy bright eyes unusual brightness shed*'. Thanks, Keats, you always have the right words for it. She pulls her hand back.

'Anyway, look, I have to go. Have to get back to the hospital then do some grocery shopping. Thanks for the coffee.'

'Thanks for dropping in. A lovely surprise.'

I see her to the door.

'What are your plans for this evening?' I ask. 'Not really a time for celebration, I suppose?'

'Oh, we always do something in the road. Our next door neighbour is hosting this year. I'll pop in for a short while. I don't expect I'll stay long; I find people's sympathy is getting a bit wearing. Is that terrible of me?'

'No, I remember the same when I lost Mary. Anyway, the important thing is, it looks as if you're not losing David, so the sympathy will soon wear off.'

'True. Let's hope so. How about you, what are you doing?'

'Oh, probably pop down to the pub, have a drink with the regulars there. Unless, of course,' I hesitate, feel like a fifteen-year-old again, 'unless you'd like to pop over here.'

'Bill, that's a sweet offer.' I wait for the refusal. 'Look, let me see how the afternoon goes. It's certainly tempting.'

She leans forward, hesitates, then kisses me on the cheek, slowly. It feels good.

I see her out. Close the door. Hope David doesn't come out too soon. Don't really want anyone looking too closely at the numbers just now, though I suppose I can smoke screen them if need be.

Still, I think I know what to do about Mr Evans and Birmingham. I need to make some calls.

Barry

'Carolson, will you take that stupid grin off your face. If I didn't think it was totally impossible, I'd have thought you'd got your oats last night. And if, by some miracle, you have, please don't tell me about it. I don't think my stomach could take it this early in the morning.'

I say nothing and try very hard to rearrange my features into an interested expression. I force memories of last night out of my tired brain and get back to the subject.

'Now, Sherlock,' Inspector Williamson fixes me with a stare, 'are you anywhere near sorting this Delling thing?'

'Sorted, actually sir. Full confession from the wife.'

Eyebrows shoot up. 'Really? So, the wife was driving?'

'No, sir. Mr Belsworth was driving but he's in hospital, stabbed at their house on the evening of the twenty-seventh when they came home.'

'Was he indeed?'

'And it looks like a revenge attack.'

'What makes you say that?'

'Delling's name spray-painted all over the walls.'

'Well done.' He sees my surprised expression. 'No, come on, credit where it's due. You've done well. Do you have all the paperwork?'

'Not yet, sir, but the confession was witnessed by the officer in charge of the case, Inspector Wedley.'

'Wedley? That tosser. Well, that case will come to nothing, you can be certain of that. You just make sure you've got the paperwork done; it's not over till it's written down.'

'Yes, sir.' I hesitate, not sure how he's going to take this.

'Actually, sir, I had the same impression about Inspector Wedley. So, since I was the officer at the original incident, I took it upon myself to do some further investigation.'

He's looking at me, frowning.

'Go on.'

'I felt there was probably some kind of connection between the gang that attacked Mr Johnson and Mr Belsworth and the Dominic Evans rally, so I made some enquiries and found that the Albion Café in Albion Street was the centre for recruiting people to come to the rally. I went in and struck up conversation with one of the organisers, a man called Jeff, haven't got any more yet. Anyway, I went along with them to the rally yesterday to get to know them and, with your permission, I can see if I can infiltrate further.'

Silence.

'So, you were at the rally, were you? We'll come back to that. Firstly, you have gone way beyond your terms of reference here and you know it. The police force is not some kind of private army full of freelancers doing what they want. We report and we do what we are told. Is that clear?'

'Yes, sir. Sorry, sir.'

'How do you know whether we already have people in that organisation? You could have screwed up weeks, months even, of work.'

I stare at the floor.

'So, don't do that sort of thing again, right. Not without checking first.'

'I just felt, it's just that I was there, I knew about it. If I'd passed it back it would just have gone on someone else's list and been forgotten.'

'Possibly, but it's not your job to prioritise our work. That said, and it's important you remember what I've just said, well done.'

'Sorry?'

'Well done. I like to see people taking the initiative, even if it means they do something bloody stupid occasionally. So, what have you found?'

'About the organisation? Not much yet, but I've told Jeff I'm happy to help out on stuff and he has my phone number.'

'OK. If he calls, you tell me straight away. Clear?'

'Yes, sir.'

'Now, about the rally. Did you see anything useful?'

'Just before the clowns appeared, I saw uniformed staff walk up several of the passages between the seats. The one nearest us put some kind of box or bag down then walked on. I think that bag contained one of the clowns, I'm guessing some kind of gas cylinder too. Probably on a remote control trigger of some kind.'

'Very good.'

'May I ask, sir, what your interest is?'

'You may. I was seconded to the O2 last night for security detail. Some lucky bugger had the day off. And I've ended up with a murder investigation on my hands.'

'Murder? I didn't see any bodies.'

'Backstage. One of Evans' minions. Probably fell off a staircase, to be honest, but we have to check. In fact,' he looks at his watch, 'I've got one possible suspect coming in here in about thirty minutes. Tell you what, when are you due to go out on the beat?'

'Twelve, sir.

'OK. Sit in on this interview then I want you to look at some CCTV of the interior of the O2, see if anything rings a bell.'

'Great.'

'Now, don't get any big ideas. You're still uniform. But do this well and we'll see.'

'Right, sir. What do you want me to do in the interview?'

'I want you to sit still and shut up.'

'Oh, right, sir.'

'Now, go and see Walker. He's got the CCTV stuff. I'll call you when Miss Cressida Huntley-Jones arrives.'

Chapter 42 – December 31st 10.30am

Jenny

I wish I could tell David all about last night. I know he'd be appalled but that would be half the fun.

I suppose that's why I went round to Bill. Wasn't true about not wanting to breathe a word. I want to shout it down Pinner High Street through a megaphone. All those people who've rendered me invisible as I've got middle-aged, I want them to stand open mouthed, as they struggle to restructure their rigid synapses. I want the WI to mutter to each other, 'Well, and she seemed such an upright person, one of us, who'd have thought it' and all feel a little shiver of envy. I will just have to settle for walking around with a big grin. I guess that's why it would be good to go round to Bill tonight; relive every moment. That, and…

'Hello, Mrs Belsworth, good to see you looking so positive.'

I'm startled to see the duty nurse smiling up at me from her desk, though, as always with medical staff, there's that slight tone of disapproval, as if I should have asked the doctor's permission before smiling. For a moment, I'm not sure how I got here. What seemed like a warren of passages two days ago now feels as familiar as my own house, easy to negotiate on automatic pilot.

'Hello, nurse. Well, got to stay positive and all that.'

'So true. And you'll be glad to know that Mr Belsworth seems to be rallying well.'

'Wonderful.' I hope that sounds genuine.

'Go on through. I think he's awake.'

'Thanks.' Down the corridor, second on the left.

David is propped up in bed. Still plenty of tubes but I see straight away that there's more animation. He looks across at me and recognition slowly widens his eyes.

'Hello, David.'

'Hello.' The voice is hoarse and barely audible but it's a voice. I feel as pleased and excited as when Nick recited The Ancient Mariner at his prep school speech day.

I hold the hand that does not have the drip in it.

'How are you?'

He nods slowly. 'Good as can be expected, in the circumstances,' he whispers.

I look up and see a twinkle in his eyes. I laugh out loud.

'I'm delighted to hear it.'

'What's out there?'

'You mean what's happening in the big wide world? Well, it's raining, it's bloody cold and the whole world's going to hell in a hand basket or whatever the expression is. And you just lazing around here.'

He raises his other hand. 'Don't make me laugh. Dangerous.'

'Sorry. No, it's just the usual boring time waiting for the final celebration to be out of the way tonight. New Year's Eve,' I explain, seeing his puzzled expression. 'Then we can get back to normality again.'

'House?'

'All cleaned up. We've stripped the wallpaper in the hall and I'll speak to Mr Binsley about coming in and putting up something else.'

'Good. Never liked it. Get regency stripes.'

I'm about to say 'Over my dead body' but realise just in time that this would be a trifle inappropriate.

'David, do you know what happened to you?'

He nods. 'Bits. Nurse explained. Have they got them?'

'Not yet. Have they said anything about when you can come home?'

'Doctor on holiday till two days.'

'OK. I guess that's the problem with this time of year. Still, gives you the chance to rest.'

His head falls back onto the pillow.

'You're tired. I'll go and get myself a coffee and come back and see you in a while.'

He nods, closes his eyes and I slip away.

So, that gives me at least three days. Might even be able to do whatever's going to happen in Birmingham. God, I hope so. Definitely going to see Bill tonight.

Chapter 43 – December 31st 10.30am

Cressida

'Cressida Huntley-Jones, here to see Inspector Williamson. I have a ten thirty appointment.'

Appointment sounds good, better than interview, puts it on a level with the doctor or dentist. Interview carries much more scary connotations.

The officer behind the desk looks at me as if I've asked him to explain some complex mathematical theorem, then sighs and picks up the phone.

'Lady to see you, sir. Name of…'

'Cressida Huntley-Jones.'

'A Miss Jones, sir. Right you are.' He indicates a wooden bench. 'Please wait there, miss, he'll be out in a minute.'

I look pointedly at my watch and sit. Beside me are copies of yesterday's *Mirror* and *Sun* and a three-month-old *People's Friend*. I decide to read the notices on the wall.

I've already seen today's papers. As soon as I woke, I was out to the newsagent, probably his first customer. Bought them all. Every one of them carried coverage of the rally. And every one majored on the clowns. *Clown Prince, Clowned in Glory, The Inflated Ego of Mr Evans* – that was *The Times*, and, even I had to admit, quite funny. None of them gave much space, if any to the bit of Dominic's speech that he was able to get out and none covered the death of Andy; too late, I guess, for them, but no doubt on the internet in the course of this morning, complete with conspiracy theories.

I tried calling Dominic, of course, but no answer. It rang, so his phone was on. I suppose he just doesn't want to talk to me. I left a message, anyway, saying I had to be here for an interview. That will get him to call back, I'm sure of it.

Five minutes late. I really hate it when people keep you waiting. So rude. I need to get back and prepare for Birmingham. I suppose, truth be told, I need to get back and see if I still have a job.

'Miss Huntley-Jones, good morning. Do come this way.' The inspector's smiling at me, all charm, as if that will wash. Not a word of apology for keeping me waiting.

He leads me into a small, dingy room with a high ceiling. I see a camera in the corner.

'Do sit down, over there. You didn't feel it necessary to bring a solicitor with you?'

'No, why should I?' And I left the only solicitor I know sulking on the sofa.

'Well, we'll see, won't we? Now, Miss Huntley-Jones, we will be recording this interview. I shall be joined by a colleague, a male colleague, but you may request the presence of a female officer if you wish.'

'That won't be necessary.'

The door opens and a rather chubby policeman in uniform comes in.

'Miss Huntley-Jones,' even I am getting irritated at my name; perhaps I should marry Nicky, 'this is Sergeant Carolson.'

We nod at each other.

'Now,' the inspector continues, 'I see that no-one has offered you a coffee.'

'That's right.'

'That will be because this is a police station and you are here so that we can decide whether you killed Andrew Woodham.'

'What?'

'Did you, Miss Huntley-Jones.'

'I… of course not. Why should I?'

'You were seen arguing with him just a few minutes before the body was found. Your whereabouts cannot be fully accounted for. And you made up some story about neckwear that would not have even fooled Sergeant Carolson here.'

'Is this the bit where I say OK, it's a fair cop, gov?'

'No, Miss Huntley-Jones, this is the bit where you tell us exactly what happened.'

I sigh, I can see that it's going to be better to tell them at least some truth about our conversation.

'OK, look, I was scared last night. It had been a very upsetting evening, what with the disruption of the speech and then, of course, Andy's death.'

'Yes, such a nuisance for you. Do go on.'

'Andy tried to hit on me.'

'Hit on you?'

'Tried to get me to go out with him after the rally, not that that would have happened, as it turned out. I turned him down, perhaps a little more harshly than I should have done, and he lost his temper, accused me of having an affair with Dominic, Mr Evans.'

'And are you having an affair with Mr Evans?'

'No, of course not.' And that is probably true, damn it.

'Why would he think you were?'

'Inspector, there are some men who just can't cope with an intelligent woman. They think that, if the boss prefers you, it must be about sex.'

'Really?'

'Andy knew that Dominic trusted me and was giving me more responsibility, so I guess he was jealous.'

'But he was a speech writer and you are…what exactly is your role, Miss Huntley-Jones?'

'Personal Assistant, researcher, organiser, whatever he needs.'

'Whatever he needs. Yes. So your jobs didn't really overlap.'

'Not in any organisational way, but Dominic Evans is a man who is going places, yes, in spite of yesterday, and there is always a certain jostling for position to be close to someone like that.'

'And have you been jostling?'

'I just do my job and it seems I do it well. And if you're implying I use sex to get where I want, I have a boyfriend with whom I live and whom I love very much.'

And who is not talking to me this morning.

'Yes, we'd better have his details. You can give them to the sergeant when we've finished. So, can you account for your time after the argument with Mr Woodham?'

'Well, I had to go and see Dominic. Ramon, the bodyguard came for me so he can tell you, then I watched the music act from the wings, then it was time for Dominic to go on.'

'Did anyone see you?'

'Well, people were coming and going. Oh, I did see Andy in the opposite wings just as Dominic got started. I remember giving him a wave.'

'Yes, going to be a bit difficult to get him to corroborate that, is it? Anyone see you after you waved to him?'

'No, some workman in overalls pushed past me, nearly knocked me over but then disappeared.'

The sergeant leans forward. 'May I, sir?' He looks meekly at the inspector, who nods.

'This workman, what was he wearing?'

'Blue overalls, I think, usual workman's stuff. And a baseball cap.'

'Carrying anything?'

I try hard to think back. 'A sort of big bag, I think. That's what hit me as he went past.'

'And can you describe this person?'

'No, I only saw him from behind.'

'Tall, short? Fat, thin?'

'Quite small, I would say, yes, slight. And I think he had long hair, there was a bit hanging down from under the cap.'

'So, it could have been a woman?'

'Well, I suppose so. You don't think of women doing that sort of job, do you?'

'Thank you.' The sergeant leans back and the inspector takes over again.

'OK. Miss Huntley-Jones. We will stop there for now. We may well want you to come in again.'

'Well, if I must. I do have a very demanding job, you know.'

'Yes, so do we.'

I stand to go.

'Oh, you are going to need to give your boyfriend's details to the sergeant here.'

'Is that entirely necessary?'

'No, I'm just deliberately wasting your time and mine.' He's glaring at me. Not a good time to argue.

'He lives at the same address as me, which you already have, his number is 07756 936756. And his name is Nicky Belsworth.'

The sergeant, who's been scribbling madly stops dead, pencil poised.

'Would he be any relation of Mrs Jenny Belsworth?'

'Yes, she's his mother. Why?'

'Just another case we are working on.'

'The stabbing?'

'Yes.' The sergeant looks nervously at the inspector then continues. 'By the way, was your boyfriend with you at the rally?'

'He was there, but in the audience. The last thing I want is to have him hanging round when I'm working.'

The inspector reasserts himself. 'Thank you, Miss Huntley-Jones, that will be all for now. We will need your fingerprints. Sergeant Carolson here will sort that out.' He sweeps out of the room.

The sergeant busies himself with the fingerprint kit and, within five minutes, I am back on the street, thankfully breathing in the damp and dirty air and hiding my inky fingers in my pocket.

Now for the second nightmare of the day.

Chapter 44 – December 31st 12.00 noon

Jenny

Funny how things only occur to you afterwards. That strange evasion of Bill's about the money, where it comes from. What was that all about? It reminded me of when I was doing due diligence, in my early banking days, how you learned to sniff out the nasty secrets.

Well, we shall see. First things first, back to the house, then the boring stuff, shopping, changing the bed. Oh, and the dry cleaners. Try to explain why my jumper is covered in dried blood. Perhaps I should just throw it away.

It's good to turn into the road and not see that awful red and white tape round the house. The house is beginning to feel like mine again. Postman waves at me, it's like some 1930's film of happy England. We'll never get that back, if it ever existed.

In the house, I take off my coat, gather up the post and head into the kitchen to make myself a coffee. Most of it is just bills, circulars and a couple of late Christmas cards, from the more distant friends, no doubt, who thought we had dropped them and then got a last minute card from us. I always feel sorry for the ones who come at the end of the alphabet, always getting caught out.

There's an envelope, square and plain. I open it. Inside is a DVD in a plastic sleeve. No markings. Picking up my coffee, I take it through to the sitting room and push the disc into the player. What I see makes me sit down very suddenly.

On the screen, slightly jerky because it's been shot, I guess, on a mobile phone, are images of me, driving out of this drive, in the supermarket, parking at the hospital and going in, walking up to Bill's door. I run it again, looking closely at what I'm wearing. All this has been taken over the last two days.

I check the envelope. There's nothing with it. I sit, holding my coffee in both hands, staring at the now blank screen. I don't understand. I mean, it's clear that someone has been following me. Stalking, I suppose you'd call it. But who? And why?

The phone rings.

'Mrs Belsworth?' Well spoken, quietly insistent.

'Yes. Who is this?'

'Mrs Belsworth, did you open your post?'

'Yes. Who's calling?'

'Sean Delling.'

The phone goes dead.

Chapter 45 – December 31st 12.00 noon

Barry

I remember reading somewhere that coincidences are glimpses out of the corner of your eye of some great Master Plan. If so, what am I supposed to understand from this connection between Cressida Huntley-Jones and Jenny Belsworth? That's the trouble with clever little sayings like that; they still leave you short of the mark.

'OK, Sherlock, tell all.'

Inspector Williamson is staring at me. He obviously knows how disconcerting those heavy eyebrows are.

'To be honest, sir, I'm not sure. It may just be complete chance but it seems strange that the name should come up in two different places like that.'

'Where do you think the connection might lie?'

I'm beginning to regret my lack of sleep. 'I suppose the only connection is the group that beat up Mr Johnson. They clearly vandalised the Belsworth's house and, if I'm right about them being the same people, they were at the rally.'

'And do you think that Mrs Belsworth was at the rally?'

'I don't know, sir. We don't know for certain that she wasn't.'

'Well, perhaps you'd better find out.'

'I'd like to, sir, but I'm on patrol at twelve.'

'So you are. Right, why don't you swing by her place after your shift? See if you can find out her whereabouts.'

'That would be a bit late, sir. I wouldn't get to her till about nine or nine thirty. That's late to knock on the door of a woman on her own, especially after what she's been through. And anyway, it's New Year's Eve. She may be out somewhere.'

'Right. I'll see if I can get you off early. Leave it with me, uniform owe me a favour. Meanwhile, did you finish looking at that CCTV from the O2?'

'Not yet, sir.'

'Right, get back onto that. I'll come and find you.'

The TV monitor room is dark and hot. I have real trouble staying awake. I force myself to look closer, seeing if I can glimpse our group and especially Salita. I was due to go round to see her again tonight, said she was off to some party and would I come. I'll have to phone and make an excuse, or see her later there. Hate having to lie to her but can't be helped. Now, back to the screen.

Right, I've found the one that covers our part of the auditorium. That must be our group there. Try zooming in but it just gets pixelated. The speech has obviously just started, everyone's staring at the stage. And there's that person in overalls, walking up the aisle. Drops that bag about half way up. Walks on to the top. Let's just run that again slowly. Whoever it is, he's finding the bag heavy. Or she. Could be. There's a way of walking there, after the bag is dropped, that could well be a woman. That Cressida said there was long hair.

The figure turns at the top and points something, the trigger, I suppose, back down at the bag. Cap's right down over the eyes. Can't see the face. But that stance seems familiar.

I wonder.

Chapter 46 – December 31st 12.30pm

Bill

'Chas, we have a bit of a problem.'

'What's that?'

'Just had a call from Jenny. Nearly hysterical. She got a DVD through the post this morning, showing film of her movements over the last two days.'

'What? Including the rally?'

'No. They've got her coming here but not to the flat or the O2. At least, if they do have it, they haven't sent it to her.'

'What do we do?'

'We have to assume the worst, that they know about us. Do you have someone you can spare to tail the tail? Not today, no point and who are you going to find on New Year's Eve? From tomorrow.'

'Of course. And, presumably encourage them to desist.'

'No. Not yet. Don't want them to know we're onto them.'

'They wouldn't if he didn't get the chance to report back.'

'Not worth the risk for now. No, we need to know who they are and where they're coming from. And make sure they don't know we're there.'

'It's OK, Bill, you don't need to teach me my job. Remember, I had you covered for years and you didn't know.'

'OK, just do it.'

'I'll have someone on it this afternoon. Is she at home at the moment?'

'Yes, she'll probably go to the shops a bit later, then she's out at a neighbour's this evening. I've told her to tell no one else.'

'Tell her to wait in until two, then go out as normal as possible. You're not planning to meet her, are you?'

'I wasn't born yesterday, Chas. Right, other things. It seems her son's girlfriend, one Cressida Huntley-Jones, is not only working for our Mr Evans but is also having an affair with him. I feel that this is information that should be shared, ideally visually, with the nation at large.'

'Nice. Leave it to me. I'll get them on to it straight away. See if we can catch the Sundays.'

I hang up. I hate having to rely on Chas, he's only going to stay nice as long as he feels there's something in it for him. Better chase up the money people. Bank holidays are always a good time to be busy.

Damn, I don't want to lose Jenny. Do I recognise a good operator or am I just being a sentimental old fool? Bit of both, I suppose. There's a bit of a spark there, I'm sure. Maybe there is life in the old dog yet. We'll see this evening and to hell with Chas and his cronies.

Chapter 47 – December 31st 4.00pm

Cressida

I get to the office by midday. Impossible to find a cab; they're all lurking round the sales in Brent Cross, not in beautiful downtown Wembley. Half of them wouldn't dare come up here, even in daylight. And no doubt quite a few are still recovering from Christmas. They should learn from Singapore. When we were out there last year they were saying that each taxi is owned by two people, who do twelve hours each, every day. That's the way to get ahead.

So, the pleasures of the tube and finally, here I am. I look through from my office to Dominic's and see it's full of people. I recognise Jack, the PR guru who has been guiding Dominic and one man from the lawyer's but not the others. They must be their hangers-on.

I give Dominic a wave; he barely acknowledges me. I sit at my desk, ensuring I'm in his sight line and get busy with the arrangements for Birmingham. Firstly, though, I need to clear all the files for last night's fiasco. One is labelled Security. I pick it up and remind myself of what was agreed.

I reach for the phone.

The conversation in Dominic's office goes on, quiet voices, urgent, irritated. I pick up snips of it, 'containable', 'sue them,' track them down', 'destroy'. Eventually, after about half an hour, they stand up. Dominic comes to the door to see them off. I don't look up from the computer, carry on tapping busily as they shake hands and go.

Silence.

'So?' he eventually asks.

I look up. 'So?'

Impatience flashes across his face. Let it, I'm not going to grovel.

'So, what did you have to tell them?'

'You got my message, then?'

'Of course.'

I take a deep breath. 'I told them that I knew nothing about Andy's death. I told them that your whereabouts were completely accounted for. I said I thought it had been an accident.'

'Good. And do you?'

'Do I what?'

'Think it was an accident? Know nothing about it?'

'Of course. Do you?'

'I think it was a warning to me. I think they killed Andy to get me to back off.'

'Really?'

'Cressida. This is serious stuff. People feel threatened by me. Otherwise, why go to such lengths? There was money behind last night's attack.'

'Hardly an attack.'

'One man dead, risk of major panic, what would you call it?'

'Good point. And that's what you'll say to the press tomorrow?'

'No papers tomorrow. New Year's Day. We're going for the Sundays. We'll put out the news of Andy's death today, then go to town on the conspiracy at the weekend'

'OK. And what do you want me to do?'

I wait, hoping the instruction is not the same as last night's.

'Well, you're certainly not going to handle security.'

So, it seems I'm not sacked, then. Time to go for an advantage.

'Dominic, I did not handle security last night.'

'You're telling me.'

'No, I did not handle security, I was not allowed to. Security was totally in the hands of the arena. I've already called them and demanded our money back. I'm guessing that entry cost was so low for the audience that very few will want refunds, so we should have some money back in the coffers.'

I tilt my head to one side and stare up at him, wide-eyed. He stares back for a moment then, thank God, starts to laugh.

'Good. Well done. I'm glad I haven't underestimated you.'

'You did but we'll let that pass, for now. By the way, the police want to talk to you. I had to give them your mobile number.'

The smile vanishes. 'You did what?'

'I may, in my distress at the time, have slightly muddled the numbers.'

He breathes out, relieved.

'Dominic, do you have any idea who's behind this?'

'To be honest, no. There's been no press release from them yet, so nothing to trace. My hunch is that it's going to be a group that pretend they're defending the rights of oldies.'

'Why do you think they're just pretending?'

'Because of the money that went into it. This is not some bunch from the local old people's home having a day out. And, if they're willing to spend this much, they must have more. Where's it coming from? And why?'

'Good questions. But no answers?'

'Not yet. I've got people on it. Someone will slip up. They always do.'

'Good. The sooner the better. By the way, talking of money, how are our funds looking?'

'OK, especially if we can get the money back from the O2. I've got plenty of people who want me to succeed, some for better reasons than others, but we can sort that out later.'

'What do you mean?'

'Oh, some want to back me because they believe in what I'm doing. Others want to make money out of what I do.'

'And is that bad?'

'Not at all. In fact, I find it easier to deal with the ones who are looking to make a buck than the fanatics. But there's always a few that will have to be jettisoned at the right moment.'

'Fair enough. Now, what do we have to do about Birmingham?'

'Lots, but not just now. There's time.'

He takes my arm and pulls me up to him, looping his hands round my bottom. I glance nervously out of the window at the office block opposite. The last day's events have made me paranoid.

'Don't worry. There's no one over there. It's New Year's Eve, for heaven's sake. Everyone sensible is at home getting ready for a party.'

'Which is where I have to be in an hour's time and you too, no doubt.'

'Oh, God, yes, Emily has organised a do where I will have to be the star attraction.'

'Come on, you love it.'

His hand travels up, lifting my skirt.

'True. Still, I'm sure we can stretch that hour to an hour and a half.'

I'm certainly not going to argue.

Chapter 48 – December 31st 4.15pm

Jenny

The phone rang again about twelve forty-five. Made me jump out of my skin but it was only Barry the policeman, wanting to come over. I put him off until five, so that I could come out to the shops. But now I'm out, I wish I had told him to come straight over. Every moment I'm longing to look round, see who's following me. I can hardly remember what I came out for.

Finally, I give up, leave Sainsbury's with my few items and walk, head bent into the rain, back to the car park. There's at least a hundred cars here. Any one of them could have a man with a camera. Maybe there are two of them. Maybe more. What if they follow me into the house?

I reach the sanctuary of the car, scramble in and lock the doors. Did I look suspiciously rushed? The whole world is rushed. And with this foul weather no one is going to move slowly.

So calm down. Calm down? Let's just list the reasons why I can't calm down. No, let's not, that would just make it worse. I jump as my mobile goes off. I scrabble for it in my handbag.

'Hi, Mum. Just calling to see how you are.'

'Oh, Nick, hello. Yes, fine, thanks.'

'You don't sound fine.'

'Oh, you know, rushing around getting provisions in. It's ridiculous, I know, with the shops only shut for one day and the corner shops open anyway but, you know…' I'm babbling.

'Yes, right. Well, just, you know, wanted to see how you were.'

'Fine. What are you up to tonight?'

'Well, in theory we're going round to some friends. But Cress has just called to say she's working late again.'

'Oh.'

'Yes. We'll be lucky if we manage to be first footers. That man's a slave driver. I hope it's worthwhile. From what little I saw of his speech last night, I'm not so sure.'

'You were there last night?'

'Yes, don't make it sound so extraordinary. I do get out, you know.'

'Sorry, no. I didn't mean… Anyway, you didn't rate him?'

'Seems a bit of a rabble-rouser. I think Cress is just hooked on the adrenalin of the whole thing. She came back in a stinking mood last night because it had all gone pear-shaped. Left me feeling it was all my fault.'

'Yes, I heard about the clowns and things. I have to say, I thought it was very funny.'

'So did I.' Nick laughs. 'Though I wouldn't dare tell Cress.'

'Anyway, darling, you have a good evening.'

'You too. As far as you can,' he adds hastily. 'Are you up to anything tonight?'

'What do you mean?'

'Um, like, are you going anywhere? I mean, I know it'll be awkward.'

I try to force my heart to slow down.

'Oh, I see. Yes, probably pop round to the usual neighbours' do.'

'OK. I'll call tomorrow and we can arrange to come round again before I go back to work.'

'Great.'

I ring off and wonder why I didn't tell him about the DVD. British stiff upper lip? Not wanting to worry him? I suspect, probably, it's just that if I talk about it, it makes it all real.

I pull out of the car park, down the slope to the road. Several other cars are coming out at the same time. One, no doubt, containing the people who are following me.

I turn onto the road, narrowly missing a car coming the other way. He sounds his horn, gives me a V sign. Working very hard to hold back the tears, I head for home.

Chapter 49 – December 31st 5.15pm

Barry

As I stand at the door, I hear an upstairs window open.

'Who is it?' The voice sounds nervous.

'Mrs Belsworth, Jenny, it's me, Barry Carolson.'

'I'll come down.'

I wait, buffeted by the wind, rain starting to ooze down my neck. It's been a long walk up from the tube and I'm in civvies, without my thick uniform coat to protect me. My only consolation is knowing that Taff Jones is having to do my shift, plodding round Wembley town centre in this weather. Such a shame.

After a few moments, I hear the chain coming off the door and locks being turned. Strange, at this time in the afternoon. She must still be freaked by the attack.

The door opens. This is a very different Jenny Belsworth. Gone is the straight look, the square-shouldered stance. She looks older, smaller, greyer.

'Come in, Barry. Would you like some tea?'

The eternal British greeting. I accept, of course. I know the procedure; give the victim something to do, keep it familiar and light. I peel off a few layers while she relocks the door and then busies herself with the kettle. Her hands shake.

'Dreadful weather out there.'

'Yes.'

'Any plans for tonight?'

She looks confused, as if I'd asked her to solve a complex riddle. She runs her hands through her hair.

'I don't know. I'm due at some neighbours but, we'll see. Maybe.'

She puts the tea on the wooden table. We sit. She jumps up again.

'Sorry, did you want biscuits?'

'That's OK. I should cut back anyway.'

'Christmas over indulgence?'

'Not really, just generally eating too much of the wrong things.'

'Right.'

There's a pause. I let it go on.

'So, er, Barry, you wanted to talk. Have you found anything useful?'

'Quite possibly. I think I've started to get in with the gang who attacked Bill Johnson and, therefore, we have to assume, you and your husband.'

She looks at me, wide eyed. For a moment I think she's going to burst into tears but I see her jaw tighten. She nods to me to continue.

'Anyway, I went with them to the Dominic Evans thing last night and…'

'You were at the Dominic Evans rally?'

'Yes, why?'

'It's, it's just that it seems everyone I speak to was there.'

'Really, who else?'

'Well, my son, for one.'

Really, is he a supporter?'

'No, his girlfriend works for Evans.'

'You say that as if you don't approve of Mr Evans.'

'I don't. Why would anyone over fifty approve of what he has to say?'

'Good point. Who else?'

'Sorry?'

'Everyone I speak to was there, you said.'

'Did I? Yes, well, I haven't spoken to many people today.'

'So, that's it?'

She shrugs.

'Were you there, Jenny?'

She stares at me, then shakes her head violently.

'Why on earth would I be there?' But there's a slight colouring in her cheeks. All I need to know.

'I don't know. Is there a reason?'

'Don't you think I've got enough on my plate without that? Good God, Sergeant, I thought you were on my side here. You're supposed to be solving one crime, not trying to invent others. I really don't need this amateur sleuthing today. I think you'd better go.'

She stands.

I remain seated.

'Jenny, Mrs Belsworth, I am working on solving your crime. But things are rippling out from it. You see…'

The phone rings. She jumps, her shoulders hunch. She does not go to answer it. This is not a call she wants.

'Are you going to answer that?'

'It'll go to answer-phone. Now, if there's nothing else.'

I get up slowly; I need to know why she's rushing me out. The answering message finishes. We both wait in silence, staring at each other. Then, a voice.

'Mrs Belsworth, Sean Delling again. I hope you enjoyed your trip to the shops. Maybe, as soon as your friend has left, I'll call again. By the way, I don't recommend the broccoli quiche you bought at Sainsbury's. Wouldn't want you to feel unwell.'

A click, then silence.

She sinks back into her chair, puts her head in her hands.

'Anything you'd like to tell me, Jenny?'

Her head shakes.

'Look,' I lean across the table towards her, 'Whoever is threatening you, you can tell me. It doesn't even need to go further. Come on, get it off your chest.'

She looks up and there are tears running down her cheeks. 'I don't know what to do,' she whispers.

'Start at the beginning.'

A long silence as she stares at the table. Finally, her head comes up.

'Earlier today, in the post, I got a DVD with pictures of me, obviously taken over the last couple of days. Then I got a call from someone, that voice there, that person, saying he was Sean Delling. They're watching me, Barry. They know you're here.'

'It's lucky I wasn't in uniform, then. Who else have you told?'

She hesitates. 'Just a friend.'

'And your son?'

'No.'

Must be some friend, to be told before the son.

'And this friend, did she give you any advice.'

A moment's pause. 'No.'

'Well. I'm going to. If you let me, I'll call in our specialist team to put a tag on these people. They won't see us but we will see them and, that way, we will be able to find the people who stabbed your husband.'

She has been shaking her head all the way through this speech.

'It's too risky. What if someone finds out?'

'Would you rather be jumping every time the phone rings for the rest of your life?' Her head slowly shakes. 'Now, wait here while I dial 1471 and see if the call's traceable. Though it's almost certainly withheld.'

As I get up, the phone rings again. We both jump. I signal to her to wait. Finally, the voice comes through.

'Oh, Mrs Belsworth, this is Sister McKenzie from Jubilee Ward. Good news, the surgeon has been in today and taken a look at your husband. He says that Mr Belsworth can come home as soon as you are ready. With tomorrow being a bank holiday and then it's Sunday, I'm arranging transport for Monday. Hope that's all right. Bye now, and Happy New Year.'

This last comment elicits a snort from Jenny.

'God, what makes her think that's good news?' She throws up her hands. 'I'm sorry, I should be delighted that David's coming back home. But I'm just not ready and with all this as well, I mean, how am I going to cope?'

'If he wasn't private, he'd be out tonight.'

'There is that. Some consolation, I suppose, but what am I going to do? I can't look after him with these people following me around.'

I suddenly remember my conversation with Salita last night.

'Look, Jenny, I know someone who, I think, might help.'

'What do you mean?'

'Someone I know who's trained in looking after people at home. I think she's free at the moment. Shall I give her a call?'

'Is she experienced? Does she have references?'

'To be honest, I'm not sure but you can check that with her. You don't really have many options at the moment.'

'You're right. Why not? Let's at least try and get something sorted.'

I fish my mobile out of my pocket and call Salita.

'Hi, Barry, how's my nerdy hunk this afternoon?'

I push the mobile closer to my ear so no sound escapes.

'Salita, hi. Listen, I'm with a friend who needs your help.'

'Another nerd need rescuing? I think I've got my hands full with you.'

'No, she's got a problem.'

'She?'

'Yeah, look, don't worry, she's an older lady.' Jenny looks up and glares at me. I look fixedly out of the window at nothing in particular. 'Her husband was stabbed last week. He's OK, or at least he will be, but he's coming out of hospital on Monday and she has no one to help her with looking after him. I was wondering, you know, what with you saying that you were trained in this sort of thing, whether you might be able to help.'

'Don't think so. I'm a bit busy doing nothing at the moment.'

'Look,' I turn my back on Jenny, 'she's in a bit of a fix at the moment. It would be really good if you could help out, just for a couple of days, maybe.'

'When did you say her husband was coming out of hospital?'

'Monday.'

'And where does she live?'

'Pinner.'

'Ooh, you do have some posh friends. Look, probably not but let's talk about it this evening. And don't make any promises, right?'

'Great. Thanks.'

'Now, when am I going to get my hands around your podgy great...'

'Um, as soon as I can. I'm on a, on a visit at the moment. I may be a bit late over but I'll be there as soon as I can.'

'Well, I'm not the patient type.'

'Ok, I'll be there. Bye.'

'Bye, Fernando.' I hear the giggle as I close the phone. I'm puzzled by Salita's lack of enthusiasm for the work but I guess that's the way it is with that group, so used to not working that they can't get their heads round actually doing something. I'll talk to her about it.

'Well?' Jenny is looking anxiously at me.

'I think I can persuade her.'

'I'll pay top rates.'

'And I'm sure she'll ask for them. Now, back to business, and I am here on official business. Firstly, these people who are harassing you. Have they asked for anything? Made any threats?'

'No, nothing. That's what makes it so scary. If they just came out and said what they wanted, I'd know what I was up against.'

'What they want, I suspect, is to scare you witless and I think they're succeeding.'

'But why?'

'Because you killed their mate. The big question is, are they going to be satisfied with just scaring you?' I know I risk frightening her even more but I need to get her to do what I want.

She gets up and draws the blind down over the dark window.

'I know. I have thought of that, you know. Thought of little else.'

'Right, Jenny. I'm going to make a call now and get a team ready to deal with this harassment. But I need your agreement.'

She hesitates. My mobile rings in my pocket. I check it. Number withheld. I let it go to voicemail.

Jenny smiles faintly. 'Seems it's an afternoon of not answering phones.'

'Don't change the subject.'

'All right. I don't seem to have a choice. And you promise me they will be discreet.'

'They're professionals. They know what to do.'

Having seen two of them strip naked after a drinking competition at the Christmas Party, I wish I had as much confidence as my words suggest.

'I'll make a call now to my boss. Is there somewhere I can do it without bothering you?'

'Without me hearing, you mean?'

'Well, that too.'

'Use David's study, across the hall, through the sitting room and you'll see it on the far side.'

'Thanks.'

Once there, I first check my voicemail.

'Barry, this is Jeff. When we were talking at the O2, you said you'd be glad to help out. I've got something for you. Salita tells me you're coming to the party at Mick's tonight. We'll talk then.'

Promising. I take out my police phone and call Inspector Williamson.

'Sir, I'm at Mrs Belsworth's house.'

'And?'

'I'm pretty certain she can tell us something about last night but there's an issue in the way. She's being stalked. They sent her a DVD of footage of what she's been doing in the last couple of days and she's getting the phone calls.'

'And who are "they"?'

'I think it's the same crowd. They called her, using Sean Delling's name.'

'So, they may know that she was involved with last night.'

Damn, why didn't I think of that?

'That's right, sir.'

'Who else has she told?'

'Just a friend.'

'Who?'

'Haven't got that yet, sir.'

'Find out. If she's told the people she's involved with, they are not going to be happy. She needs protection.'

'That's what I said to her. She's agreed to letting us tail the people watching her. How soon can we get something set up?'

'Do you know if they're still watching?'

'They phoned a few minutes ago. Knew I was here.'

'Do they know you're police?'

'Don't think so.'

'OK. I want you to stay there till I call you back. Keep your wits about you, Carolson. This could be tricky.'

'Yes, sir.'

I go back into the kitchen trying to look confident and in control.

Chapter 50 – December 31st 6.00pm

Bill

I'm checking the Radio Times to see if there's anything to pass the evening, in case Jenny doesn't come over. Just the usual mish-mash of old films and frantically over-enthusiastic variety shows.

This nothing time in the late afternoon in winter, between the sunset and getting supper under way, is the worst time. There's too much time to think. I remember my old dad, who went very deaf in his old age, used to just sit and stare at nothing in particular. Thinking. Thinking about all the ifs and buts and maybes. Not healthy. If I ever catch myself doing it, and I have once or twice, I'm up out of that chair before it traps me.

I've tried reading but that was never really my thing. I just get bored, the eyes blur and I can't remember which character is which. And cooking is always going to be a necessity rather than a luxury. Maybe I should get a dog.

The doorbell rings. I open it and Chas walks in purposefully.

'Can't stay long, got to get ready for the golf club do.'

'To what do I owe the pleasure, then?'

Although Chas lives fairly close, in the posh end of Stanmore, he's not a dropper-in. Something's up.

'I've been thinking about Jenny's little followers. I know what you said about waiting till tomorrow, but I had a couple of guys hanging around, so I thought, you know, seize the moment. They're staking her out. Looks quite slick. There's at least two cars involved, maybe three.'

Damn.

'Professionals?' I ask.

'Maybe.'

I ponder this. 'Well, if they are, and they may be a bunch of kids with nothing else to do, that's good and bad. Bad because someone is taking this seriously, good because they can be paid off.'

'Is that me dipping into my pocket again?'

'Not necessarily, no.'

'Anyway, if they're professionals, they know about the O2. And that's serious.'

'If.'

'Bill, we're going to have to cut Jenny loose. We can't risk her coming here.'

'Nonsense. She's coming here to see an old man that she rescued from a beating, a beating, incidentally, that these people administered. Innocent stuff.'

'Bill, you know how these things work. This is a possible leak. We don't even discuss it. Close it off.'

'I'll make that decision if and when I think it's right. Good God, if it blew open tomorrow, the worst they could get us for is trespass. We'd be folk heroes.'

'That's not the point of all this and you know it. I didn't get into this to be a fucking folk hero. You promised serious money and all I've seen so far is serious cost. You're going to have to deliver on this, Bill, and pretty damn soon.'

'How does ten grand by next Tuesday sound?'

'It sounds like a start and it'll sound a lot better when I see the colour of it.'

'Watch Sunday's papers. We're going public. The website's ready and the money will roll in, believe me.'

'It had better. Now, what do we do about Jenny's watchers?'

'Do you know where they're coming from?'

'Not yet. They haven't gone home yet.'

'We wait until they do. See who they meet on the way.'

Chas nods and heads for the door. I call after him.

'Chas, don't worry. You'll get your money and who knows, maybe some glory too.'

'You can keep the glory, that's for mugs. I'm happy with the cash. And, Bill, dump Jenny. Now.'

The door shuts behind him. I head upstairs to the small room that functions as my study. I pull open the bottom drawer, extract a file. It's all there. The time is coming close when I will need to put a little bomb under Mr Chas Sullivan.

Chapter 51 – December 31st 6.15pm

David

Starting to hurt a bit now. I suppose they must have had me on painkillers; probably why I've been so woozy.

Chappy this afternoon seemed pleased with me. Said I could go home. Thank God. It's weird here, not knowing if it's day or night. All jolly nice and hard-working and all that but a bit unreal. Talking loudly to me as if I'm an idiot. And always so bloody cheerful. Still, mustn't be ungrateful. They've worked hard to patch me together. Apparently I've got a few less bits than I had before but nothing critical. Must have been a nasty one. They haven't given me much detail but I suppose Jenny will know.

It'll be easier for Jenny, having me home, not trekking endlessly to and from the hospital. I'll be glad about that.

Can't play golf for a while, apparently. That's a bit of a blow. Still, maybe by the time the good weather comes I'll be back on the course. Meanwhile, there's always the Nineteenth Hole.

Ah, clatter at the door behind me. Someone coming in. Put on the welcoming smile.

'Mr Belsworth?' New face, haven't seen him before. I see what's in his hand. Oh, God, another injection. My bottom must look like no man's land by now.

I start to ease over on my side, away from him.

'Which one is it this time?'

No reply. Not the talkative type, obviously. I can understand that, hard to know what to say when you're staring at a man's bottom.

I brace myself. Feel the sting. Door behind me crashes open again.

'Stand away from the bed.' A voice, very loud, trolley goes flying, people crashing into the bed. God, that hurts. I ease myself back round. So slow. Can't do anything quickly, damn it.

There's three of them, scuffling, banging into things, one dressed as a policeman. Nurse is standing at the door, watching, aghast. What on earth is going on?

My wound is absolutely thumping.

They've got the man on the floor. He's still kicking and struggling. Handcuffs appearing. Seem to have him under some control now.

Nurse is at my side.

'Mr Belsworth, David, can you hear me?'

'Yes, of course I can.'

'Did he inject you?'

Pain's getting worse, seems to be spreading.

'Yes, I felt a prick, then chappy here came roaring in. What's happening?'

The nurse rounds on the man on the floor.

'What did you use?' Her voice seems to be echoing.

He's just staring back at her, seems to be getting further away.

So tired.

Chapter 52 – December 31st 6.30pm

Jenny

Barry comes back from David's study.

'You're looking thoughtful.'

'Am I? Sorry.'

'What did your boss say?'

'Er, he's getting right onto it. He'll call me back. Meanwhile, how about another cup of tea?'

'Do you really want one or is this just police procedure to keep the woman busy?'

'I'd love one. While you're doing that, do you mind if I check over the house?'

'If you need to. Why?'

'Just while we're waiting, just want to see how secure everything is.'

He's too casual. What on earth can his boss have said to him?

I let him go off, busy myself with the kettle. Never saw myself as the provider of endless cups of tea. Not sure how it happened. Generation thing, I suppose. I was just at the end of the assumption that the woman gave up everything for the children. The feminist writers had started to appear; The Female Eunuch was compulsory reading, but it hadn't penetrated the male middle classes of England. Still hasn't, I'd say. I remember David finding my copy. Said the cover made him feel quite ill. I had to hide it.

So many quick changes. Me, young Jen, student socialist firebrand from the inner city, suddenly transformed, first into a rabid capitalist and then a polite middle class wife and mum. I saw the disappointment in Dad's eyes. He never said anything, of course. I suppose I thought it would pass and I'd get on with my life. Then he'd be proud. Didn't know he was already dying. Never told us. Then I just sort of sank into the quicksand.

My thoughts are suddenly scattered by the crash of breaking glass from the hall. I drop the teabags all over the floor and run out. Barry's charging downstairs. The hall floor is covered in broken glass. A heavy stone is lying on the floor. There is something tied around it.

I move towards it. Barry signals to me to stay back.

'Keep out of the sight lines,' he whispers.

At the bottom of the stairs, he drops down on all fours and reaches out carefully for the stone. He waves me back into the kitchen. I duck back. He crawls after me, stone in hand.

We huddle in the corner of the kitchen. I stare at the scattered teabags as he unwraps the paper from the stone and opens it out. He passes it to me. On it are written the words 'Goodbye Jenny'.

I lean back against the wall for support, my heart thumping. He reaches into his coat and pulls out a phone.

'Inspector Williamson, now.'

We wait, feeling the seconds pass, listening for the slightest sound outside. Strange, for the first time since I put on that DVD this morning, I start to feel calm. It's as if I've been waiting for this to happen all day.

'Sir, Carolson. We have a development. A stone just came through the window with a threatening message.'

I can hear the strong voice at the other end. 'Wait,' then a shout, 'Have those boys got to Pinner yet?'

There's a pause. Eventually, he's back.

'Carolson, you're going to have to wait. They'll be another twenty minutes. Meanwhile, I'm going to send in the regulars. It's too late for subterfuge. Ask Mrs Belsworth what kind of alarm she's got.'

'It's a motion sensor,' I reply.

'Did you hear that, sir?'

'Yes. Can it isolate downstairs?'

I nod.

'Yes, sir.'

'Right, do that and go upstairs.'

I lead the way crouching across the hall. The alarm box is by the door. I reach up, press the buttons and head upstairs, Barry close behind.

'OK, sir, done that.'

'Right. Sit tight and keep your wits about you.'

We go into the main bedroom, leaving the light off. I can sense that Barry feels rather awkward.

I indicate a chair just visible in the corner of the room. 'Why don't you sit over there?'

'Thanks. What about you?'

'I'll sit on the bed.'

We sit in silence. From his pocket comes the sound of the Star Wars theme. Embarrassed, he pulls another phone from his pocket.

'Text message. Excuse me.'

He looks and laughs out loud. He sees my surprise and passes the phone across to me. The message glows at me.

To Mangoladrev the Magnificent from Demonthrust. Theodread attacks our settlement. White warriors scattered. Need succour. Be here by eight.

'What on earth is that all about?'

'It's a group of mates I play war games with.'

'War games?'

'Prehistoric, Middle Earth stuff.'

'Well, would they like a taste of the real thing?'

'Does seem a bit silly in comparison with this, doesn't it?'

'Sorry, Barry, but it's a bit silly in comparison with anything, frankly. Is it really a pursuit for a grown man?'

'To be honest, I was rather thinking that…'

He's interrupted by two sounds. In the distance we hear a police siren. Then the phone down in the hall rings again.

We wait.

The tinny voice of the answering machine creeps through the darkness. 'Mrs Belsworth, this is the hospital. There's been an incident involving your husband. I think you'd better get down here as soon as you can.'

'An incident? What the hell do they mean, an incident?'

I reach for the bedside phone to intercept the call but she's rung off. I call straight back and ask to be put through to the private wing that David is in.

Barry, meanwhile, is carefully looking out of the window. The flashing blue lights bounce of the walls of the room when he eases back the curtain.

'They're here. I'll go down and check. What's the alarm number?'

'4026. Be careful.' Then I remember the last time I said that, before David went into the house. 'Be very careful.'

The ward phone is answered.

'Jubilee Ward. Sister MacKenzie.'

'Sister MacKenzie, Jenny Belsworth here. What's going on?'

'Oh, Mrs Belsworth. Someone tried to attack your husband in the ward here. We caught him but there is a bit of a side effect. Your husband was knocked in the scuffle and needs a bit of work.'

'What does "needs a bit of work" mean? You make him sound like a car that's been dented in a traffic accident.'

'When you come in, we can tell you all about it.'

In a small hollow place deep in my stomach, something turns and twists. I can sense in what she doesn't say that this is bad.

'I'll be there as soon as I can.'

I run downstairs. Barry is at the door talking to a policeman in uniform. I recognise him as the young policeman who went round the house with me.

'Hello, Mrs Belsworth.'

'Hello.' I turn to Barry. 'Barry, listen, there's a crisis at the hospital. It seems David has been attacked. I have to go.'

'I'll come with you.'

'Oh, that's not necessary. You've already done more than you needed to. I'm sure you've got a party to be going to.'

'Not a problem. The night is young. Come on. We can take your car.'

I'm more relieved than I expected. But it's not that simple.

'What about the other people? The ones who threw the brick and followed me? We can't just leave the house with a gaping hole in the window.'

'Don't worry, madam,' the young constable steps forward. 'We can arrange for someone to patch that. If you leave me a key and the alarm details, we can, in the circumstances, look after that for you.'

'Wonderful. Thank you so much. Right, I'll go and get my car keys.'

I try to remember where my handbag is. I retrace my steps from when I got back to the house earlier. Kitchen. I grab the bag, check that the keys are in it and run back to the door.

I don't have time to think. That's a good thing.

Barry's waiting.

As we swing out of the drive, the road is clear. I send a silent message to David that I'm on my way.

Chapter 53 – December 31st 7.00pm

Cressida

Well, that's our plans out of the window. Back in time to get ready in a nice leisurely way for tonight's party and there's Nicky pacing the floor like an expectant father.

'Where the hell have you been?'

'You know where I've been. I've been at work.'

It's a good job I don't blush.

'We've got another crisis. Dad's been attacked.'
'What do you mean, attacked?'

'We're not sure of the details. Mum says it sounds serious. She phoned about ten minutes ago.'

'But how can you be attacked in hospital?'

'Cressida, I don't know. Now, are you coming?'

'What about Becca and Geoff?'

'What about them?'

'Well, we'll have to let them know we may be late.'

'We'll phone them when we know what's happening.'

'But that'll be too late for them. They'll be cooking everything.'

Nicky's staring at me. His face goes hard.

'Tell you what. You go. It's obviously more important to you than my father's life so, fine. Go. I may see you later but don't feel you have to hurry back.'

And with that he's gone, before I can even think of a witty response. I hate it when that happens.

I stand, looking around the flat. It's full of things that Nicky and I have bought over the past eighteen months. Each carries its own little story; the lamp from Leather Lane market, cushions grabbed at the Ikea sale, after we had queued in the freezing rain for half an hour. I slump onto the sofa, feeling suddenly very tired. I wish it was just the afterglow of the session with Dominic. It's more than that. To be honest, Dominic was OK but I suppose there's nothing quite like the thrill of the first time. I hardly ever feel down but just now I've got this draggy feeling. I don't like it when things are out of control.

Maybe I'd taken Nicky a bit for granted. I mean, we've had some good times. The holiday in Turkey was actually great; felt like we laughed for a whole fortnight. And lots of other silly, giggly things couples build up. Would it be as much fun with Dominic? Probably not, he's got too much to lose. Wouldn't drop his guard and be silly. Not going to see him walking down the road with a traffic cone on his head. Then again, he's going places and I'm not sure Nicky is.

God, why does it have to be so complicated? Why can't I just keep both? Actually, not a bad thought. You never know with Dominic; I expect Emily won't give up her claim easily. He certainly won't want a scandal. I'll call Nicky back and apologise.

It's ringing, good. Stopped. I've been shunted off to voicemail. Well, cheeky sod. Damn. I'll have to go out to the hospital now. No car, and taxis will be impossible at seven o'clock on New Year's Eve. Have to be the bloody tube again. It's going to take hours. We'll never get back in time for Becca and Geoff now. Probably a complete false alarm anyway. His family do seem to be getting rather addicted to excitement at the moment.

OK, coat back on. Let's get this over with.

Chapter 54 – December 31ˢᵗ 8.00pm

Barry

That's the trouble with this job. When it really gets down to the life and death stuff, there's nothing you can do. Don't think there's any training can prepare you for how you're going to feel. You just have to be the solid, strong arm and hope that helps a little.

It's clear as soon as we get to the ward that this is one of those moments. The nurse looks up at us and scurries off, muttering something about getting the doctor. She's back a minute later looking a bit shifty, saying he's tied up and will be with us as soon as he can.

Jenny's shaking. To be honest, I'm amazed she's still standing, after what she's been through in the last few hours. I think I'd be a crumpled heap on the floor by now. I get us some coffee, or at least something that claims on the machine to be coffee. She takes a cup from me but her hand is shaking so much it slops onto her fingers. She squeals and I take the cup back and put it down beside her. We wait.

She turns to me.

'Look, Barry, I mustn't spoil your evening. I'm sure you must be wanting to get away.'

I really do want to get off and see Salita but there's no way I can leave now.

Before I can answer, the door swings open and a familiar figure walks through. I jump to my feet.

'Good evening, sir. Jenny, er, Mrs Belsworth, this is Inspector Williamson, my boss on this case.'

He takes her outstretched hand and shakes it, then sits beside her in the seat I vacated. I hover.

'Mrs Belsworth, I'm here because there's been an attack on your husband.'

'I can't stand this. When will someone tell me what's happening and how he is?'

He nods. 'Strictly, it should be the doctor, but I'll tell you what I know. The attacker got into his room with a syringe.' Jenny gasps and puts her hands to her face. 'I'd sent an officer to the ward as soon as Sergeant Carolson here called me about the stone through the window. It was clear to me that this thing was escalating.'

'Escalating. That's your calm, controlled word for it, I suppose.'

'And he arrived just as the assailant had got into the room. We believe that he did have time to inject your husband but we don't know how much and what. That's what the medical staff are working on right now.'

'And David?'

'Unconscious, I'm afraid.'

Jenny leans against the back of her chair, staring up to the ceiling. I can see the tears glistening. I stand awkwardly to one side.

She looks across at Williamson.

'Do we know anything about this person who attacked him?'

'He's saying nothing but we can be pretty sure he's from the same group as the ones following you.'

Jenny closes her eyes. Williamson looks up at me and jerks his head towards the corner of the room. I lean in to her.

'Jenny, excuse me just a moment.'

She nods without opening her eyes. We move across.

'Have you left someone in charge at the house?'

'The constable who answered the call is staying until someone comes to board up the window.'

'He's going to have a long wait tonight. On top of everything else, there's a riot building up in Central London and a five other cities too, by the sounds of it.'

'Do we know who?'

He gives me a straight look. 'Who do you think?'

'Generation?'

'Asserting their rights and expressing their views on the immorality of the oldies by smashing the windows of a few McDonald's. And no doubt beating up anyone over forty-five who's daft enough to be out and about.'

'Evans?'

'Probably but you'll never pin it on him. He's got so many layers around him, he's like the dance of the seven veils.'

The door opens. A young doctor walks in clutching his white coat around him like a cloak of invisibility. We move closer. Jenny is so pale and still, it's as if her blood has stopped circulating.

The doctor clears his throat. 'Mrs Belsworth, I wonder, would you mind, would you be kind enough to come with me, please.'

Not for the first time, I'm struck by the ability of the English to stretch out a sentence. Jenny staggers slightly as she stands, steadies herself and follows the doctor out in the direction of the wards.

'Looks bad,' mutters Williamson. He checks his watch. 'Shit, I'm going to be in trouble. I'm meant to be taking the wife to a do in about twenty minutes. Still, she's used to it by now.'

'Yeah, I'm running late as well.'

'That the one that had you looking like a contented spaniel this morning?

'Yes, sir.'

'Well, we'll get you out of here as soon as we can.'

'That's OK, sir. I can hold on for a while. Mrs Belsworth's son's on his way; he can take over. Anyway, these parties don't really get going till about eleven.'

'Eleven? That's when I'm feeling ready for bed. You've done well today, lad. I'll have a chat in the new year, see if we can't get you transferred to CID.'

'Thank you, sir, that would be great.'

I see Jenny's son Nick running up the corridor, go across to meet him. He takes a moment to realise who I am.

'Ah, sergeant, didn't recognise you without the uniform. Where's my mother?'

'Just talking to the doctor. I'm sure she'll be out in a minute.'

'Do you know what's going on?'

'Not really.' I realise I'm crossing my fingers behind my back, as if this will let me off for telling a lie. 'I'm sure she'll out in a minute.'

Williamson steps forward to introduce himself. 'I had the pleasure of your fiancée's company this morning, as I'm sure she told you.'

'What, Cressida?'

'Yes.'

'Really? Not my fiancée, by the way, just girlfriend. What was it about?'

'Well, the incident at the rally last night.'

'What incident is that?'

'She didn't tell you?'

'She's been at work all day. I've hardly seen her.'

'Oh well, no matter, now's not the time. I'm sure she'll get you up to speed in due course. She not with you?'

'No.'

'Right.'

'Er, excuse me, Inspector, I'll just get myself a coffee.'

We watch Nick's hurried departure.

'Interesting, wouldn't you say, Carolson?'

'Yes, sir. Obviously not a lot of communication there. I wonder why.'

'Hardly seen her.'

'Sorry, sir?'

'Hardly seen her, he said. I mean, if he hadn't seen her at all, it would be odd but understandable. But hardly seen her. What do you discuss in the brief time you have with your fiancé, boyfriend or whatever that's more important than being a suspect in a murder case? And he obviously hasn't listened to the news in the last few hours; they released the story about three o'clock.'

We return to the seats and wait. Nick comes back in with his coffee and takes a seat some way away from us. We don't have to wait long.

Jenny reappears. She sees Nick and rushes across to him. He stands, holds his arms out. She's crying, really crying now.

'Oh, Nick, oh God.'

'What's happened?'

'Vegetative state. They don't think they can do anything.'

'How, why?'

I feel awkward, eavesdropping like this, but I suppose it's what police do a lot. Williamson taps me on the shoulder and signals that he's going to talk to the doctor. Feel even more awkward, standing on my own.

Nick sits his mother down.

'Tell me exactly what they said.'

Between hiccupping sobs, she gives him the story.

'You know he was attacked here, in the hospital.'

'Yes.'

'Well, whatever it was, I mean, what he was injected with, whatever it was, it's pretty horrible. Nick, they don't know what it is. They don't know what to do.'

'Why don't they know? It's their job to know.'

'They've been trying to find out. They're not saying much. As far as I can pick up, some essential piece of kit they need just isn't working. It's the cuts, like everything else.'

'What?'

'They've been working by guesswork. They're guessing about how to save David's life. And, oh God, I think they've just run out of time. Nick, he's all wired up to life support.'

'Why do they say they can't help him? I don't understand.'

'Something to do with how the stuff, whatever it is, has affected his circulation or his brain or something. God, Nick, I don't know why. I just know what he, the doctor, told me.'

Jenny looks up, sees me waiting.

'Oh, Barry, thanks for staying. Nick's here now. You can slip away.'

'Are you sure there's nothing I can do for you?'

She shakes her head. I walk through to follow Inspector Williamson. A nurse finds me wandering down a corridor.

'Hey, where do you think you're going?'

I take out my warrant card.

'Police. Just looking for my colleague. Have you seen him? Tall, leather coat.'

'You'll have to wash your hands with the disinfectant gel over there before you go any further.'

I do as I am told. She waits.

'Right. He's in the office down there, third door on the left. And don't touch anything.'

I knock and go in. The inspector and the doctor are standing facing each other across the desk. Williamson is talking quietly.

'So, it's a simple question. Am I dealing with a murder case or an attempted murder?'

'We don't yet know. If I was a betting man, which I'm not, I'd back Mr Belsworth being dead before daybreak.'

Williamson nods. 'Well, we've got the man.' He turns to me. 'I think we can let him stew until morning, Carolson. Sounds like we might know what to charge him with by then. OK, doc, you're going to have a busy night in casualty so I'll not take any more of your time. We'll be in touch.'

We let ourselves out of the room. Jenny and Nick are still in the waiting area. Williamson goes across to them.

'Mrs Belsworth, I am so sorry.'

'You did what you could. No doubt you're short of people too.'

'We've got the man and we'll find out who's behind this, I promise you.'

She looks up at me. 'Barry, are you going to carry on with your investigation?'

I glance at the inspector. 'If I'm allowed to, yes.'

He nods slowly. 'Yes, but officially this time. Good night, Ma'am. Good night, sir.'

Once we're outside, he puts his hand on my shoulder.

'Right, you are not to go ferreting tonight. Do you understand? This is serious, big boys' stuff and I don't want you putting your size tens into it. You keep your head down, party and ask no questions. Clear?'

I shrug.

'Is that clear?' he repeats.

'Yes, sir.'

'Good. Now I've found someone who just might, with a lot of work, make a half decent detective, I don't want him getting carved up.'

He sees my eyebrows go up at the suggestion of getting carved up.

'Oh, yes. In amongst this happy band of misguided youths are some very unpleasant people. Just you remember that.'

Chapter 55 – December 31st 10.00pm

Bill

There's something very satisfying about looking at travel brochures when it's raining outside. A cruise really appeals. Mary always wanted a cruise but prices were way beyond us. Managed to fit that small one in just before she got too ill, seven days round the Med. She loved it. Never asked how we could afford it, luckily. Wonder if she knew. The nice bits of furniture, the washing machine, even the house.

No, taboo subject. 'I'll look after the money, love. Don't you worry about it, we'll be all right.' She got her money each week for the housekeeping and a dress allowance and that seemed to work fine.

Still, time to take it up a notch now. South America looks good. All those exotic sounding names, Acapulco, Buenos Aires, Santiago. And a boat full of rich Texan widows, I wouldn't wonder. I have to admit I'm disappointed that I haven't heard from Jenny. I really thought there was a bit of a spark there. Was looking forward to a little fireside whatever. Maybe the day was just a bit too much for her. I won't text her – can't look needy. Would she have come with me? I'd have liked that but, no, too complicated. Still…

Should be able to get away in a few days. Once the money starts rolling in. And it will roll. The bits and pieces so far have been OK but I've had to share it round. That's the trouble with these share scams, too many fingers in the pie. This one will be all mine.

I flick on the ten o'clock news, not that I'm that interested, more out of habit. The newsreader has his stern face on.

'Police are out in force tonight in London, Birmingham, Bristol, Manchester, Newcastle and Glasgow as hundreds of young people associated with the new youth movement, Generate, take to the streets to express their views about the lack of work opportunities and what they see as the responsibility of older people for the current poor state of the economy.

Our correspondent David Armitage reports.'

A man appears on screen, wrapped up against the cold, with kids shouting and jeering in the background.

'Yes, John, so far the mood is quite party-like but the police say that it may turn nasty later. I have seen several older people chased away but so far no real violence. It may just be a matter of time.'

'David, I understand you had a chance to talk to Dominic Evans, the figurehead of this movement, earlier today.'

'That's right. I challenged him about the reported attacks around the country and this is what he had to say.'

My screen is filled by the smooth shiny face of Dominic Evans.

'Well, of course, I have always condemned any violence against individuals. But you can understand why younger people are so angry. Our fight is with those people who did very well out of bankrupting this country for their own gain and with the government who refuse to act against them. Those are the ones who should be paying back, which is why we want the government to impose a special tax on the over sixties.'

'Mr Evans, can I ask you about the fiasco at the O2 centre yesterday?'

'Well, I think that shows how we have some very powerful enemies here. I'd remind you that two thousand people turned out yesterday at the rally. Two thousand who care enough about

the future to want it changed. And these two thousand, this truly democratic movement, was attacked by a handful of people clearly with plenty of money behind them. Many could have died in the subsequent panic. Indeed, as you heard earlier today, one of my most trusted aides was killed.'

'Do you have evidence that the intruders killed him?'

'I don't have evidence that they didn't.'

'Will you be out on the streets yourself tonight?'

'I have some unavoidable commitments but I wish them well. This is a struggle for the future and we will win.'

We move back to the newsreader in the studio.

'Dominic Evans there, talking earlier today to our reporter David Armitage.'

Well done, Dominic, you've probably just added a good few grand to the takings. When we launch on Sunday, there will be so many scared people in this country, the money will pour in.

And then there's Chas. He knows I can't shop him to the police. He'll have as much on me as I have on him. A bit of a nuclear standoff. No, have to be more subtle than that. The only place you can hurt a man like that is in his pocket.

Well, there's plenty of people in this city of ours who would like a slice of some of his businesses. I think I've enough detail to set up a few turf wars that will keep him busy for a good long time. He'll probably realise it's me but he's not going to have the time to chase me. And I'll be a long way away.

Chapter 56 – December 31st 10.15pm

Cressida

What a crap New Year's Eve this is turning out to be. I finally get to the hospital after a really horrendous tube journey, all drunks and rowdies, and they've gone. Took me ages to find a nurse and then she wasn't exactly forthcoming.

'Are you a relative?'

'Well, sort of, I'm his son's girlfriend.'

'I'm sorry, we're only allowed to give information out to relatives.'

'But can you at least tell me how he is, you know, in general terms?'

'I'm sorry, no.'

'Can you tell me how long ago Jenny and Nick, his wife and son, left?'

'I'm sorry, we're…'

'Only allowed to tell relatives. I rather thought you might say that. Well, thank you, you've been a great help.'

So here I am, back on the bloody tube again. No reply from Nick's phone or from the house. I've called Becca to apologise. Tried to explain but she was pretty shirty, so it's back to the flat. Sent Dominic a rude text but I don't suppose I'll even hear back from him.

No point going out to the public celebrations; they've been well and truly hijacked, by the sound of it. Wonder how much Dominic really does know about that. I guess he's just channelling the unhappiness into something more useful. Good for him; give people something to hope for. And make your name at the same time.

So I'm going to be sitting on my own like Molly No-Mates. Maybe I can use it as planning time. Think through the next stages of reeling Dominic in. Mrs Dominic Evans. Mr Evans and his dynamic wife Cressida. Yes, we'll make a formidable couple but I have to get him there. There's still that Emily in the way. I met her once when she came into the office for something. Very territorial and clearly sexy. Well, I've got rid of my rivals before. Yes, I'll use the evening to formulate my plan.

And if I even start to watch Four bloody Weddings, I'll have to shoot myself. No-one can be that desperate.

Chapter 57 – December 31st 11.30pm

Barry

Williamson isn't going to like this.

I look round the room, try to make out something in the dark. Can hear the music still thumping away above me. Head really hurts.

It all started so well. I called Salita after I left the hospital, dashed home to change, and, in the end, was only about an hour late. She was still at the pub, clearly a few drinks ahead of me. Arms around my neck and a big sloppy kiss felt good. I knew most of the others from the previous night. Everyone seemed very friendly. No sign of Jeff yet but no doubt he'd turn up later.

Salita gets me a drink and then pulls me off to one side.

'So, what about this job you've got me, then? Still not keen, mind you, but I could do with a bit of money.'

'Ah, bit of a hitch. The guy isn't going to be leaving hospital for a while now.'

'Why?'

'Not sure. Relapse of some kind. Jenny says thanks and she'll get in touch when, if she needs you.'

'Jenny?'

'Jenny Belsworth, the woman involved.'

'Belsworth? Funny name. How do you know her?'

'Family friend.'

'Right. Oh, well, easy come, easy go.'

Our conversation has to be shouted over the noise in the pub. I feel uncomfortable about this and change the subject.

'Where are we going on to?'

'Just around the corner, friend of Jeff's. We'll head off in a couple of minutes. Drink up, you've got some catching up to do.'

The house is one of those three storey terraces that are everywhere in London. Paintwork on the windows and front door is peeling, parts of the pebbledash have fallen away but there's a lot of that nowadays. We all pile in. I go through to the kitchen to leave the bottle that I picked up at an outrageous price from the all-night corner shop, then fight my way back through the throng to find Salita.

The pub was loud but this is seriously louder. I push my way into two rooms without finding her and finally see her talking to Jeff on the stairs. He greets me in a friendly enough way. Maybe I'm getting somewhere here. I remember Williamson's warning and I don't push it.

'Barry,' Jeff yells, 'I'll catch you later.'

'Fine.' I'm suddenly feeling really tired. It's been a long day.

Salita leans down to me. 'What's up, big boy?'

'Sorry, been doing a lot of rushing around today. I'm feeling a bit knackered.'

'No problem. It's a bit quieter up there. Let's go and chill for a while.'

We find a room with a few people sprawled around on the floor and find ourselves a space. There's a strong smell hanging in the air that I recognise with a sinking feeling from briefing sessions at police college. Sure enough, a joint is soon making its way round. Salita takes a long drag and passes it over to me.

I shake my head.

'Come on. If I'm going to de-nerd you, you need to do as I say.'

I hesitantly take the joint from her and stare at it, wondering if my career is about to literally go up in smoke.

'Yeah, Barry, you don't just hold it in front of you, you need to put it in your mouth.'

I do as instructed.

'Now inhale, gently.'

I draw the smoke into my mouth and immediately I'm spluttering and coughing, to the great amusement of everyone watching.

Salita looks at me the way my sports teacher used to at school when I failed even the lowest bar in the high jump.

'OK, it's a start. Before you make it totally soggy, you'd better pass it on.'

I gratefully pass it to the guy next to me, who wipes the end and takes a drag.

'Feel anything?' Salita asks.

Still unable to speak, I shake my head.

'Maybe it's a bit early in your education to start you on that. Perhaps we'll go back a few lessons and line up some Tequila Slammers instead.'

'Why are you bothering with me?' I gasp, wiping my watering eyes. 'Am I some project, some experiment?'

She leans over, slips her arm around my neck and kisses me.

'No, Baz, you're not an experiment. I like you. You're nice, you're funny and, more than anything, you're honest. I haven't seen much of that recently.'

I think of all the ways I've deceived her in the last day and a half. All I can do is nod.

'Now, stop sitting there like a toy spaniel. Let's get some more drinks.'

We head back downstairs into the throng. I see Jeff in the distance and give him a wave. Get one back, which is good. The man he's talking to looks my way and seems surprised. I suppose I must stick out a bit in this crowd.

We're on our way back upstairs a few minutes later when Jeff intercepts us.

'Barry, can we have that chat now?'

'Sure, if we can find somewhere we can hear each other.'

He turns to Salita.

'Mind if I nick your boyfriend for a little while?'

'Don't keep him too long. I've got plans for him.'

Jeff signals to a door set into the triangle under the stairs. He opens it, flicks a light switch and heads down a flight of rickety stairs. I follow. So does the man Jeff was just talking to.

The cellar has been converted into a kind of den with a sofa and some chairs. Still smells musty. Jeff signals at me to sit.

'Barry, this is Mick, our host for tonight.'

'Hi.'

Mick nods back at me. Clearly the silent type.

'Now, Barry,' Jeff continues, 'I said I had something for you.'

'Sure, anything to help things along. It's a worthwhile cause.'

'Yes, as you said before. We've got a lot going on at the moment and we're looking for someone who can help us co-ordinate everything and not drop any bollocks.'

'OK. What sort of things?'

'Well, we'll go into the detail later. How much time can you give us?'

'A few hours a week, probably. I work shifts, so it'll be fine if I can fit it around that.'

'What sort of work's that?'

'Office stuff. Very dull,' I laugh.

'Shifts in an office? That's unusual.'

I'd already thought of that.

'Immigration. Out at the airport. Flights come in all day and most of the night.'

'So, you keep all the Pakis and towel heads out.'

'Sort of. I'm back room, you know, checking papers, that sort of thing.'

Jeff nods. There's silence. Finally he looks across at me.

'Not police, then?'

Chapter 58 – December 31st 11.45pm

Jenny

When Nick sees the police car outside our house, he just seems to shrug.

'Hello, what's he doing here?'

I'm surprised at his casual reaction but I suppose there's only so many things you can take in at one time. Anyway, I don't feel able to explain the events of the past day just yet. There's than enough going on for now, to be honest.

I send Nick into the house and go over to the car. The young policeman winds down his window.

'Hello, Mrs Belsworth, what's the news of your husband?'

'Not great, I'm afraid, but,' I keep talking to avoid the well-meant words of sympathy, 'we're going to be here for a while, so you can go.'

He seems relieved. Not surprising. Even a police station would be a better place to be on New Year's Eve than out here.

I step back from the car to signal the end of the conversation. 'Good night, and thank you.'

''Night, madam.'

Inside, Nick and I sit in silence at the kitchen table. I'm huddled, still with my coat on, like a refugee in my own kitchen. I'm rocking slightly, comforting, don't know why. He's made strong tea, poured out two brandies.

'Nick, one of us will have to go easy in case we get called back.'

'I think you'll benefit more than me, Mum, so I'll pass.'

I take a swig. If David were here, he'd be saying, 'Don't swig it, savour it.' Well, sorry, David, darling, this is a swigging moment.

The heat of the alcohol fills my mouth, a promise of softer edges and oblivion. That would be nice but not now. I think of David in suspended animation, lying in some anonymous bed like an exhibit, and my heart lurches again. Why was I so worried about having him home? Now that prospect is vanishing, I feel robbed. Robbed of the chance to look after him, to be needed. To be a wife, a partner. All the suburban values that I've fought off for years come charging in, just when it's too late. The mind is a perverse little sod.

'Nick, I wonder if we should be here, whether we shouldn't be back at the hospital.'

'They said we could go home, that nothing would happen.'

'Or they wanted us out of the way on a busy night.'

'Mum, we can go back, right now, if you want.'

'Do you mind?'

'Not at all.'

I take another swig, get up. Nick's phone rings again. He looks at it, presses a button and puts it back in his pocket.

'Cressida?'

'Yeah.'

'Won't she want to know what's happening?'

'Probably.'

'Right.'

'Shall we go?'

My boy is getting a backbone. Good, though it's sad that he doesn't have her downy breast to rest on right now. Life's a bitch and so, it seems, is she.

He glances at the door on the way out.

'What happened to the glass?'

'Oh, accident. Tell you later.'

As we pull out of the drive, I take a good look around. No cars in any direction. No lights follow us down the road.

In my head, I hear Bob Hope and Bing Crosby singing 'We're off on the road to Morocco.' Why? What random synapses linked arms to generate that memory? Not a song I particularly liked, ever, now it's stuck, rolling around my head with no way out. I start to hum, trying to get rid of it. Nick gives me a worried look.

'Sorry,' I smile across at him. 'Nerves.'

'Go for it, Mum. Anything that helps.'

Chapter 59 – December 31st 11.55pm

Barry

'Not police, then.'

The question hangs in the air like a wasp.

'Police? No, of course not. Immigration, separate department, separate ministry, come to that.'

Control the breathing, keep eyes steady, voice light.

Jeff's still doing the slow nod. 'It's just that Mick here says he saw you today, out in Pinner.'

'In Pinner? Well, yes, I was there this afternoon. Visiting an old family friend, friend of my parents.'

'And who would that be?'

'Lady called Jenny Belsworth.'

'Right.' Another long pause. 'It's just that, shortly after you turned up at her place, the Old Bill appeared in force. We just thought there might be a connection, you know.'

I shake my head vigorously. 'No, no. Someone threw a stone through her window, so she called the police. Don't think they found anyone.'

Jeff looks sharply at Mick. 'A stone through her window?'

Mick shrugs, a slight shake of the head. Jeff turns back to me.

'Someone doesn't like her, then.'

'Probably kids. They'll know her husband's in hospital, so I guess they're looking for mischief.'

Mick leans forward and breaks his silence. 'What was it you did again?'

He's surprisingly well-spoken; not what I expected. 'Immigration, checking papers.'

'Right, so you'll know about the P463, then.'

'P463?'

'The form.'

'Oh, yeah. Sorry, there are so many, I get mixed up. That'll be the one for temporary entry.'

'Actually, Barry, that'll be the one I just made up.' He stands and steps back. 'We're going to leave you for a while, Barry. You just make yourself comfortable. Don't even think about going anywhere. Oh, and we'll have your mobile, please.'

I put it into his outstretched hand.

Mick moves forward so he's standing right in front of me. He leans in, a hand on each arm of my chair. I smell the beer on his breath. He grins at me. Very suddenly, his head comes forward. He butts me full in the face.

His forehead catches me just above the bridge of the nose. An explosion of light, colour, pain. Through it, I hear Jeff.

'That'll do for now, Mick. Plenty of time later.'

I scrabble in my pocket for a handkerchief, find only a well-used tissue, hold it to my nose. I can feel the blood pouring either side of it over my hand. The light goes off and I hear a key turn.

Put my head back. It doesn't seem to help. I try sniffing but that really hurts. Pinch my nose. That hurts even more. There must be blood everywhere.

I sit for a while and try to think, only hear my heart thumping, louder than the thump of the music upstairs. Suddenly there's an explosion of sound from upstairs, cheers and whistles, and I realise that it's midnight. I wonder what Salita's doing. I feel more alone than I can ever remember.

The damp of the room seeps into me but no ideas do.

After about half an hour, during which I alternate between mopping my nose and realising that I'm in serious shit, I hear a scrabbling noise.

Rats. Oh God. These houses must be full of them. I lift my feet off the floor and tuck them up onto the chair. I thought I was scared before. Now I'm really scared. The scrabbling becomes a scraping. How can rats scrape? What would they scrape with? Confused, I stare into the darkness. A patch forms on what must be the opposite wall, still dark but lighter than the area around it. I hear a whispering voice.

'Baz?'

'Salita, that you?'

'Come over here.'

I make my way across the room, tripping over something that adds a badly grazed shin to my list of injuries.

'You haven't got a torch, have you, Salita.'

'Sure, and a brass band so we can be absolutely certain they spot us. Now get over here.'

I realise that the opening is some kind of coalhole, probably covered by a metal plate. It's high on the wall and I can't get a grip. I stumble back across the room to get the low table I tripped over. I find it with my other shin, drag it across and balance on it. I get my purchase and wriggle out. Salita grabs my collar and pulls me through.

'Bloody hell, Baz, you took a punch there.'

'Head butt.'

'Come on, let's get you out of here.'

We cross the rubbish-strewn yard as fast as we can, into a passage that runs behind the houses. Running, crouched, trying to ignore the overpowering smell of urine, we head for the lights at the end.

When we reach the main road, she pulls me back.

'Right, how far away is your flat?'

'About two miles.'

'Well, you can't go there looking like that. Listen, do you remember where my place is from here?'

'Yes, I think so.'

'Right, here's a key. Get yourself there.'

'What are you going to do?'

'Back to the party before I'm missed. Now go. I'll see you later.'

Chapter 60 – January 1st 12.15am

Bill

Well, that's it. Another year over. I think I preferred it when I was knee deep in other people's blood and vomit, back in the good old days on the force. At least then you weren't just an onlooker. Saw my face in the mirror just now. Funny how being old just creeps up on you. Well, not funny, not really.

Feel sorry for those lads out there trying to deal with the riots. Nasty night they're having. They'll be cursing their luck and wishing they were in front of the tele, I suppose.

Strange old world, all of us wanting to be somewhere we're not. Sad that Jenny didn't make it. I thought she had more fire. Maybe she just got caught up with David or her neighbours.

Not a bad film, though, helped along by a couple of whiskies. Reminded me of those old Ealing comedies. Bit nearer the knuckle than they used to be, of course, but that's the way it is. Maybe next year I might get a bit of the old permissive society myself.

Yes, this time next year. Next New Year's Eve, Acapulco, Rio, who knows? And not on my own, either.

Maybe with Jenny, be worth the risk after all. If I can just prise her away from that dreary husband, that is. Stranger things have happened.

And, on that happy note, Bill, old chum, off to bed.

Chapter 61 – January 1st 8.00am

Cressida

Well, happy New Year to me. That dark grey sky out there is exactly how I feel. Why the hell I'm awake this early I don't know. Thumping head, serious need for liquids, sense that I'm going to explode in all directions any minute. Yes, that'll be it.

So, it's me and an empty flat. Well, whoopee. Oh, and a detailed plan of how I'm going to get what I want. Though, looking at it this morning, it starts off pretty detailed, all carefully drawn columns and neat writing but the second half, which coincides, I would say, pretty accurately with the second bottle of champagne, gets a bit wobbly.

There's a bit here that seems to be a detailed plan of how I was going to dismember Emily, with drawings and diagrams. Best lose that one, I think.

Where the hell is Nicholas? How dare he stand me up? I'll have to swallow my pride and call again. First, I think, major caffeine injection, get the voice going again. Not sure why I'm so hoarse, though I think I remember singing along to Bruce Springsteen at one point.

Let's see what's happening in the outside world while I come round. Where's the remote? Ah, here it is, on top of the fridge.

The television leaps into life. I hurriedly turn it down.

'In our city centres this morning, bargain hunters mingle with cleaners tidying up after last night's riots. Windows were smashed and cars set alight as police battled through midnight to contain the revellers who became rioters across several cities. Police believe that the rioting was co-ordinated and blame Generate, the youth movement. Its leader, Dominic Evans, was quick to deny the allegations.

There's Dominic, looking gorgeous as ever. God, I wish he was here now.

'You have to understand that feelings are very, very strong among young people today. We really do feel let down by the older generation. It's unavoidable that that anger may sometimes come out in an inappropriate way but I emphasise that this is nothing to do with me or my team.

Looks like Birmingham on Tuesday's going to be big. I'll need to get back onto that as soon as I can.

In a separate statement earlier this morning, Mr Evans announced his engagement to television presenter Emily Wright....'

What? Whoa, back up there. Engagement? No, no, this can't be right. Excuse me, that man is mine. And, as the man said, I get what I want.

Right, where's all that work from last night? There must be something in there. Maybe I should get that dismembering stuff out of the bin. God, Dominic, I knew you were a shit but I didn't know you were a sneaky shit, going straight from our rumpy on the desk to sweet little Emily with a ring in your pocket.

Cressida, you've been played along, my girl. Well, no one does that to me. If there's any playing to be done, I'll do it. More serious planning to be done here.

Meanwhile, I need to get rid of this nasty feeling that I might, in the last few hours, have gone from two men to none.

Where's that coffee?

Chapter 62 – January 1st 8.15am

Jenny

Empty.

Just empty.

You read in all those Russian novels and what have you about people prostrate with grief, rending their clothing, beating their breasts.

I can't feel any of that. Is it the famous British self-control? I'm terrified of feeling nothing and terrified of feeling anything.

Nick's beside me. Holding my hand. We're together but apart, each contained in a kind of bell jar of grief. I don't know how long we've been sitting here. I need the loo. Seems such a mundane thing, when something so enormous has happened. Is this what they mean by 'life goes on'?

I'm so glad that we decided to come back, even if it did mean sitting surrounded by drunks most of the night. Seems being a private patient goes by the board when half the population is bent on self-destruction. And when the patient is in intensive care.

I saw the paperwork, had to sign it. Time of death, six forty-eight a.m. I'm told a lot of people die in the early hours of the morning. Must be something to do with that Chinese stuff about circadian rhythms. The worst of it was not being able to hold his hand or anything. They were still trying to find the antidote but it seems whatever it was just wiped out his liver and then his heart. I wonder if they knew from the moment it happened that he would not survive. I'll never know, I suppose.

I look across at Nick. 'I'm just going to the loo. Then I think we can leave.'

He nods. 'Paperwork's all done for now, I think.'

I stand up and stretch. At least they let us be with him after… afterwards. In one way that was very good, calming, just sitting with the silence. Remembering. Then of course you realise that this isn't David any more. Never will be. And a sort of vast endless emptiness just seems to blanket everything.

I've been trying to remember good things, happy times that would keep him alive in my head. Trouble is, it's all a blur at the moment. I can remember, of course, all sorts of events but they don't seem to connect with David. He must have been there, definitely was there, but there's a bit of a shadow where he would have been. I'm tired, it will get clearer, I'm sure. I hope.

We can't arrange anything today, with it being a bank holiday, but the hospital say that's not a problem, that they can keep him. I just hate the idea of him being on his own.

We step out into the first day without David. The rain has stopped and there's quite a dramatic sunrise, with pale green streaks across the horizon and heavy clouds. But none of it really matters.

Chapter 63 – January 1st 10.00am

Barry

I can't see at all out of my left eye. I know this because I can only just see out of my right eye and when I close it, nothing.

There's the blurred outline of Salita's room, the light through the curtains, the weird posters on the wall. I can't see my watch to check the time. Last night slowly comes back to me. After all those warnings from Williamson, how am I going to explain to him that I didn't push it, that it was just bad luck that someone recognised me? At least it confirms that they were the ones stalking Jenny. Still got to prove it, though.

Something's moving, God, something's moving. They've found me. They're coming in. The door swings open.

'Morning, Baz. How's my battered hero this morning, then?'

'Salita. Thank God. I thought it was…'

'The nasty men? No, just me. Let's take a look at you.'

She kneels on the bed and turns my face to the light.

'You'll live. You won't win any beauty contests for a week or two but, let's face it, that wasn't really in your stars anyway, was it?'

'But how about you. Did you go back to the party?'

'Oh, yes.'

'Did they suspect anything?'

'Dunno. Time will tell, I suppose. By the way,' she fishes in the pocket of her jeans, 'Here's your mobile.' She tosses it onto the bed. 'They won't miss it.'

'What did they say?'

'They didn't find out you'd gone for quite a long time; too busy drinking. Then, when they eventually checked, they were, it has to be said, a trifle displeased. Words to the effect of "oh, bother", as I recall.'

'Thanks. Thanks so much. I don't know what would have happened if you hadn't come for me.'

'I do. That's why I came. I tell you, you wouldn't be worried about not being able to see clearly, you'd be wondering where your head was.' I feel a shiver down my back. 'That Jeff was always a shit, even at school. Tried to beat me up one day. I was only ten, but I knew where to kick a boy. He didn't try that again.'

'Look, Salita, there's something I think I really should tell you.'

She puts her head on one side.

'Is it confession time, Baz?'

'I am a policeman.'

I pause, waiting for the news to sink in.

'Well, no shit, Sherlock. Baz, sorry to disappoint, mate, but I knew you were a policeman within two minutes of talking to you.'

'Was it really that obvious?' I feel deeply disappointed.

'To me, certainly, but I've got special antennae for that sort of thing.'

'What gave me away?'

'Hm, where to start?' She ticks off on her fingers. 'Well, there's the shoes, highly polished, the haircut, short sides and floppy, not having a good reason for how you'd come to be in the Albion in the first place, the use of phrases like "that's really interesting" or "as a matter of fact', knowing what to do when the clowns caused such a panic at the stadium.' She pauses. 'That do for now?'

'Are you going to tell everyone?'

'Not much point, seeing as they already know.'

'I suppose, good point. So, I don't understand why you paired up with me then.'

'Paired up? I hadn't realised we were playing rounders. Baz, I've told you why I fancy you. Stop fishing.'

'But you said you liked my honesty and I wasn't being honest with you.'

'There's more to honesty than what you say.'

'I don't understand.'

'That's what I like about you.'

My head's hurting and I'm obviously not going to get any further.

'Got a mirror? I need to see what I look like.'

'Sure?'

'Yes.'

She shrugs and goes off to the kitchen, returning with a small hand mirror.

'Ready?'

I reach out for it. It's a shock. My nose is at least twice its normal size and pushed off to one side. Bruises of red, yellow, blue and black surround each eye. The eyelids are swollen and closed over my left eye. What I can see of my right eye is very bloodshot.

Salita's watching me. 'And that's after I cleaned you up.'

'When did you do that?'

'When I got back, about three. I'm not surprised you don't remember. You were barely conscious, slumped in that chair over there. And talking of barely, I took your clothes and washed them.'

I look down under the covers. She's taken everything. She sees my embarrassment.

'No, I didn't have my wicked way with you, more's the pity.'

'Well, if you promised not to try and kiss me…'

'We'll see. First things first. Let's get some food into you. Bacon and eggs do you?'

I attempt a grin. Even that hurts.

'I'll give it a go.'

Chapter 64 – January 1ˢᵗ 3.00pm

Jenny

I've slept. Why do I feel guilty about that? A couple of catnaps at the hospital, otherwise I haven't had any decent sleep for, what, thirty-six hours. I feel I should have been holding a vigil of some kind. Sorry, David.

There was that brief moment when I woke, before I remembered. I felt light, rested. Then it all came piling back in like a great black wave. And I drowned. Just put my face into the pillow and wept. I'm sure that won't be the last time. Supposed to make you feel better, it says in the magazines. It doesn't.

I don't know what to do, now I'm awake. What time is it? God, three in the afternoon. I can smell bacon.

I wrap a dressing gown round me and go downstairs to the kitchen. Nick is standing at the stove jiggling a frying pan. He looks up, embarrassed.

'Sorry, Mum. I didn't mean to wake you.'

'You didn't. It's OK.'

Awkward silence. Neither of us knows what to talk about. The only subject is so immense that saying anything else seems almost blasphemous.

Nick nods at the pan. 'Um, would you like some? Eggs. And bacon.'

'No thanks. I'll just make myself a coffee.'

'In the cafetiere on the table. I just made it.'

'Thanks.'

'Do you mind if I...do this?'

'No, no, of course not. You need to eat. I'll have something later, something healthier.'

We both grin. Then stop grinning.

'So,' Nick ventures as he decants his fry-up onto a plate. 'What do we do today? I mean, is there anything we're supposed to be doing?'

I take a swig of the coffee and feel the heat scorch down to my stomach. 'No-one's working till Monday, maybe Tuesday, then it'll be funeral arrangements, I thought we'd use Harpers.' It sounds so matter-of-fact, as if we were organising a drinks party. 'And we'll have to get onto the lawyer about the will. That can wait too. Then I suppose there'll be a thousand letters to write.'

'I'll stay and drive you round.'

'Don't you need to be back at work on Monday?'

'I'll just tell them. Compassionate leave.'

'Thanks.'

The phone rings. Nick looks enquiringly at me and I nod towards the receiver. He goes across and picks it up.

'Hello... Oh, yes, hello. Yes, this is Nick Belsworth... That's right... Really? Yes, I see... Right, thanks for letting us know. Is there anything we can do about that?... That would be fantastic, really helpful. About five? Fine. Thanks again... Yes, bye.'

'Who was that?'

'That inspector from last night, Williamson. He says that the evening news will be carrying the story about Dad. We should be ready for the press to come running.'

I'm shaking my head. 'Oh, God.'

'No, no, it's OK. They'll send someone round, keep them at bay. But the phone's going to start ringing.'

'We can leave it on answer.' I look out at the pouring rain, which is back with a vengeance. 'And if anyone wants to stand out there in this weather, good luck to them.'

Nick attacks his plate with enthusiasm. It makes me realise how hungry I am. I get up to go to the cupboard for some cereal. Just then the doorbell rings.

Nick raises a hand to me and goes to the door, still chewing.

'Check who it is first,' I whisper. I don't think he hears me as I hear the door opening.

'Oh, hi.' He sounds surprised but not in a good way. Then I hear the other voice.

'Well, I thought if you're not going to answer my calls, I'd better just come and see you face to face.' The unmistakable tones of Cressida. 'And now I'm soaking wet and I've had to take a taxi from Harrow. You need to pay the cab, please Nicky. Twelve pounds.'

She walks in past Nick to the kitchen, leaving him to go out in the rain to the waiting taxi.

'Hello, Jenny, how are you. Have you been holding my Nicky hostage?'

'Sorry?'

She takes off her coat and shakes it. 'I haven't heard from him since this time yesterday. I went to the hospital to find you but you'd gone and they wouldn't tell me anything. I seem to have spent the last twenty-four hours on tubes with smelly, drunken people, spent last night, New Years Eve, on my own like some sad sack. How is David, by the way?' For the first time, she looks at me. 'What?'

She turns from me to Nick, who has come back into the room.

'What?'

Nick looks at me. I realise I have to speak.

'Cressida, David died last night.'

She's the first person I have had to tell. Each time you say it out loud, it becomes a little more true.

She staggers, puts her hand out to Nick. He hesitates for a moment then takes it.

She gazes at me. 'Oh, my God, oh, Jenny, I'm so sorry. And here's me bellyaching about nothing.' Tears start in her pale eyes. 'I'm such an idiot. I should have known something was wrong. What happened? He seemed to be recovering so well.' She drops into a chair.

I can't answer. Nick takes a deep breath.

'He was murdered.'

'What?' Her voice is barely a squeak.

'It seems that the people who attacked him here at the house came back to finish the job. Some kind of injection.'

'Oh, my god. How dreadful. Did they catch anyone?'

'Yes.'

'Jenny, is there anything I can do to help? Anything?'

'To be honest, there's not much to do. We're in that awful hiatus while we wait for the rest of the world to get back to work.'

'Well, can I stay, lend a hand around the house?'

I glance at Nick. He gives a non-committal shrug.

'Doesn't Dominic Evans want you in the office?' I enquire as innocently as possible. She has the good grace to blush.

'If he does, he can whistle for it. This is more important. Let me put the kettle on.'

I quieten the voice inside me that is longing to tell her to go away. The comforting closeness between Nick and me is crumbling with every second that she is here, moving, talking. I shiver. It's as if a bitterly cold wind has blown the front door open and is swirling through the house. Not her fault, I suppose. How could she know?

'Tea or coffee?' Cressida calls from the sink.

'I've got a coffee on the go, thanks,' I reply.

'Nicky?' The voice is hesitant; she's asking about more than hot drinks.

'Thanks, I'll have another coffee.' He smiles across at her. That's my boy, always making others feel better. I remember about my hunger and get the cereal pack from the cupboard. The mixture of bran and dried fruits tastes surprisingly good, as if I have never eaten it before. Wonder if that's shock or hunger.

'Right.' Cressida puts Nick's coffee down triumphantly and looks round. 'What's next to do?'

Chapter 65 – January 1st 3.30pm

Bill

Feel surprisingly well today, considering how much less there now is in the whisky bottle. Good to know I can still do it.

I'll phone Jenny later, wish her a happy New Year. In fact, I'll phone her now.

'Hello.' Man's voice. Must be the son.

'Hello, er, Nick. This is Bill Johnson. Is your mother there? Happy New Year, by the way.'

'Oh, hello. Just a minute.' A hand goes over the phone and stays there. Something's up. Am I persona non grata for some reason? Has someone said something?

Nick's voice comes back on the phone. 'Bill, I'm afraid she can't talk to you at the moment. I'm sorry.'

I force a laugh. 'Hope it's not something I've said.'

'No, it's just that… Sorry, hold on a minute.'

What the hell's going on?

'Bill.' It's her voice now.

'Jenny. Is something up?'

A dry laugh. 'You could say so, yes. Bill, they came back for David.'

'What, in the hospital?'

'Yes. Bill, he's dead. They killed him.'

Forty years as a policeman kick in. A hundred questions pour into my mind. But this is not the time.

'Jenny, I'm so sorry. I really am. Listen, we will get them, you know that, don't you? They'll bloody pay for this.'

'It's OK, the police are onto it. They caught the man who did it.'

'Police? Ha, you should know by now that you can't rely on them any more. There'll be a lot of talk and no action.'

'Bill, it's OK, really. Enough's enough. Leave it to them. That young guy who came round to your place, he's on the case and seems pretty good. I don't want any retaliation. Nothing. Two people are dead and one of them's my husband.'

I can hear her voice cracking.

'Jenny, OK, I understand. But if they let you down, just let me know.'

'I know, thanks but… well… you know.'

'Sure. Listen, I'll leave you in peace for now but if there's anything, anything I can do, just call me.'

'Of course. Thanks, Bill, I will.'

'You do that. Bye for now.'

'Bye.'

I hang up. The bastards. To do that to someone so… so, well, you don't do that to one of my team. You don't do that to Jenny. I can sense the red mist rising, the way it did sometimes when I had a hit and run or a child molester in the interrogation room. In the good old days before there were cameras everywhere. Whatever Jenny says, they are going to pay. That moon-faced idiot of a sergeant isn't going to crack this, even if he gets permission from his do-nothing bosses. Time for a bit of detective work, I think.

Chapter 66 – January 1st 3.45pm

Cressida

Funny, even in a weird situation like this, it feels good to be part of a family. I guess that's the thing when you're from my kind of world. Parents abroad, boarding school, farmed out for the half terms, jetting here and there, all looks very glamorous but when you get there, sitting among all that luxury and servants and stuff, you'd like nothing more than beans on toast, giggling with some friends round a kitchen table.

Well, here's the table and, I hope, here are the friends. Not much giggling tonight, obviously, and I'll pass on the beans on toast; my tastes have evolved a bit since then. But seriously, even though I'm on my own here in the kitchen, I don't feel alone. Do I just give up on Dominic? Let bag of bones Emily have him? He's probably all washed up now anyway, after that fiasco. Nicky's sweet and gentle and kind, which makes him a bit of a wimp, but, whatever, he's safe and he's here.

'Penny for them. Isn't that what they say?'

I jump, turn to face Nicky, who's silently come back into the room.

'They're worth a lot more than that. No, I was just remembering your dad, the way he talked and so on. It does seem so strange, doesn't it, not to hear him again.'

'Mm.' We share a silence. I move closer, put my arms around him.

'I'm here, Nicky.'

He rests his head on my shoulder. It feels very nice. I can smell his aftershave. That's Nicky, even on a day like this, shaved and smart, hair brushed, teeth cleaned. No designer stubble for him.

Jenny comes in, stops in the doorway.

'Oh, sorry, am I interrupting?'

'No, no, of course not,' I reply with a smile. Yes, actually, but can't say that. 'Now, what can we do for you?'

'Nothing, Cressida, really. We can't do anything until tomorrow. I think we need to think about something to eat. There's cold meats and cheese in the larder and plenty of veg. That do everyone?'

'Great. Lovely. I'll prepare some veg.'

'No. Really. I need to stay busy. Why don't you two take a walk? I think the rain has stopped.'

'OK, mum, sure, we'll do that.'

We'll do what? Back out in that? It's winter out there, I've only just thawed out. Oh, I see. Reconciliation moment. Clever, Jenny. Get us out there, needing to huddle together and all will be well. Nice. Good to know you're on my side, too. Worth investing a few shivery moments, and I can be very shivery.

We trudge up the drive, wrapped up against the cold, the only sound the crunching gravel under our boots. Nicky is hunched into his blue overcoat; no scratched and stained Barbour for him, always the City Boy. His hands are pushed deep into his coat pockets. I loop my arm through his. He doesn't look at me but he doesn't pull away either. We walk on in silence into the road. The whole world seems deserted. A car engine starts up the road just ahead of us, a sudden sound that makes me jump. I feel foolish.

'Sorry,' I mutter.

'What?'

'For being jumpy.'

'Oh.' I don't think he'd even noticed.

The car drives past, its windows misted up.

'Nicky, I'm really sorry, you know, about being a bit of a bitch after the O2 and then, last night, about the party and so on.'

A slight shrug.

'It's just that, you know, after the whole thing with the clowns and Andy's death...'

He stops dead, making me stumble.

'What?'

'Andy's death. You must have seen it on TV.'

'No. When would I have seen TV in the last two days? We've avoided any news programmes, anyway, didn't want to hear reports about Dad. Go back a bit. Which one was Andy?'

'You know, Andy Woodham, the little fat speechwriter who kept trying to hit on me.'

'I remember you telling me. And he's dead?'

'Yes, fell off a high staircase at the O2, it seems. That's why I couldn't get out to meet you, I had police and everything to deal with.'

'Shouldn't Dominic have done that?'

'He'd gone already.'

'Yes, I bet he had.'

'And then I had to go to the police station, which was really horrid.'

'Police station. When?'

'Yesterday morning, on my way to work. They really grilled me. Seemed to think I had something to do with his death.'

'You should have called me. I could have come and helped. You shouldn't be in there without a lawyer.'

'I didn't think you'd want to. After, you know, the way I'd been to you.'

A slight smile. At last.

'I wouldn't have wanted to. But I'd have come.'

'My knight in shining armour?'

'Well, knight in a grey suit, really.'

I snuggle closer. 'That'll do.'

I feel him thawing, leaning slightly towards me. I feel more than triumph, relief as well. That's interesting.

A spat of rain hits my face.

'Oh, oh, time to turn back. Race you to the first gin and tonic.'

I start to run. After a moment's hesitation, he follows. Thank God.

Chapter 67 – January 1st 4.00pm

Barry

Wasn't looking forward to this. And with good reason. Williamson is glaring at me from behind his desk. I'm still aching from getting patched up in the police surgery. Those boys seemed delighted to have someone to practice on. I had to stop them swathing my whole head with bandages; just a couple of plasters which, I hope, are discreet but almost certainly aren't. Could have called in sick. I suppose no-one's going to believe that on New Years Day. The silent glaring continues. Bugger it, I wish he'd say something.

He gets up, walks round the desk, towers over me. Reminds me of last night. In the cellar. Not a nice feeling.

At last, and in a voice that is so reasonable it's more scary than being shouted at, 'So, let me be sure that I understand this. The last thing I said to you last night was to stay out of trouble. Yes?'

I nod.

'Sorry, didn't hear that. Yes?'

'Yes, Inspector.'

'And when I said that, remind me of your reply.'

'I said that I would do as you said, sir.'

'Right. You're sure?'

'Yes, sir.'

'Absolutely sure?'

'Yes, sir.'

'Are you certain I haven't remembered it wrong? You didn't say, "Interesting point of view, Inspector, but I plan to do the exact opposite and get my face rearranged in the process"? No chance that you said "Inspector, you know nothing and I am so much wiser and more experienced in these matters than you"?'

'No, sir.'

'Then why the fuck did you do something so irredeemably stupid?'

'Don't know, sir.'

'Carolson, this not fourth form maths. "Don't know, sir" is not an answer, it's a snivel. Do I need to repeat the question?'

'No, sir. You see, sir, after I left you I was due to meet Salita, my, er, girlfriend and we went to this party. Jeff, the man I told you about, the ringleader, was there. He said he wanted to talk to me and next thing I know I'm in a cellar and his mate is headbutting me.'

'So this so-called girlfriend of yours set you up.'

That hurts. 'No, sir, absolutely not. I'm sure she didn't. I mean, she was the one who rescued me.'

'Rescued you?'

'Yes, she got me out of the cellar and took me home.'

'And you, no doubt, stuck to your cover story with her, in spite of being semi-conscious and scared shitless.'

'Well, um, not exactly, not, you know, totally.'

'Really. Do tell.'

'She knows I'm a policeman. But, to be fair, she had already guessed.'

'Right, Of course, we must be fair. If she'd already guessed, that doesn't count, does it? So, let me get this right. This girl, about whom you know nothing except where the important parts of her body are located, knows you're a copper. This man Jeff, who runs a gang who beat up people at random and is almost certainly behind the murder of David Belsworth, also knows you're a copper. Pretty good night's detective work, wouldn't you say, Carolson?'

'Yes, sir. Um, no, sir.'

'So, can you think of any good reason why I should not recommend that you are kept on foot patrol, nights only, specialising in cold wet nights, for the next forty years?'

I feel like crying. 'No, sir.'

'Right answer, Carolson. Now bugger off home and come back when you look less like Quasimodo.'

Chapter 68 – January 2nd 8.45am

Jenny

Sunday, bloody Sunday. Always had an ambivalent attitude to it. Day of rest for everyone except Mum, who spends half the day sweating to prepare a giant lunch and the other half getting everyone ready for Monday. I was always ceremoniously placed in an armchair after lunch, 'Mum's Time', while everyone else washed up, for which I was clearly expected to be very grateful. Then I'd go and do the pans that they always managed to miss.

Not much of a dawn today. Just grey and cold. I know, been up since six watching it, waiting for the light to creep in, apologetically, the way it does at this time of year. Like a schoolboy without his homework. Still, at least we'll get some papers today. They will no doubt come through the door with a mighty crash in half an hour or so. No sound from the others.

My need to get some time to myself yesterday afternoon seems to have backfired. They came back intertwined, disappeared soon after our makeshift supper and I haven't seen either since. Should be grateful for the space, I suppose. Left me to field the phone calls. Only two papers called in the end. Just shows how commonplace these things have become. Usual stuff, 'how do you feel?', 'what do you remember about him?' Such stupid questions, I had to just say no comment. I mean, where do you start with questions like that? And where do you stop?

No, I just have a feeling that the Nick and Cressida thing will end in tears. Still, that's life, tears. Oh shit, here I go again, getting weepy. Come on girl, get a grip. This too will pass, life goes on and all those clichés. Trouble is, clichés don't really help. They don't change the fact that I'm sitting here and am going to sit here every Sunday morning for the rest of my life, on my own. Am I wallowing in self-pity? You bet your life I am and why not. If not now, then when?

Wonder if I can call Bill. It's early, but I'm pretty sure someone like him would be up and about by now.

I pick up my phone and find the number. After a moment's hesitation, I tap his name. It rings.

'Hello.'

'Bill?'

'Jenny, hello.' I feel absurdly pleased that he's recognised my voice. Trouble is, I can't think of anything to say.

He fills the silence. 'How are you today? Absurd question, I know, I've been just where you are now. But I also know how it ebbs and flows.'

'I… it's… I don't know. Can't really find a way to describe it. I'm just sort of hollow.'

'Hollow, yes. Good word. Look, is there anything I can do? Do you want to come over here for a break? I mean, I'm a bit busy today but I'd be glad to see you.'

'Busy? Is this planning for Birmingham?'

"Um, yes, that's it.'

Why was there a hesitation there? There's something else here.

'Come on, Bill, what are you planning?'

'What? Nothing, really.'

'OK.' I let it go for now. 'Look, about Birmingham, I really don't think I can join you, given, well, everything.'

'No, I'd rather assumed that. I'm sure we'll be OK.'

'Is it the same gang, with Chas's people? We seemed to work well before.'

'Probably, yes. Anyway, don't you worry about that. You focus on yourself.'

'Sure, and thanks for the offer of a bolthole. I may well take you up on that.'

'You're welcome. Just give me a call before you come over – I may have to pop out.'

'Of course. Bye now.'

I ring off, puzzled. There's an undertow there. It's as if Birmingham isn't going to happen. What isn't he saying? Or is it just my fuddled mind?

More coffee. That's the answer to most things in life. House fallen down? Have a coffee. Broken leg? Have a coffee. Lost the cat? Have a coffee. Lost your husband…

God, what was that crash? Oh, papers, a bit early today. The double thud, *Mail on Sunday* for me, *Sunday Times* for David. For David. For David.

He was so embarrassed by my taste in gossipy rags. Used to make me hide the *Mail* if anyone came round. I really hated its politics, think I just kept having it to irritate him. Poor David. Who's suddenly, with a flick of a switch, become a past tense.

I go through, push the *Times* to one side, the others can have that later, I'll have the easy one. Looks like a nice big lurid headline. *Good 'Eavens, Mr Evans*. Nice. Where are my glasses. Right, here we go. Oh. Oh dear. That does put the cat well and truly among the pigeons.

Chapter 69 – January 2ⁿᵈ 9.00am

Bill

Excellent. Chas' boys have done a good job on this one. I think I like the *News of the World* best with '*Dirty Dom and the Blonde*', good traditional, lip-smacking stuff, though the *Sunday Mirror's* not bad with its '*Dominic's Party for Two*'. The pictures are good; it's amazing what a digital camera can capture nowadays, considering they were shooting from the building opposite. They've even had to put little stars over some of the more intimate bits. Must have been quite a debate in the news room, 'We can show those bits of hers but have to cover up those bits of his,' that sort of thing. The *Sunday Sport* are already advertising the video on their website, '*The Politician and his Plaything - Uncut, Uncensored, the Full Monty*'. Pay per view, no doubt, with Chas getting his share.

I wonder if that girl is going to be relieved or cross that she's only named as Mystery Blonde. You just don't know nowadays, some people want fame however it comes. Porn stars end up with their own shows on TV. I'm glad I'm getting away from here, I really am. I just don't get it any more.

That was my doing, the Mystery Blonde bit. Didn't want to embarrass Jenny, not with everything else she's got on her plate. Can't tell her, of course, well, maybe one day. Poor Jenny. I just wish there was more that I could do for her.

I wonder if this will finish Evans. Not guaranteed, might even make him a bit of a hero. Even if it does do for him, there'll be more of them popping up. One thing's for sure, it will help the subscriptions to roll in. Couldn't have timed it better.

I pick up the *Sunday Telegraph*, '*Evans caught in flagrante*', not very inspired, and turn to page ten. It's a discreet little ad but it works.

FIGHT BACK!

Our great country is falling into the hands of violent extremists.

None of us is safe and those of us who are older are most vulnerable.

We have a choice.

Either we cower in our homes, afraid of going out onto the streets of our own country or we can stand and fight back.

We have already struck one blow. Help us to strike more often and more effectively.

Send your subscriptions now to www.agefightback.co.uk

An ad in five of the main papers this morning – Chas felt the *Sunday Sport* would undermine our credibility and he should know – and an online campaign that will be sending out messages to every AA member and everyone on the Saga mailing list. The people who know these things reckon we will have reached sixteen to twenty million people over forty-five by this evening.

They reckon on a two percent response. I think we'll get more, what with the fear that is everywhere. Even at two per cent, twenty five pounds a time is going to get us a nice eight to ten million pounds coming in. Chas gets his money back, plus a hundred percent and I'm left with enough to keep me in wealthy Texan widows for the rest of my natural. They really ought to tighten the laws up.

I call Chas.

'Happy New Year, Chas.'

'Looks like it will be. Like the ad, by the way.'

'Good, I like the photos. I think we may have stuffed Mr Evans for now, though no doubt some other self-important little upstart will come along soon enough.'

'Not our problem, old son. Our work here is done, as they say.'

'Yes, give it till the end of the week and we can close up shop and head for the wild blue yonder.'

'Or in my case, back to the golf club.'

'Now, the banks are all arranged. It's going straight offshore, no questions asked. It'll cost us about five per cent of the total but it's worth it.'

'Right. I'll pick up mine in Spain. I'll be over there in a week or two.'

'Visiting old friends?'

He laughs. 'It's like the old days down Bermondsey Road over there, I tell you. Mind you, they're all complaining about the cost of living. It's getting really tight for some of them.'

'My heart bleeds.'

'Just 'cos you didn't nick them in time.'

'Maybe.'

I think back. Most of them bought their way out anyway. I've a very nice fridge freezer in the kitchen that got one villain his free pass.

'How come you never took that route, Chas?'

'Me? I love this country. Wouldn't go anywhere else in the world. I've got a picture of the Queen in my study to this day and heaven help anyone who disrespects her. Anyway, changing the subject, Jenny. What are we going to do about her?'

'What?'

'I mean, they have film of her coming to your door, Bill. There's an issue there.'

'Chas, there's more. This is the other reason I called. David, her husband, he's dead.'

'Is he? I thought he was getting better. Well, I'm very sorry and all but I don't…'

'Chas, they killed him. It'll be in tomorrow's papers, no doubt. They got into the hospital.'

'Shit, they're better than I thought. OK, listen, Bill, it's really bad for Jenny and all, but it's not our fight any more. We're out of this, we've got what we wanted, or will have by tomorrow. Let someone else deal with it.'

'I want them, Chas. We know who they are and I want them dealt with.'

'Then you'll have to find them without me. Bill, you're letting your emotions get in the way here. Think back, mate. You're a copper, emotions are a luxury you can't afford.'

'I'll pay. Find me someone, Chas. If you're not going to do this thing for me, find me someone who can do the job.'

'I'll get back to you. But I'm out of this.'

The phone goes dead. I should have known. The one thing you can be sure of with Chas is that he'll let you down in the end. Well, OK, if that's how it has to be. He should have learned by now to do what I say.

Chapter 70 – January 2nd 10.30am

Cressida

There are few places in this world colder and more lonely than a station platform. Maybe it's all those old films of lovers parting in billows of steam, maybe it's just because that's what they are, cold and lonely. This one certainly is. It's high up and the straight track coming up to it seems to funnel the wind right into your face. And it's starting to rain again. How very appropriate.

I don't think I could have buggered things up any more comprehensively if I'd tried. This really is PhD standard buggering up. Even thinking back an hour, seeing Nicky's face, makes me squirm. I'm not the squirmy type but, oh, God.

Such a lovely night. I don't know what it was that made us so up for it. Nicky's grief about his dad, maybe, they say it works in funny ways. But it was more than that. We were close. I think that was me, just dropping the barriers. We were just so together.

I popped into the shower while Nicky went down for some coffees. I came out all ready for more, just a towel wrapped well, draped around me, and there he was, with the newspaper in his hand. And that weird look on his face.

'You look as if you've just swallowed a swarm of wasps. What's up?'

He just throws the paper onto the bed. I can see straight away, of course. I look up at Nicky, shaking my head. I just can't think of anything to say. Unfortunately, he can.

'I think you'd better leave.'

'Nicky, I…'

He holds up his hand.

'Leave. Now. Please.'

And he just walks out of the room, leaving me with the paper. I take it between my thumb and finger, like it might bite, and pull it slowly towards me. There's pages of it. My face isn't too clear but no-one can have any doubt. I feel nausea soaring up inside me and just make it into the bathroom before throwing up. Shaking, I clean myself up, do my teeth again and stagger back to the bedroom. I pull on my clothes, check myself in the mirror – very bad idea – and get ready to go downstairs.

There's no sign of Nicky, thank God. He knows to do the right thing and keep out of the way. The door to the kitchen is open and Jenny is at the sink. I take a step into the room. She turns.

'Jenny…'

She looks at me. One eyebrow raises, eyes narrow. I can't hold her gaze, look down at the floor.

'I… I'm sorry,' I mumble and dash for the door and out.

Now the freezing platform. My legs are shaking, I don't know whether from the cold or the shock. I stare at the rails in front of me. Tempting. Two steps, a jump, a big flash and that's that. Just shut down the whole thing. That stupid bastard. How could he be so careless? I told him. It's as if he wanted to be watched. Maybe that's his thing. Well, I'll never know.

I'll have to leave the flat, of course. It's in Nicky's name. Where the hell will I go? I can't think of anyone who would want to share. Most of my friends are partnered off and the last thing they want is me around the house, distracting their men. There's got to be something other than going back to living with Mummy and Daddy. Daily doses of disapproval and disappointment. I can feel tears starting. No, I don't do that.

'You look as if you've had as rough a night as me.'

A coarse Welsh voice, full of last night's booze. I look up. A man in a ragged overcoat tied up with string is staring at me, his mouth open in a toothless grin. I glare back.

'Fancy a cup of coffee?'

'No. Go away.'

'Go on. Does wonders when you've been shagging too much.'

'What? Look, just fuck off and die, will you?'

He just grins back at me. How did he get onto the platform? Don't they have any security any more?

'Just ride up and down all day, I do.'

I ignore him. He pulls a newspaper out of his coat pocket and unfolds it.

'Get thousands, you could.'

'What?'

'Sell your story. Got a thing for faces, you see. Always did have. So did my mother before me.'

I can hear the sound of a train coming in behind me but can't turn round. He leans in towards me, tapping the side of his nose with his finger. I get a full blast of his breath. That and the sight of the filthy broken nail nearly makes me throw up again. He's laughing now. The doors slide open. I run down the platform to the next carriage and dive in. I look out as we pull away. He's not there. I ease myself out of my seat and peep into the next carriage. No sign of him. Did I imagine him? What is happening to me?

The carriage is nearly empty. I slump onto a seat, creep into the corner and hug my coat around me, watching the suburban back gardens flashing by. Is this how it's going to be from now on? Infamous as the girl in those photos? I don't think I can do that. I really don't.

My phone rings. Nicky! I fumble in my pocket, finally find it and drag it out. I can't see the display, my eyes are too blurry. I flick it on.

'Hello.' I can hear the hope in my own voice.

'Hello. It's Ramon.'

'What?'

'Ramon. Ramon Rodrigues. Mr Evans's bodyguard.'

'Yes, yes. I know who you are. What do you want?'

'I need to talk to you.'

'Why?'

'It's about Mr Evans.'

'Obviously it's about Mr Evans. What else would we have to talk about?'

'I need to talk to you.'

'So you said. So, talk.'

'Not on the phone. Can we meet?'

'No.'

'It's really important. Please.'

I sigh. It's not as if I have anything else to do.

'OK. When?'

'As soon as possible.'

'Today, then. Meet me at two at the office. No, not at the office. We'll meet at the Starbucks on the corner of Old Street and St John's Street. Two o'clock.'

'Thank you.'

'This had better be important.'

'It is. It is.'

Chapter 71 – January 2nd 11.30am

Barry

I've got the hang of it now. If they stare at my face, just stare back. Then give them a big grin. That soon stops them. I know I'm a pretty horrific sight right now; I suppose most people think I've been in some drunken fight. There's enough of those around nowadays. Better get another coffee. I've been nursing this one for an hour now. Weird having nowhere to go. Life's been so busy and, yeah, exciting, over the last week or so, it's like I've suddenly stepped off a winding path and over a cliff. Just free fall.

Tried calling Salita but voicemail. I wonder what she's up to. Think I'll go round to her after this next coffee. No, I'll go now. She's just round the corner, after all. Seize the moment, carpe thingummy, as that film said, whatever it was.

Out in the street it's drizzling again. There really is nothing to recommend this time of year. No wonder so many people die in January, you just can't believe it's ever going to change, that you'll ever be warm again.

Oh, bloody hell. Thank God I didn't leave one minute earlier. Jeff and his gorilla friend, heading in the direction of Salita's. I duck into a shop doorway, watch them turn the corner, scamper after them. I can hear Williamson's voice in my ear, 'What idiot thing are you doing this time? Don't you ever learn?' Well, sorry, sir and all that but this is important.

Ahead of me, they turn down the alley towards her flat. I get myself into the shadows and peer round. They are stopping at her door. I hear the murmur of Jeff's voice into the intercom, the door buzzes and they go in. I race down the alley and catch the door just before it clicks shut. I can hear their footsteps on the bare stairs, then Salita's voice. She sounds pleased to see them. Doesn't she realise how dangerous they are?

The lights are on a timer. I wait for the darkness and slip in, feel my way up the stairs. Rubber-soled shoes, thank goodness, so I can move quietly.

Her door is flimsy, it's easy to hear what's being said.

'So, boys, what can I do for you?'

'That so-called boyfriend of yours. Where is he?'

'No idea. Not that bothered, frankly.'

'Think we've scared him off?'

'Oh, yeah. He was whimpering like a baby. He's a very ordinary policeman and we all know how brave they are. Not.'

I can't believe I'm hearing this.

'Right. And he fell for the brave rescue?'

'Totally. I told you that was best. I mean, what were you going to do with him stuck in Jeff's cellar? He'd have just been an embarrassment.'

'I'd have let Mick play with him for a while.'

'Jeff, I remind you, he's a policeman. Don't fuck with the law, rule one. Keep out their way and you can get away with murder.'

'I know. We already have.' Loud guffaw, must be from Mick. 'Now, listen, Salita, if he turns up again, you keep him away.'

'Don't worry. He's history.'

'Right. Just make sure he knows it.'

I hear them moving around and realise they are about to leave. I look round frantically and see that the stairs go up towards the roof. I clamber up and crouch, making myself as small as possible. The door opens and the two men come out.

'Hey, Salita, now you've finished playing with the opposition, maybe you ought to try a bit of the home side.'

'In your dreams, Jeff. I told you in Year 10 you weren't my type and I still mean it. This is strictly business.'

'You don't know what you're missing. Prime English beef, this is.'

'Yeah, right. Chipolata, maybe.'

A grunt from Jeff and the men are off down the stairs. Neither of them looks round, thank God. I sit, not knowing what to do, not wanting to do anything. The worst of it is that bloody Williamson was right again. I've been set up like a complete amateur. Don't know why I ever thought I'd make a detective.

I think I'll go back for that third coffee.

My phone starts to ring, loud and clear, the Star Wars theme seeming to fill the space around me. I crush it into my pocket but it still blares out. I drag it out to turn it off, briefly see the name on the display before it goes.

I look up. Salita is standing there with her phone to her ear.

'Anything you want to ask me then, Barry?'

Chapter 72 – January 2nd 1.30pm

Jenny

'That was your sister on the phone. She's got as far as Bristol. Going to be here about six.'

'Right, we'll make up a bed for her, though I suppose she'll want to sleep on the floor or in a hammock or something.'

I've finally coaxed a smile out of Nick. Doesn't last. 'You know, Mum, I think I knew. About Cressida.'

'Really?'

'Yes. There's something in the pit of your stomach, you know, that tells you that something's up. Just didn't want to hear it, I suppose.'

'No.'

'I mean, I'm sure you found her all very sweet and suitable but there was something, you know, not quite right.'

'Uh, huh.'

'Did you ever get that feeling with Dad, you know, that he was messing around?'

'Good heavens, no. Your father was much too transparent. He'd blush if he'd had a dirty thought about Angela Rippon. Silly old…'

The sentence ends in a sob. Out of nowhere. I get up quickly from the table, go to the sink, start washing up. Got to refocus when things suddenly overwhelm.

'You never told me what happened to the front door, the broken pane.'

Dear Nick, changing the subject, though I wish he hadn't changed it to that one. I'd pushed that whole thing out of my mind, what with, with everything else.

'Oh, that. Yes, well, I suppose I ought to tell you. You know the whole Sean Delling thing and Dad being attacked and the graffiti? Well, on Friday, I found out they were following me. They'd filmed me everywhere I went.'

'God, that's really horrible. I thought you sounded strange when I called. You should have said.'

'Yes, I should. Sorry.'

'So what happened?'

'That young policeman, Barry, you know, the one at the hospital, he came over. Then they threw a brick through the window. Barry got the police here fast and I think that scared them off. Anyway, I've heard nothing since.'

'Bloody hell, Mum, you really have been through it.'

'Yes, been quite a week, one way or another.'

Nick comes up and gives me a hug from behind. 'Is there anything else you haven't told me?'

The cup I'm washing slips from my fingers, splashes back into the bowl.

'Steady, Mum. You OK?'

'Yes, yes, I'm fine. Just, you know, distracted.'

Nick takes me by the hand and turns me round.

'What else, Mum.' I shake my head and try to get back to the washing up. He holds my arm.

'I know you, Mum. There's something you're not saying. Last week, you were really buoyed up. Something was going on. I thought it was weird, what with Dad being in hospital...' He stares at me, wide eyed. 'God, it's not another man, is it? That guy who keeps phoning you?'

'No, Nick, it's not another man. I don't do that sort of thing, never have.'

'Sorry. But it is something, isn't it.'

I sigh. 'You're getting to be quite a good lawyer. Pity you work on such dull stuff all the time.'

'It's not dull and don't change the subject. Come on, sit down, I want to hear this.'

Meekly, I follow Nick to the table and sit. Actually, it's a relief, having the chance to talk. Secrets can be really exciting for a while, then they seem to become just sort of constipated and you're longing to be rid of them. And I suspect I won't be hearing from Bill again, judging from the last phone call. Couldn't get off fast enough.

'Now, Mum, tell me.'

'Well, you remember the O2 Centre, you were there, last Wednesday?'

'Of course. The clowns and all that. It was…' I watch, I have to admit, with some pleasure, as Nick's features change. He's looking at me with something like respect. 'The clowns. Was that you?'

I nod.

'But, how? I mean, there was serious money behind that. And the organisation it needed.'

'Are you suggesting I can't organise things?'

'Hey, don't get all feminist with me.' His expression changes suddenly, a frown like when I used to stop him watching television. 'God, Mum, how could you? People could have been killed.'

'Oh, I don't think… I mean, there was no risk, they were just inflatables.'

'There was a stampede, Mum. Several had to be treated. People could have been trampled to death. What were you thinking?'

I don't know what to say. For a moment, I'm cross with Nick for taking the pleasure out of it. Then I start to realise what he says is true. I'd just seen it as a fun way of dealing with Evans. Did Bill realise? Probably. God. I find I'm sitting on my hands, staring at the table like a schoolgirl in front of the headmaster. This will not do. I look up.

'Nick, while I concede there was an element of risk that I hadn't really thought about, no-one was badly hurt and the point was made. That little creep got his comeuppance. You of all people must be pleased about that.'

'Yes, Mum, thank you for reminding me that he's been screwing my girlfriend.'

'No, that's not…'

'Listen, you may be in big trouble. These phone calls and the brick, did it occur to you that they might be about the O2, not just the earlier escapade?'

'No, they can't be. No-one can connect me with the O2. The others made sure of that.'

'Mum, they've been following you. Do you know how long for? They could have followed you to the O2.'

'No, the DVD was only from Friday.'

'The one they sent you was only from Friday.'

'Well, yes, but…'

'But what, Mum?'

A long silence hovers round us.

'You're right. I don't know.'

'I think you should tell the police.'

I'm staring at the table again. 'I think they already know.' My voice sounds small, distant.

'What?'

'Nick, please don't shout at me. I just can't stand that.'

'Sorry, sorry. But it was a bit of a shock. Tell me.'

'When Barry was here, just before the brick came through the door, he virtually accused me of having been there.'

'Why?'

'He didn't say. We were interrupted by one of the phone calls and then, well, everything else.'

'Right, let's go back a bit. How did this all start? How did you get involved?'

'Nick, I'm sorry but I'm not going to tell you.'

'Mum, I can't help you if I don't know.'

'I know and that's why I'm not going to tell you. Look, you're a lawyer, you're bound by certain rules and ethical codes and stuff like that. If I tell you who else is involved, you're going to have to do something about it, go to the police and so on.'

'That's not actually how it ...'

'No, Nick. I know you. You're the most decent and honest person I've ever met and I love you for that. I'm not going to burden you with the knowledge. I will sort this out. The police have no evidence against me, I'm sure of that. They're just fishing.'

'Even if that's true, what about the thugs that followed you? And the brick?'

'It's been thirty-six hours since the brick and nothing else has happened. I think they got what they wanted with your father.'

'You hope, you mean.'

'Yes, I hope. I hope. Hope is all I have, Nick, and not much of that, frankly. Good God, everything any of us does is based on hope, isn't it. That will have to do for now.'

'And the people you pulled this stunt with?'

'They're OK.'

'Mum, you're in the public eye. You've had policemen outside your door, reporters at your gate. Do you really think they will be happy about that?'

I shrug, trying to look more casual than I feel.

'What are you going to do now, Mum?'

'Wait, I suppose.'

'Then I'll wait with you.'

'Nick, you don't have to.'

'I know, but I will. I said I'd stay over anyway, to help with tomorrow's things, with the undertaker and lawyer and what have you. All the more reason to, now.'

I feel my throat tightening, take a very deep breath. 'Thanks. I really do appreciate that. '

'Right. But this is not going to go away, Mum.'

'Don't think I don't know that, but one thing at a time. Now, help me get some lunch together.'

Chapter 73 – January 2nd 2.00pm

Bill

It's cold out there. Still, had to do my reconnaissance. Can't brief someone without the facts. I should know. Now I'm back home, warming my hands around a nice cup of tea. Time to check on how everything's progressing.

I like the fact that people think anyone over fifty can't work a computer. Gives me a lot of freedom. I wouldn't say my fingers exactly fly over the keys but I can get there soon enough. In fact, I'm looking at a lovely screen full of numbers. It's only two o'clock and already I've got over three million. Forget Children in Need, this is Copper in Need and thank you, British public, you've responded wonderfully. Like I knew you would.

At this rate, I'll be gone by Tuesday. Damn, phone's ringing.

'Hello.'

'Bill, Chas.'

'Oh. Hello.'

'How's it looking?'

'Good. We're already just over the million.'

'We're hoping for better than that, aren't we?'

'Give it time. I reckon by midweek we'll be there.'

Grunt from Chas. Then he clears his throat. 'I've been doing some asking around for you. Your request earlier.'

'Oh, yes.'

'Someone will call you. Name of Taggart.'

'Taggart? Bit unimaginative.'

'Whatever. I don't want to know. OK?'

'Fine.'

'And don't go wasting any of my money on this.'

'Don't worry, you'll get what's due.'

'Right, I'll see you midweek.'

And he's gone. He's slipping, our Chas. Used to be much more suspicious. Must be the good living. Well, not for much longer. I turn back to the screen and check again. Already up another fifty thousand. Time for a celebratory scotch, I think.

Phone goes again. Perhaps it's Jenny. I take my drink and pick up just before the answer machine cuts in.

'Hello.'

'This is Taggart.'

'Good. Have you been briefed?'

'Not fully.'

'Right. There's a café, Café Nero, just off Albion Street, SW 8. Be there at five thirty.'

He rings off without answering. I press 1471. Number withheld. Of course. I go upstairs and take money out of the bedroom drawer. Two thousand should do for now. Learnt a long time ago to have money to hand. Make it all untraceable. Into an envelope in the inside pocket, then down to the hall and pull on my coat.

Chapter 74 – January 2nd 2.00pm

Cressida

When I come up from the tube at Barbican, my phone bleeps with a message. I flip it open. From Dominic. 'Don't come to office. Will call.' Nothing else. Not signed, nothing. So, that's it. Six words and that's it. He won't, of course. Call. They never do. I look up past the tall towers at the heavy grey sky. Thank God it's not sunny, couldn't cope with that.

I walk up the street, weirdly quiet at this time of year, no roaring lorries or clattering taxis. The wind has come up now, blowing into my face like an insult, bringing tears to my eyes. Not proper tears, though. Funny thing is, well, funny strange, I don't feel like crying. Think I'm past that, somehow. Maybe later, sometime in the dark hours. Something to look forward to.

Ramon's waiting as I walk into the warmth of the coffee shop. He stands as I approach the table, awkwardly holding out his hand. I shake it briefly. He looks past me, over my shoulder, as we shake. Hate that.

'So, skinny latte, please, Ramon.'

'Sorry? Oh, oh, right. Back in a minute.'

I sit and stare out of the window as he hurries to the counter. All round me, newspapers. They seem to be surrounding me, whispering at me, like those girls used to at school. I should be grateful to Ramon that he didn't have one in his hand. Probably too thick.

Eventually, he's back.

'So, what is it that's so urgent?'

He looks cautiously round, then leans in towards me.

'Oh, for fuck's sake, Ramon, stop the 007 crap and tell me.'

'Sorry, Miss Jones.' I don't correct him about my name. 'It's like, about that night, you know, Wednesday or whenever. When Andy died.'

'Yes, and a lot of good you were.'

He sits back, offended. Good. 'Well, you know, my job was to protect Mr Evans, not the whole team of you.'

'Whatever. What about it anyway?'

'I know how Andy Woodham died.'

'So do I. He fell off the staircase. Big revelation.'

'No, Miss Jones. That's just it. He didn't fall, he was pushed.'

'Pushed? Who by?'

'By Mr Evans.'

I stare at him, open-mouthed. Don't know what to do with my body, where to look. My phone rings in my pocket. I jump, pull it out. It's him, Dominic. It feels like he's watching us. I flick it open, holding my hand up to Ramon to shut him up.

'Hello.'

'Hi. How are you?' The warm, creamy voice wafts into my ear.

'How do you think?'

'Listen, we need to talk but can't meet, obviously.'

'Obviously. What about?'

'What?'

'What do you want to talk about, Dominic?' Ramon is on his feet at the mention of the name. I signal him abruptly to sit down. 'About your engagement, perhaps? Do tell me what you'd like me to get you from the wedding list, won't you.'

A dry laugh. 'What engagement. That's out of the window.'

'So it's back to the reserve team is it?'

'No, it's not like that. I can explain.'

'You know, I really hate it when a man says "I can explain". Usually means the opposite, in my experience. What are you going to explain? How you hot-footed it to bone-bag Emily while you were still sticky from screwing me? I'd love to hear that one.' I'm shouting. I'm aware that the few people in the coffee shop are all staring. Ramon is looking out of the window, wishing he were somewhere else, no doubt. The man behind the counter is edging towards me. I don't care. 'Did you have her too, Dominic, that evening? How did we compare? Scores out of ten?'

There's silence at the other end. Then a click. Damn him. I wanted to hang up first.

The manager is at my side.

'I'm sorry, madam, I must ask you and your companion to leave.'

'No problem. Your coffee's shit anyway.'

I stalk out onto the pavement, followed by a crouching, deeply embarrassed Ramon.

'What's up, Ramon. Didn't you think that ladies talked that way?'

To my surprise, he grins widely.

'To be honest, Miss Jones, you just gone up in my estimation.'

I nod briefly. To be honest, I think I've just gone up in mine too.

'So, tell me what you know.'

'About Andy?'

'Of course about Andy. Why else would I be talking to you?'

'When he came off stage, Mr Evans, you know, Andy kind of pulled him off, remember? Well, I was there, at the side and I come forward to take him out to the car. You remember, we had to go up them metal stairs at the back to get out. Well, we're nearly at the top and Mr Evans, he wants to go back on stage again and Andy and I, we're pushing him up the stairs to get him away before anything else happens. Like, we didn't know if there was going to be bombs or something.'

He looks at me, seems to be looking for some kind of approval. I shrug.

'Anyway, we're up there, quite high up and he, Mr Evans, he's suddenly like "No, this is my big moment, I'm going back". And there's me above him trying to hold him back and there's Andy below him like, blocking his path and Mr Evans is like "Get out of the eff-ing way" and he gives Andy this big shove.'

Ramon stops, stares across the road at nothing in particular. I can see that his eyes are shiny with tears. He's shivering.

'Then,' he takes a deep, juddering breath, 'Then Andy's gone. He's like, tipped over and lands on the floor below. I look around and there's no one watching so I grab Mr Evans and hustle him up the stairs and away. We get to the car and he just grabs the keys from me, jumps in and he's gone. Yells at me to stay and sort it. Yeah, right, I think. I mean, you know, I really thought he was something special, someone who could change things for people like me. But he's just the same as them all, isn't he? Anyway, that's when I came to find you.'

We stand, huddled on the pavement. I wish I'd brought my coffee out with me. Might have been shit but was at least hot.

'Why are you telling me this, Ramon?'

'It's conscience, I guess. I'm a Christian man, brought up that way. I just, you know…'

I stare at him. 'He's fired you, hasn't he?'

'Sorry?'

'He's fired you. If you were that Christian, you'd be talking to the police, not to me. He's fired you.'

Ramon looks at the ground, then nods silently.

'Why?'

'I don't exactly have legal papers to be here. He didn't want the hassle of someone finding out.'

'When did he know about this?'

'He's always known.'

'So, what else?'

'How do you mean?'

'Well, if he's always known, why now, why suddenly does he fire you?'

'I'd rather not say.'

'I'd rather you did.'

'I don't think you want to know, Miss Jones.'

'Let me be the judge of that.'

He hesitates, a slight, irritating smile on his face. 'After speeches and that, Mr Evans would like, get visitors.'

'Of course, he's a popular man.'

'No, I mean like, lady visitors, you know.'

'Oh.'

'Well, there was usually more than enough calling round, you know what I mean, so I kind of thought, well, maybe I should get my share too. I used to be a roadie and that was the kind of system then. Roadies got the spares, you might say.'

'You're telling me that the groupies Mr Evans didn't want, you took?'

'Yes, except it started to kind of work the other way round. I'd sort of filter off a few before they got to him.'

'A few?'

'There was plenty.'

'And he found out?'

He nods.

'Why didn't I know about all this?'

'We always found stuff for you to do straight after the speeches, remember?'

I do remember. Scurrying around, sorting things out with the hall owners or whatever, being the dutiful Events Manager, feeling important and valued. By the time I was done, Dominic was usually gone, to have a well-earned rest, so I thought.

I glare at Ramon. Don't like him, don't trust him but, as they say, my enemy's enemy is my friend.

'What do you want, Ramon?'

'He's going to shop me, probably already has, get me out of the way. I'm going to be going back to nothing. That's not fair, Miss Jones.'

'So, you want to get your own back. And who do you think is going to believe you?'

He shrugs. 'It's what happened. Anyway, it doesn't matter whether anyone believes me. The suspicion would always be there.'

'You've thought this through, haven't you?'

He nods. Again the little grin.

'And how do you expect me to help?'

'You know how things work, how to get this story out. You could even say you witnessed it.'

'And you think I'd destroy the career of the most promising politician in this country, do you?'

He looks shocked. So he should.

'Miss Jones, he's two-timed you, he's fired you, he's spread you across the Sunday papers, and I do mean spread, lady. You not going to tell me you're still hot for him?'

'You're a vulgar man. And he hasn't fired me. I've quit.'

Yes, I suppose I have, one way or another.

'So, are you going to help me or are you going to let him get away with it?'

'I don't know. I need to think about it. I've got your number. I'll call you.'

'When?'

'I don't know.'

'I could be picked up any time and be out of the country.'

'I know. I need to think about this. OK?'

He spreads his hands. 'I have no choice.'

'That's right.'

I turn and walk back to the tube. I've got a lot to think about.

Chapter 75 – January 2nd 12.00 noon

Barry

Back in the flat, her arms crossed, she's staring down at me. At least she's made me a cup of coffee. In silence. I take a sip. Burn my mouth. Some dribbles out past the bruises. Snort from her. Seems I can still make her laugh, then.

'So, Mr Detective, like I said, is there anything you'd like to ask?'

'Yes.' I try sounding defiant. 'Those guys and what you were saying. I heard it. What was that all about?'

Her stare doesn't waver. 'That was all about saving your life, if you must know.'

'Yeah, right. Telling them I'm a cop and a wimp.'

'They know you're a cop, remember. And would you rather I told them you were shit hot and coming back for more?'

'No, but…'

'But nothing, Baz. I tell you, you were so sodding lucky they didn't see you here. We wouldn't be having this charming conversation. We'd both be having a conversation with the slime at the bottom of the river.'

'But you're in with them. You planned my fake rescue.'

'Sod me, Baz, are you sure they didn't take your brain out last night as well. Now, listen carefully. I'll make it as simple as possible. That was a real rescue. I persuaded them to let you go. You heard what Jeff said. You'd have been Mick's plaything. And, let me tell you, Mick breaks all his toys. He may be a nicely-spoken lad, but he's a bit of a psycho. And as for me being in with them, as you put it, do you think they would have been so nice if they'd seen you here? I'm a watched woman now and you don't know how much that pisses me off.'

Even I'm starting to see that she has a point. Or am I? I'm feeling so confused, the bit of my brain that does the thinking seems to have shut down completely.

'Salita, I'm sorry. I'll go.'

'Derr. What if they're out there? You just going to give them a cheery wave as you walk by? No, Baz, I'm stuck with you for a while. But as soon as it's clear, you are going away and you're going to stay away.'

I nod dutifully. Suddenly, Star Wars fills the room again. Her eyes widen.

'Do something useful, Baz, change that bloody ringtone.' She stomps away and stares out of the window.

I scrabble the phone out of my pocket.

'Hello.'

'Sergeant Carolson, Barry? It's er… it's Jenny… Belsworth.'

'Oh, hi. What can I do for you?'

'There's something I'd like to discuss with you. Or, at least, my son would like me to discuss with you. I was wondering when you might be able to come over.'

'Is this police business, Jenny, because I've been temporarily stood down. Took a bit of a beating last night.'

'Oh, oh, I am sorry. What happened, or are you not allowed to say?'

'In the line of duty, as they say. Following up on that lead. Got myself into a bit of a spot.'

I hear Salita snort again. She's turned to listen.

'I see. Been rather eventful for both of us, then.'

'Yes.' I want to offer my condolences but can't find the right words. Maybe face to face later.

Silence.

'Look,' I say, 'I'm a bit tied up at the moment,' another Salita snort, 'but I could get out to you later. Say about seven.' I raise an enquiring eyebrow in Salita's direction. She shrugs.

'Well, if you're sure. I mean, I don't want to get you into trouble or anything.'

'Oh, believe me, you couldn't get me into any more trouble than I'm already in. I'll see you about seven.'

I end the call.

'Who's that?'

'That woman I told you about, Mrs Belsworth, remember, the one who might have wanted some help with looking after her husband. Well, he died, was killed in hospital. It was on the news.'

'Yeah, I think I heard.'

She sounds surprisingly casual. I'm about to tell her of my suspicions about Jeff, about the connection with Belling, about Jenny's probable involvement with the clowns but I don't. Trust no one. That seems to be the best motto from now on.

'So, do you think I can get out of here?'

She sighs. 'I'll go down and see if it's clear. If I don't come back up, stay here.'

'OK.'

I wait, listening to her footsteps on the stairs. The outside door slams. After a couple of minutes, she's back.

'OK, you can go. Don't go up past the café, obviously.'

'Obviously. I'm not looking for trouble, you know, even though it might not seem that way.'

'Right.' She puts her hand on my shoulder. 'Look after yourself, though.'

'Sure, you too. Um, will I see you again?'

'Not for a while, Baz. Wouldn't be clever. I'll call you.'

I nod. I know what 'I'll call you' means. She grins and kisses me on the cheek.

'Don't worry, Baz. You'll see me again. Sometime.'

I give a little wave and head down the stairs, thinking how pathetic I am.

Chapter 76 – January 2nd 5.35 pm

Bill

5.35. He's late. Unprofessional. Unless, of course, he's already here, watching. I'll just have to wait, nurse this very expensive coffee.

Ah, phone ringing, here we go.

'Hello.'

'Mr Johnson? Taggart.' The voice is polite, soft-spoken. 'I'd like you to leave the café and join me in the Starbucks in Milton Street in five minutes.'

'How will I know you?'

'I'll know you.'

There's a click. Doesn't waste words. I like that. I drain the coffee, not wasting it at that price, and head out. The icy wind catches me as I turn the corner. I will be so glad to get away from here.

The Starbucks sign beckons. Look around, can't see anyone watching. Good, if I can see him, don't want him. I go in, order a hot chocolate this time, just to ring the changes, find a table at the back where we can't be seen or overheard.

He slips into the chair opposite me. Ex-army, I'd say, forty-ish. Good. Don't trust the young ones, they do it for the thrill. With these older guys, it's just business.

'So?' he looks across at me.

'Know about Generate?'

'Of course. Dominic Evans?' His eyebrows go up.

'Not him, tempting though it is. Local level. A group that works out of the Albion Café, round the corner. Damaged a friend of mine.'

'And...?'

'I need a permanent solution to the leader.'

He nods. 'Any ID of him?

I pass over the photo that I printed out.

'I took this earlier. Not great, I'm afraid, the café was dark. That's him, the weasely one, with his minder. Name seems to be Jeff.'

'Minder too?'

'Optional, if it makes it easier.'

He studies the photo. Nods.

'Just so there's no misunderstanding here, you want this Jeff taken out, permanently?'

'That's it.'

'Six thousand. Half now, half later.'

'I can give you two thousand now, rest on completion.'

He stares at me, pale blue eyes unblinking.

I spread my hands apologetically. 'The banks are shut and the cash machines have run out. Always happens this time of year. Don't worry, you'll get it.'

Unless I'm on a plane first.

He holds out a hand and leans forward. 'Mr Johnson, I always collect my debts.'

I smile, shake it. 'Of course, and I always pay mine.'

I pass over the envelope, which disappears into his coat. He picks up the photo, folds it carefully and slips it into the same pocket.

'I'll be in touch,' and he's gone.

I realise that my heart is pounding, not a good idea for a man of my age. Must be out of practice.

Chapter 77 – January 2nd 6.00pm

Jenny

Really not sure about this. Nick's sitting opposite me, looking like the wrath of God. Hardly blame him, of course. Bad enough to have your girlfriend playing away, without her vital dimensions and technique being the topic of conversation around the coffee machine in every office in the country tomorrow.

That's not all, though. He's determined that I should 'confess all' as he puts it, to Barry. Hoping they'll do the decent thing and drop charges because of what he gently calls 'the circumstances'. We'll see. Don't think it's in Barry's gift, frankly.

And on top of that we've got Fiona arriving any minute. My Gran always used to say 'This house is like Waterloo Station' whenever she came to stay. People coming in and out. Love it, usually. Just not now. Wonder if it will ever be like that again.

Still, be lovely to see Fiona. Been a while, last time a bit awkward with David's comments about scroungers and that strange man she brought. Don't think I could ever get used to calling someone Merlin. Wonder how many piercings she'll have this time. It's the tongue stud I don't get. Must make eating so uncomfortable.

'So,' need to break the silence, 'is Fiona going to ring when she gets to the station?'

'That's right, if the phone's working there and hasn't been vandalised again.'

'And if it has?'

'She'll have to swallow her socialist principals and take a taxi.'

'Right.'

He goes back to the paper. Don't think a *Sunday Times* has ever been read so thoroughly. Not in this house, anyway.

Must be something I can do. I'm awash with tea, don't need to cook, can't focus on the paper. As if I'm in suspended animation, kind of conscious coma. Tried the TV, just irritated me.

I jump up. 'I need some fresh air. Going for a walk round the block.'

Nick looks out of the window. 'Rain seems to have eased. Want me to come with you?'

'No, you stay warm. I'm just feeling a bit stir crazy.'

'OK.'

Outside, wrapped up, I breathe deeply. Must remember to do this every day or I'll become a house mouse. Maybe join The Ramblers, get myself a stripy jumper and a bobble hat. Maybe not. Can't help feeling nervous as I step out of the gate but there's no cars lurking. The street lights shine down on a quiet street. No one around. All the sensible people are indoors. I set off at a quick pace. After a couple of minutes I see a bedraggled figure with a backpack stumbling up the road towards me, long hair across her face. She's wearing some kind of embroidered sheepskin coat. And is that a tattoo? My daughter. As always, I have a flashback to the pretty little girl in her smart school uniform, proudly showing me her certificate for good attendance.

She lurches towards me and I can see she's crying. I hold out my arms and she sinks into my shoulder, sobbing.

'I know, darling,' I murmur.

'Bastard fascists,' she sobs. 'tried to throw me off the train just 'cos I didn't have a ticket.'

I'm shocked by the Cornish accent that she seems to have adopted.

'I told 'em,' she wails. 'I said my dad had been killed and that but they still gave me a fucking fine.'

'Why didn't you call from the station? Nick would have collected you.'

'Bastard phone was bust. No taxis.'

'Come on, let's get you into the house.

The warmth envelops us. We shed layers. I hang mine up, Fiona's hits the floor. She blows her nose on a shredded tissue. Nick comes out of the kitchen.

'Hi, Fi.' He gives her a big hug. Good to see.

'Hi, big bruv. How's the world of capitalist oppression of the masses?'

'Great. How's poverty and degradation?'

'Sod off and put the kettle on.'

'Already done. Come and sit down.'

We gather round the kitchen table. Like old times, but not. Fiona produces some herbal tea bags from a deep pocket. Apparently drinking tea oppresses the workers.

'Even Fairtrade?' I ask hopefully.

'Western conspiracy to make us feel better.'

'Oh, right.'

A silence falls over us as we all remember why we are together. Nick clears his throat.

'Fi, we've, er, got meetings with the lawyer and the funeral people tomorrow.'

'Right. God, all seems so real now. I mean, you know, you want someone to say, sorry, all been a mistake and that but it's not going to happen, is it?'

I take her hand. 'No, love, it isn't.'

She sits, silent, brow furrowed but no tears. If this was the TV, she would cry on my shoulder at this point. But things are never that orchestrated. I didn't cry at Dad's funeral. Wept buckets afterwards. Still do, sometimes.

Nick brings us back. 'And there's a few more things you need to know about.'

'Wassat, then?'

Nick looks across at me. I nod.

'Well, you know that big fuss at the Generate rally last week, at the O2.'

'Yeah, that was so funny. Really stuffed it to that pompous git.'

'Yes, well, I was there and…'

'You were there? You don't support that toad, do you?'

'No, I certainly do not. I was there to, well, to help someone out.'

'Hey, did you see the papers today? Looks like our Mr Dominic…'

I come to the rescue. 'Look, we're getting off the subject and we haven't got long. What Nick is working up to,' deep breath, 'is that I was involved in the clown incident.'

Fiona looks at me, mouth open. Not an attractive sight. Dentists must be scarce in Cornwall.

'You, Mum? You were behind…? You?'

'Is that so surprising?'

Really, children are such bigots.

'Wow. Rock on, Mum. I mean, respect. R-E-S-P-E-C-T.'

'Yes, well, it's not that simple, is it, Nick?'

Nick takes his sister's hand to get her attention. 'In a nutshell, the local Dominic Evan supporters club, aka Generate, were almost certainly the ones that killed Dad and have been harassing Mum.'

'Harassing?'

'Threatening phone calls, filming her in the street and sending her the DVD of it, culminating with a brick through the glass in the front door. Thing is, I suspect that they know about Mum and the O2, so I don't think they've necessarily finished yet.'

'Wow, Mum. That is seriously unfair. I mean, you're entitled to your view.'

'Fiona, listen,' I struggle to know where to start, 'I don't know how it is in Cornwall but up here, like most of the big cities, it's something close to open warfare between Generate and my generation. Except that only one side is fighting. That's why I felt I had to do something. But, as things are, "seriously unfair" doesn't really come into it. I took them on. They're fighting back. It hurts. That's how it works.'

'So, what's going to happen?'

'There's a young policeman who's been very helpful and supportive…'

'You're not going to get the fuzz involved. You don't seriously think they can help, do you? I mean, we may be a bit behind in Cornwall but even we know the fuzz are no bloody use. Nick, this is you, isn't it? Can't you stop being a bloody lawyer for just one minute and realise? They're not the middle class's best friends any more.'

I watch Nick's mouth tighten. 'So, Fi,' he snaps, 'I suppose you have a better idea.'

'As it happens, I have.' I'm intrigued to hear the Cornish accent gradually disappearing. 'Sell the house.'

'What?'

'Sell the house. Get right away. You don't need all this space anyway. Just forget them and bugger off round the world or something.'

Nick's eyebrows shoot up. 'Thought you didn't approve of international travel, air miles and so on.'

'Nick, I'm trying to make a serious point here. No, I don't approve but this is Mum we're talking about. She's in danger. The plod can't or won't help. What are you going to do? Stand guard with your trusty pea shooter?'

I'm impressed. Yesterday, I would have put any money on Nick having better ideas than Fiona. But he's not giving up.

'So, you think Mum should just run away, do you?'

'Too bloody right, I do. Better to live to fight another day, eh, Mum?'

'Oh, I'm so glad someone has at last asked what I think, even if it was rhetorical. Thank you for remembering I'm here too. Actually, Nick, I think Fiona has a good point and I believe you do too.'

He has the good grace to grin and hold his hands up. 'OK, just hard to accept from Fifi the Circus Clown here.'

Fiona bridles. 'There's nothing wrong with being a clown, I'll have you know. It's an ancient and honourable profession, unlike being a lawyer.'

'Children, children, can I just drag you back to reality? What about this idea? Just disappear. I can put all the important stuff into storage and we can get Jaggers to put the house on the market.'

I look around the room. Since David retired, I've been feeling that the house was more a burden than a refuge. And since the attack, even more so. Couldn't have said such a thing to David, of course. The immovable object on that topic. Said he'd be carried out feet first. Didn't know how true that would be.

Nick leans forward. 'If you're sure, Mum. It's a big decision.'

'Actually, it's quite a small decision. Big decisions are when you've got lots of choices. I haven't. Look, I'll sleep on it.'

'One thing, Mum,' says Nick. 'Barry, your policeman, is going to be here any minute.'

'Damn, I'd forgotten about him. Well, we'll just tell him there's been a mix-up. Give him a cup of tea and send him on his way.'

'May not be that easy.'

'But it may be. Let's just see. Now, Fiona, go and get yourself settled. You're in your old room, of course.'

She and I stand. And we are, in that second, thrown into a different world. A deep boom from just outside, deeper and louder than I have ever heard. Table, cups, everything shakes. Glass from the window comes flying in. I feel as though I've been hit by a giant wave. I stagger back. I see Nick pushed down across the table. Fiona spins across the room, hits the sink unit, slumps to the floor.

Then, as suddenly, a deep silence. My ears are ringing. I call out to the others.

'Are you OK?'

Fiona stirs, looks up. There's a dark red mark on her cheek.

'Think I'm OK.' Her voice sounds thin and high. 'Are you?'

I nod. Look over at Nick. He's staring back at me, wide eyed, hands still spread across the table.

'What the hell was that?'

'I don't know. A bomb?'

He gets unsteadily up, eases towards the window. Light is flickering through.

'Be careful, Nick, please.'

He nods, ducks down.

'Upstairs, everyone,' he commands.

We scurry up. I take a tissue to Fiona's cheek: glass has scratched her, though it seems to have missed anything important.

'Any more cuts?' I ask as calmly as I can manage.

She shakes her head. 'Don't think so, I'll check.'

Nick grabs the phone in the bedroom, flings it down again.

'Dead.'

Takes out his mobile, dials.

'Police. Yes, there's been an attack, maybe a bomb. Holly Cottage, Hamilton Avenue, in Pinner.'

As he's talking, I edge towards the bedroom window and peep out from behind the curtain. The front garden is lit brightly. In front of the house, the Volvo is burning from end to end.

Beside the car lies the body of a man, spread-eagled on the ground. Even from here, I can see blood across his face and on the ground by his head. And leaning over him, Barry, our friendly policeman.

Chapter 78 – January 2nd 7.30pm

Cressida

These guys never seem to sleep. Thankfully. Even given me a coffee this time.

Blank room, grey and green paint, no carpet. Williamson sitting opposite me, waiting.

I stare at the table, covered in scratches. Smell of stale air and old coffee. Am I really going to do this? Seemed so logical. No point going straight to the papers. Their libel lawyers wouldn't have let them touch it. So this was the only way. But, but…

Eventually, he gets impatient.

'Miss Huntley-Jones, I really –'

'Please. Please, you make my name sound like a swear word. Can you just call me Cressida?'

He waves my request away. 'It's seven thirty on a Sunday night. I haven't seen my wife for thirty-six hours, I'm tired, hungry and the only good thing about the situation is that I've missed *Strictly Come Dancing*. I would really appreciate it if we moved on from the discussion about the etiquette of names.'

'I'm sorry. It's just, you know…' I see the look on his face and peter out.

He stares at me. 'So?' An eyebrow raises slowly.

'I'm sorry, it's just difficult.'

'Miss… madam. You said on the phone that you had information about the death of Andrew Woodham. Shall we move on to that topic?'

I nod. This is it, in at the deep end. 'Do you remember a black guy, a bodyguard?'

'Yes.'

'Well, he called me, asked for a meeting.'

Why is this so difficult to get out? I should be glad to be putting the boot into Dominic. But it's really closing the door on all that, I suppose. Williamson looks pointedly at his watch.

'I met him this afternoon. He had been with Dominic, Mr Evans, after he had to leave the stage. He told me that he and Andy were escorting him up that metal stairway at the back when Dominic decided to turn back and go on stage again. The others tried to stop him and in the confusion, Andy fell from the staircase.'

I stop, breathless. Williamson sits, nodding slowly. The silence seems endless.

At last, he moves and takes a deep breath. 'So, you are telling me that Mr Evans pushed Mr Woodham off the staircase.'

'No, no. I mean, not in that sense.'

'In what sense?'

'In the sense that you meant.'

'Did I mean any particular sense? What do you think I meant?'

I'm beginning to feel like a rabbit who's just met up with a python.

'I, well, you might have been implying that Dominic pushed Andy off deliberately.'

'Did he?'

'No, not as far as I know. I mean, I wasn't there, of course, but the way that Ramon explained it, well, it sounded like a simple accident.'

'A simple accident. I see.'

I'm nodding like one of those nasty dogs you see in the back of old people's cars. He continues to stare at me.

'Yes, exactly,' I fill the silence. 'Why would it be any different?'

He leans forward, his head close to mine. I wonder how my breath is. 'You see, Miss… Cressida, the thing that puzzles me is how someone can topple off such a wide staircase. As I remember it, there was plenty of space for two people to pass.'

'I think Andy and Ramon were trying to stop Dominic going back down. Holding him back, you know.'

'Yes, I can see how that would be very annoying for Mr Evans. Enough to make anyone lash out.'

'Oh, he, no, really, he does not have a temper. I mean, I work, worked for him, I would know.' Feel like crossing my fingers behind my back.

'Major rally, launch of the next step on his road to power and world domination, totally ruined, made to look a fool. I think I'd be a trifle peeved, wouldn't you, Cressida?' Smiles at me. Wish he wouldn't. I'm starting to feel I should have stuck to Huntley-Jones, after all.

I look at the floor, feels like the safest thing to do.

'I wasn't there. I can't speculate on such matters,' I mutter.

'No. Perhaps I'd better have a chat with this Ramon.'

'Yes,' I say, a little too eagerly. 'He's waiting outside, I can call him if you'd like.'

'Please do.'

Fumble the phone out of my bag, misdial twice before I get it right.

'Hello.'

'Ramon, can you come on in. They'd like to talk to you.'

'Are you sure this is a good idea?'

'Don't you wimp out on me now or you'll be on the next plane out.'

'OK. I'm coming in.'

I end the call and look up at the Inspector.

'He's on his way.'

'What's his full name?'

'Ramon Rodrigues.'

'Wait here.'

I sit, sip the coffee. Cold. Try to stop my hands shaking. Fail. Well, that's it, girl. Boat's well and truly burned. You'll never work in this town again and all that. Sorry, Dominic. We could have been a wonderful power couple but you blew it. Or I did. Not sure any more.

Tired. Suppose I can go back to the flat tonight. Nick will be with his mum, cosy family time.

If they ever let me out of here.

Oh, fuck.

Chapter 79 – January 2nd 8.45pm

Barry

I mean, Pinner. It's the place where maiden aunts live and cosy TV programmes about jovial vicars are based. Not a place where cars blow up and people get shot.

OK, I never liked Jeff but that didn't mean I wanted him dead. As I've just explained to Inspector Williamson.

Not a happy memory. Sitting in his car outside the Belsworths' house. Blue lights flashing all around. Fire engine, Ambulance. Those guys do love a drama.

'So, Carolson, you do seem to turn up at the most unfortunate places, don't you? Unfortunate for you, that is.'

'Yes, sir.'

'I suppose you have an explanation.'

'Yes, sir.'

'And I suppose I have to listen to it.'

'I had a call from Mrs Belsworth. She wanted to see me. I told her I was off the case but she seemed, well, a bit desperate. Something she had to tell me, she said, or that her son had decided she had to tell me.'

'So, you thought this would be your glory moment when you solved the case and we would all realise what a great detective you were.'

'Something like that, sir, yes.'

Looks surprised at my honesty. Well, what have I got to lose? No, wrong question. Lots, actually. Job, reputation, freedom.

'Then this Jeff appears and it all goes horribly wrong.'

'No, sir. He was already there. I mean, I was walking up from the station and I turned into their road, the Belsworths', then I hear this loud bang and, a few seconds later, this car comes racing past me.'

'Did you see who was driving it?'

'No, sir, seemed to be wearing a hood or maybe just had his collar pulled up.'

'Registration number?'

'Got that, gave it to the patrol guys. They'll be checking with the DVLA.'

'That's something, I suppose. Then what?'

'I run up to their house and the car's on fire in the drive. Really ablaze. So I get on the phone, call up help.'

'And then.'

'Well, I go towards the house, to see if they're OK, and just sort of trip over this body on the ground. Didn't recognise him at first.'

'Really? I'd have thought his face would be imprinted on your brain.'

'He'd been shot through the head, sir. There was a lot of blood.'

'Your first corpse, Carolson?'

I nod. He grunts.

'OK. You obviously didn't kill him.'

'No, sir, of course I didn't. I mean, why…?'

He holds up his hand. 'Don't need an explanation. I mean, not really the killing machine kind, are you, Carolson?'

'There are many ways to be a good policeman without being cold hearted and callous, sir.'

He stares at me for a long moment as I watch my career walk away from me. Finally, he looks out of the window.

'Thank you, Carolson. I'll bear that in mind. Now, there's work to be done. Since you're here, you might as well make yourself useful.'

'Really?'

'Oh, for God's sake. Yes, really. We're understaffed and even you are better than nothing. Just. As it is, I've had to leave a very interesting discussion with the charming Miss Cressida Huntley-Jones. But more on that later. Now, chase up those guys for an ID on the car number you got. What about the family?'

'The medics checked them over. Shaken up, sir, but basically unharmed. The house hasn't been too damaged by the fire, just some scorching and a window blown out, so they're staying there.

'Has anyone been allocated to stay with them?'

'Don't know, sir. I'll check.'

'You stay.'

'Yes, sir. Thank you, sir.'

He's staring at me again. Now what?

'Well, get on with it.'

'Yes, sorry, sir.' I scramble out of the car.

Standing in the drive. Foam creeping up over my boots. A chaos of hoses, the blackened Volvo still burping the occasional wisp of smoke. I go up to the door and ring the bell, then realise the door is open and the house already full of people.

Nick is sitting at the kitchen table with a girl I don't recognise. She has a large bandage on her cheek. One of the policemen is with them. He's looking cross.

'Look, that's all I know,' Nick is saying. 'I can't see through walls, you know. There was no warning, just this great bang.'

The policeman looks at Nick with the standard Metropolitan 'I don't believe you' face. I move in.

'That's OK, Constable. Inspector Williamson has asked me to liaise with the family.'

That stopped the 'who the hell are you' moment from the young constable. He grunts and closes his notebook. I lean over to the girl.

'Barry Carolson.'

She stares back at me, ignoring my outstretched hand. Puzzled, I look across at Nick.

'My sister, Fiona. She has a traditional hippy view of the police, I'm afraid. Sorry for the rudeness.'

She swings round at him. 'Don't you apologise for me, Nick. Don't you dare. You know nothing about what the filth are up to, sitting in your lawyer's office. You should get out into the real world.'

I pick up a trace of some kind of West Country accent. Nick shrugs and turns away.

'No, Fiona, if I may call you that? There's some truth in what you say. The police may not have always done what they should, especially in the last few years. But we're not all the same, you know.' She sniffs, not an easy thing, I guess, with those rings in her nose, but I think I detect a slight thawing. 'How's your mum?'

She looks at Nick, who signals to her to speak. A moment's hesitation, then she replies.

'She's with the medics right now. I think this might have been one thing too many. I'm taking her away, soon as I can.' She looks at me defiantly.

I nod. 'Good idea.'

'You're not going to stop me?'

'No.'

She stares at me again. 'What happened to your face?'

'Beaten up in the course of my duty.'

'Who by?'

I let the question go. The answer's too complicated.

'I see,' she arches her eyebrows. 'Being the mysterious one, are we?'

I laugh it off. 'No, sadly I'm a man of deceptive shallows.'

Don't quite understand the expression, saw it written somewhere. Seems to work, though. Get a small smile.

'Look, I've been allocated to stay with you as long as necessary.'

She freezes up again. 'Long as necessary just finished. You can go. We can cope very well, thanks.'

Nick focuses back on us. 'Fi, that's enough. It's Mum's call whether Sergeant Carolson stays, not ours.'

As if on cue, the door opens and Jenny comes back into the room. I'm shocked. She looks ten years older than when I last saw her. I stand, she looks at me but seems to look through me.

'Oh, it's you. Hello.'

Nick gets up and moves to her, guiding her to a chair. She sits, heavily, stares at nothing. Fiona reaches out, takes her mother's limp hand.

'Mum?'

Jenny turns slowly towards her daughter.

'Fiona, let's get out of here.' The voice is quiet, flat. 'Let's just pack a case and go. I really can't stand it any longer.'

'Sure, Mum, if that's what you want. It's a bit late to get back to Cornwall tonight but we can go in the morning.'

'No, not the morning.' Jenny is shaking her head vigorously. 'Now. We have to go now.' Her voice rises to a shout. 'Don't you understand? I need to get out.'

Fiona glances nervously across towards her brother, who is watching his mother closely. He leans in towards her.

'Mum, we can go to my flat tonight. Remember we have meetings with the funeral director and the lawyer tomorrow.'

'Stuff the funeral director and bugger the lawyer. And bugger you. I want to be away, out of here. Do you understand? Out.'

Nick glances across at me for help. I feel out of my depth too but have to make some kind of contribution.

'I suggest that you let tomorrow look after itself,' I venture. 'For tonight, it's fine for you to go to Nick's flat as soon as you like. I'll make sure everything's OK here. Fiona, why don't you go and help your mother pack?'

Fiona looks at me with what I hope is gratitude. She jumps to her feet and helps Jenny out of the chair.

'Come on, Mum, let's get your essentials together.'

Jenny glances across at me, almost shyly.

'At least someone here knows what I want. Thank you, Barry.'

I see Nick wince but wait till she's out of the room.

'Don't take it personally, Nick. It's shock.'

'I know. Still hurts a bit, though.'

'Let's go and talk to the medics. Find out what they advise.'

We find the two paramedics loading their equipment back into the ambulance. I know them by sight from a couple of traffic accidents.

'Mrs Belsworth seems very shaky. What do you recommend?'

'Who's asking?'

'Sergeant Carolson.' I flash my card. 'We worked together on that smash in Lithestock Road about a month ago. Remember?

'Sorry, sergeant. Didn't recognise you without the helmet. We've prescribed a sedative. Given her the first one, which should take effect in the next few minutes. Her son here will need to keep an eye on her, though. This could pass in a day or two or develop into a full-blown breakdown.'

'What should I look out for?' Nick's voice shakes slightly.

The younger medic smirks. 'Easy. If she's normal, she's OK. If she's not, she's not.'

'Look,' I cut in, 'You probably don't know what Mrs Belsworth has been through in the last few days so I won't report you for that. I will rephrase Mr Belsworth's question, though. What do you recommend we do about a woman whose husband has been murdered, who's been threatened, stalked and now physically attacked in her own home?'

I keep my voice steady but only just. The older of the two steps forward, putting himself casually between us and his colleague. He addresses Nick, not me.

'Sorry, mate, out of order. Been a long day. Have you got a good GP?'

'Yes, Dr Shaw, he's known Mum since I was a kid. Known us all.'

'Get an appointment with him as soon as you can. He'll know her history and he can treat her or refer her on. Most important, though, don't let her be brave.'

'How do you mean?'

'I know these kind of women. They are brought up to keep things bottled up. My mum was the same. I sometimes think the Americans have got it right. Let it all hang out. We can be our own worst enemies.'

Nick nods. We say good night and walk back to the house. He's shivering.

'Nick, as you know, I've been allocated to stay with you. What do you want?'

'I think we just want to be quietly together tonight, just the three of us. My car's round the side. Will I be able to get it out, past all this lot?'

'I'll make sure it's clear.'

'Thanks. Oh, and, Barry…' that's the first time he's used my Christian name… 'you came here for a reason tonight.'

'I think that can wait. I'd say that the car being burnt out neatly draws the line under the Delling death. As for the other matter, you know, the police always have in mind whether a prosecution would be in the best interests of society as a whole. It may not look like it sometimes but we do. If you can get me the names of the leaders of that little escapade at the O2, I think we can probably call it quits.'

'Thank you.'

'No guarantees, of course. I'm not the final decision maker on this, I'm just the humble sergeant.'

'Of course.'

'And, Nick, we haven't had this conversation.'

He gives me a lopsided grin.

'What conversation?'

'Exactly. Now, go and look after your mum.'

Chapter 80 – January 2nd 9.00pm

Bill

I look around the bedroom. This house has been home for a long time, over thirty years. So many memories. Mary has been in every corner, still is, has walked on every thread of this carpet. Old conversations hang in the air like cobwebs. There's a few of those too. Housework was never my thing. I do my best. Mary wanted me to be sure and keep clean.

I take a good swig from my whisky. Calm the lump in my throat. Been a long time since I cried. There have been moments. When the bed feels too empty, the kitchen too silent. Comes at you in a great rush. Strange really, all those years, all those horrific sights on police work, those bloody stupid people killing themselves and others. Kids. Never made me cry. Made me angry, bloody angry. I suppose that's what got me through. Even when we found out we couldn't have kids, Mary and me. She cried, of course, for a long time. Tried to hide it from me but I knew. But not me.

Was almost a relief to know I could cry. And it helped. Once I got past the, I don't know, the embarrassment, I suppose. Even though no one else ever saw. Just embarrassed myself. I was brought up under the 'boys don't cry' rule. Don't be a cissy.

But still, hard to say goodbye. I wonder if Mary will come with me, or whether I'm leaving her behind here. Wouldn't want that. Even if I find that rich Texan widow. Need someone to talk to. There's Jenny, of course, maybe in a year or so. Strange that I've heard nothing more from her. Probably for the best.

Anyway, enough of all this. Get on with the last bits of packing. Just about done. Don't need much. Sunny climate.

Cab's going to be here in half an hour. Then the midnight flight. Sounds dramatic. Isn't really. Just the next stage.

Raise a glass to Gerry too. Feel bad about leaving the poor sod but he didn't seem to even know I was there when I looked in yesterday. Made me want to stay, fight on. But that's not the point. What's done's done.

They'll probably confiscate the house. Shame but still. Nearly six million on its way to a nice little account in the Caymans. Palms greased, no problems. In, what, eighteen hours, I'll be sitting in the sunshine. Hope it goes to a nice family. Like the Patels. Bound to be Asian. Once they get into a neighbourhood, that's it. Still, not my problem.

Doorbell. Cab's early. Well, I'll tell him to wait. I'm not going to be rushed. This is important.

I open the door. Two people I don't know, standing in the dull evening light. But I know they're police. Unmistakeable. One steps forward.

'Mr Johnson?'

'Who wants to know?'

He takes out his warrant card.

'Inspector Stephenson. May I come in?'

I hope they can't hear my heartbeat.

'No, sorry. I'm really busy. Not a good time. Can you come back later?'

I start to close the door. His foot blocks it, same old trick.

'Sorry, Mr Johnson. This won't wait.'

'I assume you have a warrant.'

He nods.

'Show me.'

He takes a familiar document out of his pocket. My heart sinks. What do they know?

'Come in then, but make it quick.'

They follow me into the lounge. See one of the cases.

'Going away, sir?'

'Yes, going off in the morning to see an old friend in Yorkshire.'

He nods slowly. He's enjoying this. Must be certain of his facts. Or bluffing. I wait.

'Do you know a Mr David Singleton?'

I'm surprised. They may be wrong.

'No. Never heard of him.'

'You may know him by a different name.'

'What's that?'

'Taggart.'

Clever. Get them relaxed then hit them. He's staring straight at me. Grey eyes. Unusual. Small scar just to the side of the left one. Unblinking. He knows. Even with all my years of practice, I can't disguise the reaction. The body does its own thing.

It's over. I hold up my hand.

'Well done. How did you know?'

'He's one of ours, sir.'

Chas. Talking to the police. Never thought he'd go that far. Bugger. Losing it, that sense that kept me going for so long. But he'll not get a penny. He won't know where to find it. And those letters that I put in the post today are going to keep him very busy. Bastard's not going to have time to play golf for a while.

I nod. 'Chercher la femme. That's what they say, isn't it? I was doing someone a favour. Never a good idea.' I go to get my overcoat, taking the chance to run my finger round the inside of my trouser waistband to the hidden pocket. Yes, still there. I turn back to them. 'Right, shall we?'

They follow me out and I lock the door. And say goodbye to Mary. But not to the money. Not yet.

Chapter 81 – January 3ʳᵈ 9.00am

Jenny

My head's spinning. Dizzy. Focus, focus. No, can't. What's happening to me? Where am I? Look round the room. It seems to sway as I look. Drunk. I feel drunk. But I don't remember…

Have to get out. Out. Away. Ease open the door. Into the corridor. I do know this place. But it's not right. I shouldn't be here. Feel like I'm wading through jelly. Quite funny, that, wading through jelly. Where's the way out? Voices. I can hear voices. Got to be careful.

That looks like the outside door. Nearly there.

'Morning, Mum. How you feeling?'

I freeze. Can't turn round.

'Mum?'

I make myself turn. Oh, thank God. I know her. Fiona.

'Fiona,' I'm finding it hard to talk. Words slur. Throat tight.

'Come on, Mum, come and sit. We're just making some tea. Come through and sit down.'

She holds out her hand. I take it and she leads me to the sofa. I feel like my own grandmother. Fiona calls out.

'Nick, Mum's up. Put the kettle on.'

Nick. Right. The fog's clearing just a little.

'Why am I here?'

'Don't you remember?'

I shake my head.

Fiona looks at me. Eyebrows knit together. 'Must be those pills. They said they would knock you out a bit.' She leans forward, articulating clearly. 'This is Nick's flat. We came over last night.'

'Don't shout at me, Fiona. I can hear perfectly well.' I see a little grin. Not sure why. 'I know that. I know it's Nick's flat. Last night?'

I force myself to remember. The fog closes in again. Nick comes into the room, hands me a tea. My hand's shaking. I put it down quickly.

He leans in towards me.

'Do you remember what happened yesterday?'

'Not really.'

'Well, we thought it would be good to have a night here and you and Fi were planning a few days in Cornwall together.'

'Cornwall? Why?'

'Just to take a break. But we have to do a couple of things before you go.'

I take a sip of my tea. And, as I swallow, the fog clears. Suddenly and terrifyingly. Memories come flying at me like debris from an explosion. Explosion. I start to shake, tea spills over my hand. Nick quickly grabs the cup. My whole body's shaking. Fiona holds her arms out. I fall towards her.

And I remember. The car. The explosion. The dead person. The ambulance men. I remember it all. I don't want to but I remember. Tears come. I can hear myself wailing. Can't stop. Fiona is holding me tight. It helps, but not enough.

'It's OK, Mum. It's OK. You've had a horrible fright, on top of everything else. It's OK. Let it out.'

Don't know how long I stay there. Somewhere, in the distance I hear the doorbell. I look up. John Shaw. Dr Shaw. He puts down his bag and sits beside me, on the other side to Fiona.

'So, Jenny. Been in the wars, I hear. Let's have a look at you.' He turns to the others. 'Would you excuse us for a few minutes?'

As they scurry out, he takes my pulse, wraps that band thing round my arm for my blood pressure. I can't stop the tears but they seem to be slowing down a little.

'All right, Jenny, I want you to stand up for me.'

I lever myself up off the sofa. Realise I'm still just in my nightie. Go to cross my arms in front of me and wobble badly. He takes my arm and guides me back to the sofa. Takes a little torch out of his case and shines a light in my eyes.

'Mm. Right. Jenny, we've known each other a long time. You know that I will always be straight with you, don't you?'

I nod, not sure what's coming but feel it will not be good.

'You've had a real beating. Nick told me about it when he called me this morning. You've been incredibly brave and very resilient, which is what I expect from you. But you need a break. You need to get right away.'

'What about David's funeral? I need to sort all that out.'

'That can wait for a few days. I can have a word. I'm sure that David would agree with me if he were here. Nick's here and you can do most things by phone if you need to.'

'But I can't just leave him…'

'Jenny, listen to me. Your responsibility now is to yourself and no one else. You're going off with Fiona as soon as you feel up to the journey. She's arranging a hotel you can both stay at. Nick has said he will drive you down.'

I sit and try to think this through, dab the tears from my eyes.

'Why can't I think straight, John? I feel as though someone has taken out my brain, minced it and shoved the bits back any old how.'

'That will be the medication they gave you yesterday. I checked with the ambulance crew on the way over and they gave you something pretty powerful. Basically, wanted to knock you out, so you could sleep. I'll prescribe something a bit gentler.'

'Thank you. Not Cornwall, though.'

'Sorry?'

'Not Cornwall. It's too far. And I really don't want to see how Fiona's living, not at the moment. I might want to tidy it up.'

He smiles. 'OK, as long as it's away from the familiar places for a few days. Sort that with the kids.'

'I feel as though I've got flu.'

'That's the shock. It will pass.'

'When?'

'That's up to you. If you do your usual supercharged belting around doing stuff, it will take a long time. If you just stop and give it space, a few days will make a big difference. Look, you're going to have bad dreams for quite a while, maybe the odd panic attack. But it will get better. Meanwhile, best to have some company.'

Company. Not something I've had to think about for thirty something years. Often longed to be alone for a while. But that was when I knew that there'd be someone at the end of it.

I'm sitting there nodding like a mechanical doll. But at least I know where I am.

John stands up.

'Right, I'm going to give this prescription to Nick to get as soon as he can. And you are going to take them. They will make you feel a little light-headed and you shouldn't drive but they will help.'

'Mother's little helper?'

'If you like. But you are going to have to admit for once that you need some help. And accept it with good grace.'

'Yes, sir.'

He smiles broadly.

'Right. Lecture over. Come and see me next Monday after you've had your break.' He turns and calls out 'Nick, Fiona.'

They appear from the kitchen. They look pale, scurry gratefully in. No matter how old they are, still kids when their world wobbles.

'Right. Nick, here's your mother's prescription. Fiona, you'll need to change plans a bit. Your mother shouldn't have the long journey to Cornwall just now but she does need to go away and can leave tomorrow morning. Any questions, just call me.'

He gathers up his things briskly and heads for the door. Nick goes with him. I hear a murmured conversation.

I feel as if someone's cut my strings. As if I've been shoved out of the driving seat of my own life. I should be really angry about that. Actually, I don't seem to mind.

Chapter 82 – January 3rd 9.30am

Cressida

I am so hungry. I've just realised I haven't really eaten since the day before yesterday, if you don't count the odd muffin. And that one at Baker Street yesterday was definitely odd. Better get myself downstairs to the restaurant before they close the breakfast buffet.

Still, managed to sleep. At last. But God, that was the day from hell. I really thought, once I'd given that inspector the whole story I would be able to get a bit of space. Start to plan what I do next. Given that I can't do any of the things I was doing yesterday. But no. It's like there's a couple of wicked devils up there or down there or wherever they are, and they've decided to pick on me and it's 'right, what can we throw at her next?' I just wish they'd pick on someone else for a while. Like Dominic, though I suppose they've already got their claws into him. Or Nick. No, not Nick. It's not his fault I'm such a cow. Not really my fault either. Just the way it turned out.

That thing at the police station was weird. One minute that Williamson's locked into me like I'm the only person in the world, then there's a knock on the door. He's obviously not pleased. He leans back.

'What?'

A helmeted head comes round the door.

'Sorry, sir, but I think you'd want to hear this.' Welsh voice. Never did like the Welsh. Can't remember why, now.

'You'd better be right, or you'll be hearing stuff you'll wish you hadn't.'

He levers himself up out of the chair and goes out, closing the door behind him.

He's back in less than a minute.

'You'll have to excuse me, Cressida, something's come up that demands my urgent attention. Sergeant Jones here will take the rest of your statement and that of Mr Rodrigues. Jones, there's a man waiting outside, in front of the station, big, black guy, built like a brick shithouse, answers to the name of Rodrigues. Bring him in and sit him down in Room 6, find out what Miss Huntley-Jones has to say then interview him.'

I butt in. 'Are you saying that I have to go through all this again with this man?'

He smiles, a cold smile.

'That's right, Miss Huntley-Jones. Weren't rushing off anywhere, were you?'

'No, but…'

'Good. Well, I am. Goodbye.'

'When do I hear back from you?' I call after his retreating body.

'When I'm ready,' the voice floats back.

Silence. The Welshman and I eye each other, him nervous, me making sure he stays nervous.

'Well,' I finally say, 'aren't you going to collect Mr Rodrigues?'

He jumps as if someone's stuck a pin in his bum and hurries off.

Well, that all took forever. I had to wait between sentences as he laboriously took notes of everything I said, even though the tape machine was still running. Maybe I shouldn't have mocked his accent. And I suppose suggesting he might be better with chalk and a slate was definitely a wrong move. He slowed down even more after that. Really, some people are just so sensitive.

Finally, finally, I got away and headed back to the flat. Our flat, I was going to say, but not now. Not any more. It felt weird opening the door and going into the emptiness. I mean, it was not any emptier in the sense of having no furniture or anything. Just that sense that something has gone. An atmosphere, a feeling. Sad.

Still, poured myself a strong gin and sat down, flicked through the channels, settled for *Antiques Roadshow*. God knows why, most boring show on television, all those people hoping that Aunt Masie's piece of junk is worth a million.

I was quite enjoying watching the disappointment on their faces, when there's a noise outside and I hear the key in the lock. I'm up like an electrocuted cat.

Nick walks in.

'Oh.' That's it. All he says.

We look at each other, as Fiona Bruce witters on about candlesticks behind me.

'I… I'm sorry. I didn't think you'd be coming back. You said…'

'Well, things have changed. There was an attack on the house.'

'What?'

Behind him, Jenny appears. She looks terrible, barely alive and she's supported by a younger woman, dressed like something off children's television and with a big plaster on her cheek.

Jenny doesn't seem to know I'm there. The younger woman looks at me.

'Who's this?'

'It's OK,' Nick replies, still looking at me. 'She's just leaving.'

I start to reply but think better of it. I'm not very sensitive to atmospheres usually but I can see that this is not a time for a debate.

'I'll get some things from the, er, bedroom.'

As I leave I hear the other woman whisper, 'Nick, is that…?'

'Not now,' his quick reply, 'I'll explain later.'

Yes, I bet you will. But how much will you leave out? Most of it, I hope.

I pack an overnight bag and slip out as quickly as I can. They are fussing over Jenny and don't really notice me.

I don't say goodbye.

It takes me two hours to find a hotel that doesn't look as if it's got bed lice and actually has a room available. And having to put up with the stares from behind the counter. Well, I suppose, young girl, good looking, if I say so myself, with just an overnight bag. Bound to make them suspicious. Finally end up in somewhere that describes itself as a boutique hotel, which seems to have become an excuse for overcharging for cramped rooms. I can only manage a couple of nights at these rates, then I'm going to have to arrange something. I just wish I knew what.

Right, down for that breakfast. I just hope they're not one of these places that just does muesli and beautifully arranged fruit segments. I could kill for a full English.

Chapter 83 – January 3rd 9.30am

Barry

I watch the grey streaks of condensation run down the canteen window, hands tight around my coffee mug. Monday morning. Back to normal for the rest of the world. Seven o'clock alarms, dragging themselves off to the tube or whatever, back to their warm offices after a nice long rest. Jealous? Of course I'm bloody jealous.

Actually, no. Not one of them has experienced what I've been through in the last few days. While they were comatose in front of their TVs, overdosed on Bristol Cream and Quality Street, I've been beaten, fired, reinstated, investigated a hit and run, a murder, an arson attack and another murder. In a weird way, I've quite enjoyed it. Not the bollockings, maybe, but the rest. Felt involved, useful. Hell of a learning curve and still, maybe, a chance of a CID posting. And Salita. Another learning curve. Wonder if I'll ever see her again.

Bruises are fading. I could just about recognise myself in the mirror this morning. Maybe the odd scar will add a bit of interest. Bit of a pudding, to be honest, my face, like a full moon on a foggy night. Needs livening up a bit.

I look around the room, watch tired policemen stand in line for breakfast or slump over a coffee. Like all these jobs, pilots, firemen, whatever, ninety-five percent tedium, five percent excitement. Been rather the other way around for me in the last few days.

'Hello, Bazza, boy, look at you then.' The irritating Welsh lilt of Taff Jones. 'Been auditioning to be a crash test dummy, then? Heard you'd lost an argument with someone's fist. Didn't realise you'd lost quite so bad.'

'Hi, Taff. Lovely to see you too.'

He sits down.

'God, I had a belly full yesterday. Where the hell were you?'

'Out on a case. With Williamson.' That'll show him.

'Williamson? He was here, with me.'

'After that. I called him in. Murder case. In Pinner.'

'In Pinner? Seriously?'

'Yeah, that's what I thought. Seems there's nowhere safe nowadays.'

'Anyone I know?'

I shake my head, look out of the window to the carpark outside.

'Anyways,' he ploughs on, 'I got lumbered with some stuck-up cow, works for that Dominic what's his name, you know, the one who got caught with his trousers down. Evans.'

My heads spins back round.

'Evans? You mean Cressida Huntley-whatsit?'

'Something like that. Why, do you know her?'

'Yes.'

'Well, perhaps I shouldn't tell you about it. Might prejudice something.'

Toad. Might put me at an advantage, you mean.

'That's fine,' I counter, as casually as I can. 'I guess it was something about the death of Andy Woodham.'

Taff's attempts to hide his frustration give me the best moment of the day so far.

'Anyway,' he mutters, 'Right bitch. Still, got my own back, see. Made her…'

'Carolson!'

The voice that whiplashes across the canteen can only be from Inspector Williamson. I'm on my feet.

'Come here. I need you.'

He's already off down the corridor and I hurry after him, trying to ignore the grins, whistles and 'Here boy' calls from the others. I catch up as he turns towards the interview rooms and stops.

'What kept you?'

'Sorry, sir,' I gasp.

'Right, listen. In there,' he points to Interview Room 1, 'is a man you know, one Bill Johnson.'

It takes a moment for the connection. I try to interrupt to ask why. He holds up his hand.

'All in good time. He was brought in yesterday afternoon by John Stephenson. Now, here's the funny thing. Johnson had a contract out on Jeff Smith. Or thought he had. Turned out he'd briefed someone from Special Branch on the hit. Inadvertently, of course. He was grassed up. And Smith's dead anyway. Could have saved himself a lot of trouble and money. Funny old world.'

'I understand, sir, but I don't see what it's got to do with me.'

'Seems our Mr Johnson was running a scam. Those ads in the paper at the weekend about the oldies fighting back. We're pretty sure they were from him. Except there will be no fight back. He had a one-way ticket to the Caymans in his pocket. Trouble is, we don't know where the money is and my guess is that other people will be looking for it. We've sent a team in to look through his computer but we need to get a move on.'

'OK.'

'Right, this is where you come in. Judging by what he said in the ad, he's also the brains behind the O2 fiasco. Which means he's connected to Jenny Belsworth, more than just the Boxing Day incident. From what he said to Stephenson, he might even have a bit of a soft spot for her. I want you to dig, see what you can find out about his involvement, who else was in there with them. It may take us somewhere.'

'OK, sir. Shall I go in now?'

'Of course. Unless you've anything more pressing.'

'I'll just take a couple of minutes to get my brain in the right place, sir.'

'Whatever. I'll be watching the monitor. There's a button under the table. Press it when you want me in.'

Wish I'd had time for another coffee. I'm going to need all my wits about me with this one. Ex-copper, he'll know all the tricks. Still, I think I know where the weakness might be. I push the door open.

He looks up at me. Steady pale eyes. Must have scared the shit out of villains back then.

'Mr Johnson, I'm Sergeant Carolson. We met before, when you were attacked.'

'Yes, I recall.'

'Would you like a coffee?'

'Thank you, that would be nice. I'm sure if you just signal to the camera, it will come. White, two sugars.'

I do just that and take a seat opposite him.

'So…' I start.

'So.' There's a soft mockery in the voice.

'A lot's happened since we met last.'

No reaction.

'Yes, Mr Belsworth was killed. I'm surprised you didn't read it in the papers.'

He looks steadily at me.

'And, of course, Mrs Belsworth's been in the wars as well.'

I wait. Not a flicker.

'Still, the doctor says she should pull through. With rest and quiet. Away from everything.'

I can feel his temperature rise from three feet away. A fractional move, but every muscle has tensed. I let the silence hang.

'Doctor?'

'Yes, after the explosion.'

'What explosion?' The voice is slow, soft, pulled out of him in spite of himself.

'Mr Johnson, how well do you know Mrs Belsworth?'

'You could say she saved my life. I wouldn't want anything to happen to her.'

'So why did you put her in danger by involving her in your little escapade at the O2?'

He looks at me, a slight smile on his lips.

'What explosion?' he repeats.

'Mr Johnson, let's swap secrets here. After all, you are up for attempted murder and embezzlement; I don't think you've a lot to lose by telling me about the O2 incident. I was there, by the way. Nice.'

'If you could find out something about that incident, and I'm not saying I know anything about it, what would you most like to know?'

'Who the organisers were.'

'And what would you be prepared to give for that information?'

'Full details on Mrs Belsworth's state of health.'

'And whereabouts?'

'I don't know her whereabouts.'

'You'll need to explain that.'

'She's going away for a few days. I don't know where to.'

He sits, nodding slowly.

'You heard of a chap called Charles Sullivan?'

'No.'

'Used to answer to Charlie, only Chas or sir nowadays. Before your time, I expect. Ask some of your older colleagues. Pillar of the community over in Stanmore. Big house, Bentley, golf club membership. I think he will be able to shed some light.'

'OK. Anyone else?'

'Just foot soldiers. Not worth your while.'

'Perhaps we should be the judge of that.'

'And perhaps not.'

Another staring match. I can see that I've got all I'm getting for now.

'Thank you, Mr Johnson. I think I'll go and see what happened to your coffee.'

I head for the door.

'Carolson.'

I turn.

'Jenny Belsworth.'

'Oh, yes. Sorry. Arson attack on the house. Car was blown up. No serious physical injuries, but I suppose it was just the last straw. She's on medication and going away for a while.'

'Thank you. And, by the way, well done.'

'Thank you, sir. But I don't think you told me anything you weren't planning to tell.'

He shrugs and turns away. I go out into the corridor. Williamson emerges from another room.

'Good. That's a start. And especially useful as I've just been told that Johnson's computer had already disappeared by the time our guys got to the house. I suspect our Mr Sullivan could tell us something about that.'

'Do you know him, sir?'

Williamson nods. 'Pure Teflon. Still, we can make life unpleasant for him. Put the VAT men onto him. Usually persuades people to toss us a couple of minnows. Who knows, he might slip up, if we push him hard enough.'

'Can I say, sir, that sounds a bit unambitious. Surely….'

The hand goes up.

'You'll discover, Carolson, and I'm surprised you haven't already, that some things take a little longer. Your Mr Johnson in there, for example; there were stories about him being on the take for years. Now he's heading for a cell. Patience, lad. Invisible in the young and bloody pointless in the old. Now, there's something else for you, something we might actually be able to get a quick solution on. You remember Mick, the gentleman who rearranged your face?'

'Not likely to forget, sir.'

'Right. We've brought him in. His prints are on the car you spotted leaving the area last night. Seems there was a turf war going on within Generate and our friend Jeff was a bit pizza.'

'Pizza?'

'All promises and no delivery. Mick got a little impatient, decided to take some executive action. Oh, and by the way, that Delling boy. Seems he and Mick had a bit of a thing going. Apparently, Mick, or Michael, as he likes to be called when away from the hoi polloi, likes a bit of rough. Hence the personal vendetta. The lad with the syringe in the hospital just came clean; he was paid by our friend Mick. Go into the observation room. You can see how it goes.'

'I have to say, I'm all for police impartiality and all that, but I'd be very glad to see him put away.'

'I didn't hear that.'

Williamson nods, points me to the door and disappears down the corridor. I go into the darkened room. A slight figure on the far side turns and comes towards me. There is a shock of recognition before she speaks.

'Hello, Baz. Told you we'd meet again. How you been keeping?'

Chapter 84 – January 3rd 11.30am

Cressida

That's the trouble with cash machines. They tell the truth. The bit where it says 'balance available'. Or not available, in my case. It paid out twenty pounds but somehow made me feel like it was doing me a favour. So, no money, no job, no home. Not a great way to start the year. Time for drastic action.

I press the number on my phone, feeling as if I've just triggered the guillotine onto my own neck. Three rings and it's answered.

'Hello.' The voice that strikes fear in tradesmen and pins waiters to the wall.

'Hello, Mummy, it's Cressida.'

'Oh. Hello, dear.'

I plough on into the silence.

'Mummy, is it all right if I come to stay for few days.'

'Um, well, I suppose… Why?'

'Oh, you know, just need a tide me over.'

'What about what's his name, that pleasant boy from the suburbs that you brought over at Christmas?'

'Nick? Oh, that's sort of over.'

I can feel the exasperated sigh crackle over the airwaves and hit me right between the eyes. How does she do that?

'I see. Well, I suppose so. You won't be able to have your room, I've got my tapestry loom set up in there, but I'm sure we can put you up for a few days. I suppose you'll be going to work anyway during the day.'

'Yes,' I hastily reply. 'So, is that OK?'

'When did you want to come over?'

'Soon as I can, really.'

'The Richmonds are here to play bridge this evening so don't come before nine thirty.'

'OK, Mummy. Thanks.'

'Yes, well, see you later then.'

'Yes, bye, and thanks,' but the line is already dead.

I look at my watch. Half past eleven. Ten hours to kill with the remains of the twenty quid. Limits the options. I scroll through the names on my phone but I don't really want to talk to anyone. Either they're going to be happy, which will make me even more miserable, or they're going to be miserable too, which I really can't deal with just now.

The phone vibrates in my hand and the sound of the Beyonce ring tone yells across the street. What was I thinking?

'Hello.'

'It's Ramon. Thanks for nothing, lady.'

'Sorry?'

'They gonna kick me out. Just 'cos I got no visa.'

'Oh, I'm sorry about that.'

'Yeah, right, sure you are. You with the posh voice and the big rich family. Like you give a shit.'

'No, really. I'm sorry. You did the right thing, coming to me about Andy. But don't they want you to be around while they investigate Dominic, Mr Evans?

'Yeah, I know who Dominic is, lady, even if I didn't screw him personally. They'll keep me as long as they need me, then it's goodbye London, hello, Jamaica. I know how they work. How you all work. So that's why I phoned, to say have a really shit life.'

The phone goes dead.

Bit late to wish me that, Ramon.

Cinema across the road is advertising half price tickets for the afternoon show. Only three hours until that starts. I look in my purse again. Just enough money left for a sandwich and a few hours warmth. I try to avoid seeing what's actually showing. And fail. Armie Hammer in a whimsical romcom or Emma Stone being brave. What a mind numbing choice.

Chapter 85 – January 3rd 11.30am

Barry

'Salita?'

'That's right, well done. So, that beating didn't totally destroy your brain after all.'

I close the door to the observation room behind me and move forward into the dimly lit space.

'But, what… I mean, why…?'

'Bit of problem with the language, Baz? Have a think for a minute.'

I look through the two-way mirror to the scene beyond. Mick is slumped in a chair, looking defeated. A policeman leans over the desk towards him. The door opens and Williamson walks in. I know what I'm looking at, just don't know why I'm looking at it with her. She sits back down, relaxed as if she was in her normal surroundings.

Then the penny drops.

'You're a cop.'

She grins at me. 'I think the correct response is usually "you may say that but I couldn't possibly comment".'

'So, you were onto this lot all the time.'

She shrugs a sort of yes.

Thoughts tumble into my head.

'So, you must have known about them going to the Belsworths, Jeff and Mick. Why didn't you stop them?'

Again the shrug. 'Some things you have to just let happen.'

'She's on medication, Mrs Belsworth.'

'I know. But she's alive.'

'Was there a chance of her not being?'

'Funny old times we live in, Baz.'

I look back through the window. Mick is talking, waving his arms at Williamson. I turn up the sound.

'…bloody stitch up. Yes, OK, I was there, but I didn't shoot him. He's a friend, for fuck's sake.'

Williamson just stares back. I turn to Salita.

'Did he shoot him?'

'Probably,' she replies calmly. 'Not a nice man, our Mick. Jealous type. On the other hand, there was another bunch following them, quite professional. Got a bit crowded, what with us following the others following them. So, who knows? We've got enough to nail pretty boy in there, and that's nice and tidy. Anyway, Baz,' she comes over and puts her arm round my shoulder, 'how you been?'

I don't know how I feel about her touch. Part of me likes it, part wants to step away.

'OK,' I nod. 'Good, actually, in spite of all the bad bits.'

It's her who steps back.

'Am I one of the bad bits?'

'I don't know yet. I mean, I'm kind of guessing that you linked up with me so you could keep an eye on me. Because, well, knowing as you did that I was police. So, have I been just kept on a lead here?'

'Initially, yeah,' she replies, offhand, as if I'd just asked her the time. My heart sinks. 'I couldn't have you running around getting underfoot. But I remind you, you did get your oats, something that, I'm thinking, doesn't happen to you that often. And that didn't have to happen, that's not part of the training, whatever you see on the tele. There's many other ways I could have got you out of the way. No, strange though it may seem, I fancied you.'

'Past tense?'

'Not necessarily.'

A voice comes over the speaker. Williamson's blunt, direct tones.

'You didn't like the way it was going, did you, Mick. You wanted more fighting, thought Jeff was getting all the praise while you did all the dirty work.'

'Bollocks.'

'Who was it, Mick? Who gave you the gun? Who put you up to it?'

Salita leans over and turns the sound down.

'Hey,' I object.

'Don't worry, I know how it ends. This one will worm its way right back to that nice Mr Evans. We've a couple of his people who are being very helpful. Funny thing is, Evans seems to think that Jeff had something to do with the clowns. Now, I wonder how that happened.'

I feel out of my depth on so many levels. I grab for a lifebelt.

'That thing you said then…'

'What's that, Baz?'

'The bit about not necessarily.'

'Oh, yes. Well, that depends, doesn't it?'

'Does it? What on?'

'On you, Baz.'

'How do you mean?'

'Can you take it?' The teasing voice has gone. 'Not knowing where I am or even who I am. Not being able to ask. All those usual bits of chat, how was your day, what are the people like that you're working with, let's all meet up after work, all that, out of bounds. Never quite relaxing. Thinking, like you did just now, that it might have been me who shot Jeff. Yes, you did, don't try to deny it. Think about it, is that what you want?'

I think, but can only remember how good I felt being with her. I nod. 'I'm up for that.'

Her serious face dissolves into a grin.

'Right answer. Good. God, what a fucking relief. I thought you'd just dump me and walk out.'

'Never crossed my mind. Well, not for long.'

She thumps me playfully on the chest. Still hurts.

'One question, though,' I gasp.

She looks warily up at me.

'What do I call you? I mean, Salita's not your real name, you told me that.'

'It'll do, though, won't it, until you come up with something better?'

'Where did you find a name like that?'

'You ever been to Spain, Baz?'

I shake my head, realise that I'm going to feel confused for as long as this girl is near me.

'Well, it's everywhere there, the word. Means 'way out'. Quite appropriate, really. Except I spelt it wrong, should have been a d. What the hell, sounds better like this. Anyway, enough of that.' She looks up at me, one eyebrow raised, 'We have some catching up to do, my chubby little friend. Do you think that door locks?'

Chapter 86 – January 3rd 11.30am

Bill

Walls. That's it, now. Walls. No space, no wandering down the road, no pop to the pub. Camera watching my every move. I don't think I want that. Seventy-two now. Can't be less than a ten stretch, even with a good lawyer and good behaviour. They'll want to make an example of me, no doubt. And what's the point in getting out when you're eighty two, just at the point when you can benefit from having a hospital in the same building?

Poor Jenny. Damn, I'm a stupid bugger. Why did I want to go and get that nice girl involved in all our shenanigans? I know she was looking for an adventure, but I bet she's not now. Face it, Bill, you messed her life up. Great work. And you know why. You just wanted her around. Thought maybe a little magic spark might happen. Ha! You're a washed-up bent cop, hardly a fantastic catch.

So, look at the options, Bill, like the good cop you are, OK were. What's the likelihood of bail? Fifty/fifty at best. They'll want to know where the money is first. I could give them a fistful, I suppose, a million, even. All in separate accounts, easy to do. Give them Chas's share; there's a nice irony about that. The man who claims to be so generous, giving it all to the police. Yes, there'd be some satisfaction in that. But that's giving the money away. Wasn't that the whole point, the money?

Say I got a deal. Easy enough then to get a passport, get away. But then what? Spend the next however many weeks, months, years waiting for Chas's man to come knocking at my door. Won't be a Special Branch substitute this time. Two and one, they call it. Two to the chest, one to the head, dead before you hit the floor. Not such a bad way to go. Better than ending up like a cabbage, like poor old Gerry. But the waiting. Knowing it could be any morning, any passer-by. Someone said on the radio the other day, 'I'm not afraid of dying, it's the bit leading up to it that scares me'. No, I don't think so. Can't start being scared at my age.

Even the idea of the rich Texan widow is starting to pall. After Mary. No way I'm going to get that again. She'd probably end up nagging me to wear those Bermuda shorts and put the toilet seat down all the time.

Odd. It all seemed so straightforward only a couple of hours ago. Being in the swing of things, I suppose, all about the right now, not the future. Oh, for a life of sensations rather than thoughts. Good old Keats again. Another one of his. Wrong on this one, though, John. It's focusing on the sensations rather than the thoughts that gets us all in the shit in the first place. Look how we both ended up.

No, I really can't be arsed with the whole thing.

And the money. No doubt Chas will have got hold of my computer by now. Lot of good it'll do him. There's nothing on there and the one I did all the work on is at the bottom of the canal. Oh, he's going to be really cross. Anyway, it's all taken care of. They've got their little list, the bankers. They know, if they don't hear from me for a month, they know what to do. There's going to be a few charities around here getting some unexpected windfalls. Hope they get to keep it. Should do. It's supposed to be untraceable. The bankers, no doubt, will get their chubby little hands on a chunk of it but there should be enough left. What do you think, Mary? Do you approve of your stupid old man, after all? Have I done enough to jack it in?

If you were me, you'd be saying 'see you soon, love'. Not sure if I believe all that stuff. Be nice though. Very nice.

Where's that bloody coffee. Typical. Still, I can use it as an excuse to get to the toilet. All I need is a few seconds on my own and I can still pull rank to get that. Thank God they're so bloody awful at searching folk nowadays. Must be all the PC rubbish about not invading people's space. This little pack of pills I've been carrying around, they missed that. The man said they're supposed to be quick. And painless. Let's hope so.

Chapter 87 – January 5th 3.30pm

Jenny

Fiona's voice is raised against the wind.

'You know, Mum, you could come down to St Ives. I mean, once the house is sold and all that. There's a great vibe down there.'

I weigh up the attractiveness of this proposition. Even in my state, which I'm aware enough to know that most people would describe as befuddled, it takes no more than a couple of seconds, great vibe or no great vibe.

'Fiona, that's a lovely suggestion, but I really don't think you want your mum cramping your style down there.'

I shout my answer, even though she's sitting next to me, so I can be heard over the wind that clatters round us like a class full of overexcited children.

'Oh, that's not a problem…'

'No, I'd be out of place among all you younger… whatever you are.'

'Hippies, Mum. Good old fashioned hippies. And proud of it. Anyway, there's other old people, I mean, older, you know, more, like, grown-up…'

'No, really, I couldn't. I mean, you've established your way of life, which is, I'm sure, just right for you, but I think I'm looking for something a bit different. Besides, I'd still want to be within striking distance of London. Just not in Pinner. Not after all…'

My hands start to shake. Fiona puts her hand on mine without a word and sits, staring out at the grey sea. It was the same earlier, when Nick called. Calm voice, bless him, the perfect lawyer, telling me about arrangements for David. Next

Wednesday. Gives me a week to get myself as together as possible, even if it's only a temporary, string and sellotape fix, just enough to get me through those terrible few hours. The public goodbye, all acting as if we are just waving someone off for a holiday, being British and agreeing that it's the perfect weather for it.

I wonder, not for the first time this morning, what we must look like, me wrapped in seven layers and Fiona in pink and yellow striped dungarees, a beany rammed down to her eyebrows and a bobbly wool sweater that smells strongly of its previous owner, which was probably the sheep. The only people brave or foolish enough to sit out on the promenade. At least the wind has dropped but the damp air is still creeping into my bones.

Her suggestion and my answer nag at me. What do I want? I know what I don't want. That house, that life, W.I and rose gardens.

I try to explain. 'To be fair, it's been a great place, Pinner, for you kids to grow up and it's served us well. Good people and a real, genuine sense of community. The trouble is, I don't think I want a sense of community any more. I mean, I don't want to be a hermit or anything but I just want to be anonymous for a while, not Jenny from Holly Cottage, David's widow, the woman who was... just me, just Jenny. Reinvention, maybe. Or back to something I was. I don't know.'

Fiona nods. I think she understands, hope so. She's brighter than she lets you think, that one. I look around. Brighton always looks a bit sleazy and at this time of the year, with the grey sky bearing down on us and the sea undulating in that arrogant, threatening way, it has little to recommend it. No, inland, I think.

Could go back North but I think I've been gone too long. Been Southernised, as they would say. As I used to say.

So, a small ordinary house, like a thousand others. Sounds good. I could get back into finance, not full time, of course, maybe one of those debt advisors. There's certainly plenty of need for that nowadays, growing by the day. Maybe do some writing. Always enjoyed that when I was younger. Dad wanted me to be a journalist. Might make him proud of me at last, from wherever he's watching. I'd like that.

'Come on.' I gather my clothes around me and get to my feet. 'This is just a bit too bracing. Let's go and get some coffee.'

I start to walk towards Starbucks. Fiona takes my arm and steers me across the road towards a dowdy greasy spoon café.

'Not supporting American cultural imperialism even if I am freezing my tits off.'

'Elegantly put. I'm so glad we paid so much for your education.'

And I laugh, we both laugh, for the first time, it seems, for a very long time, for a lifetime. Passers-by give us a worried look. And I know, I'm suddenly certain that somewhere, some way from here along a road with a lot of potholes, it will be OK again. Not fantastic, not totally liberating, but OK.

And that's enough for now.

RESPONSE

If you have enjoyed this book, do please post a review on Amazon. Indeed, if there's something that you haven't enjoyed, do let me know. It's all learning.

You can reach me via my website phillawderwriter.co.uk

Thanks for reading.